CH01004485

ISBN E Book: 979-8-9856019-3-0

ISBN Paperback: 979-8-9856019-4-7

ISBN Hardback: 979-8-9856019-5-4

For permissions email: nemo.noman.outis@gmail.com

Though this book is in part based on historical accounts, it remains a work of fiction. Though many modern groups and individuals have since adopted the names, titles, and symbols of this time period, any similarity between the characters and groups portrayed in this work and any modern individual, religion, or group is coincidental.

Cover art is derived from Adobe Stock Images. Extended licenses were purchased.

To the tyrants and monsters of my time.
Of which there are many.
You who see yourselves as wolves before the flock.
Beware,
For among the sheep lay mild-mannered dogs
Who will kill and die in their defense.

I, Anonymous

*George is of the saints whose names are justly
reverenced among men but whose actions are
known only to God.*

Pope Gelasius
The Canonization of Saint George

WHAT FOLLOWS ARE THE legends of old, as they are told, and
the history, as it is known.

History records that when Rome fell, the western world
descended into darkness. We know little of the time that
followed the fall of that empire. The deeds of this age are
lost. What few records were kept, have, for the most part,
been destroyed by the decay of time and the fires of war.
However, there are truths passed down from that time that
neither flame, nor sword could destroy.

What is remembered, is that in a time of greed and
contempt, there were those who stood against the darkness.

At times, these heroes were victorious and drove the
armies of greed and destruction back to the shadows.
However, there were also desperate days when the forces
of evil ground the armies of justice to dust. Defeats that

left slain heroes, broken shields, and ruined nations in their wake. Yet those who survived the chaos kept the stories of the brave few alive.

Their legends have echoed through the ages.

This is why all have heard of George the Dragon Slayer, King Arthur, and the Knights of the Round Table. Their stories refreshed and renewed constantly over the centuries, while tyrants like Emperor Justinian and the Vandal King Gaiseric are forgotten by all but the footnotes of history.

It is the storyteller's sacred charge to keep such legends alive.

For when the mighty seek to smudge the heroes out of history. When the chronicler and the journalist record more lies than truth. It falls to the jester, the poet, and the playwright to remind people of the honor of courageous knights, the cruelty of tyrants, and the existence of monsters.

I write to preserve the legends of yesterday in hopes that others to come will record the legends of today.

For tyrants are feared, then reviled, and soon forgotten. Yet, for as long as men and women tell stories, legends will never die!

I am Outis, I am No Man, I am Nemo.

I Anonymous, to the tyrants of today and to the tyrants of tomorrow deliver this warning, passed down from ages long ago. Beware the eagle, the lion, and the bear. For the valiant will resist you.

LOOK. EVEN NOW ... THEY ARE COMING FOR YOU!

Prologue

Ambrosius Aurelianus

Valley of Annwn
October 31st 456 AD

All the settlements were brought low with the frequent shocks of the battering rams; the inhabitants... both priests and people, whilst swords gleamed on every side and flames crackled, were together mown down to the ground ...
Some of the wretched remnant were consequently captured on the mountains and killed in heaps. Others, overcome by hunger, came and yielded themselves to the enemies, to be their slaves forever, if they were not instantly slain ... Some repaired to parts beyond the sea ...
Others, trusting their lives, always with apprehension of mind, to high hills... dense

forests and rocks on the sea, remained in their native land, but in fear ...
That they should not be utterly destroyed, they took up arms and challenged their victors to battle under Ambrosius Aurelianus. He was a man of unassuming character, who, alone of the Roman race, chanced to survive in the shock of the storm ... To these men, by the Lord's favor, there came victory.

Gildas Sapiens, 542 AD
De Excidio et Conquest Britanniae

AMBROSIUS AURELIANUS HAD BEEN a hunted man his entire life.

He had been hunted as an infant by Roman assassins for the crimes of his grandfather Constantine. Then by the Cambrian King Vortigern for the simple inconvenience of his existence. Now, the Saxons hunted him.

For years the Saxons had ravaged the island of Britain. Plague and war had drained the Romano Briton's strength. Now, there was no army, nor fighting force of consequence, with the power to resist the invaders. Nor were there any tribunes or captains to lead such a force had it existed.

All that was left was Ambrosius, the last vestige of the old Roman aristocracy in Britain, and a few desperate rebels willing to follow him. However, these were refugees, river folk, and woodsmen. There was not a fighter among them.

And, what was he?

His mother might have been a princess once, but the woman he remembered had not lived in a palace. She had been the wife of a wool merchant. Ambrosius was his father's son. He had been a shepherd, a hunter at best... he was no warrior.

True, he protected those hiding in the wilds, as best he could, because what else do you do when you find starving women and children in the woods. For this, he was hunted. However, by fortune, fate, or perhaps the will of God, he had eluded his enemies for years.

Now, need drew him to the dark valley of death. Here he hoped to find the last men on the island with the means and the skill to break the Saxon lines.

Walking through the mist down into the valley below, he yelled out. "I come on an errand of justice, driven by a matter of oath, for my home and land,!"

"Only those who seek death come to the Mists of Annwn," a rough voice said ahead of him.

"I... I seek the soldiers who fought under Emperor Constantine the Third," Ambrosius stuttered, mustering his courage as he forced himself to walk forward.

"Then, you seek the dead. Go search the mud of the River Rhine or the ditches of Hispania. That's where you will find them. The Romans have left this island, their cities lie in ruins. Rome is gone, it will never rise again," the voice said.

"I was told that some who had crossed the channel with Constantine had returned. That they might be found here."

"Constantine's bloodlust and greed for power dragged all who believed his lies to darkness and death. He is dead and beyond further justice. Why seek you deserters? There is no one to pay you any bounty for our heads. Or do you come seeking vengeance for crimes committed before you were even born? Leave this place! Let the dead rot in peace." The speaker said as three riders in black Roman armor came out of the mist.

They were old men, but their mounts were young and strong. The giant beasts chomped at their bits in a way that indicated the violent temperament of horses bred and conditioned for battle.

The leader of the trio wore no helmet. He was bald, scarred, and grizzled from years of battle, and on his harness hung a string of human scalps, the grizzly trophies swaying in the damp breeze.

Ambrosius heard the soft twang of arrows being nocked to bowstrings in the fog as the two mounted guards leveled their lances at his chest.

"From the scalps on your bridle, I take it that you are Respendial, King of the Alani and Sarmatian tribes of Britain," he said, mustering his courage before the fearsome trio.

"I am a king no more, and I go by the name Riothamus now. As I have said. This is the valley of the dead. To come here is to seek death. Leave this place or join the dead," the scarred horse lord said, turning his mount back towards the mist.

"I would hear your story," Ambrosius said.

How badly he wanted to hear that story. Needed to hear it. He wanted answers. Answers to questions he had asked his whole life.

Why did his homeland now lay in ruins?

Why had his parents been slaughtered?

Why had his grandfather left Britain a hero, only to fail and fall?

For almost a century, the Sarmatian and Alani auxiliaries of the *Ala Petriana* had defended the coasts of Britain against foreign raiders. Their massive Scythian warhorses the only cavalry in the West capable of breaking the shield walls of the Saxon infantry.

Yet, how did men who for generations drove their mounts against Saxon shields and Pictish spears, in defense of a land

and people not their own, end up deserters hiding in the hills?

There must be a reason!

"My story!" the man said, wheeling his horse around to face Ambrosius. "You come to this valley; you know my name. Therefore, you must have heard the story. We are traitors, murderers, and deserters. We are those who abandoned our oaths to commander, empire, and land. Those who turned on our comrades, slayed our brothers, and returned home while others marched on and died. These crimes curse us. They bind us. As they bind our families and all of our blood."

Ambrosius was suddenly very aware that, as he was, it would take no effort for these men to kill him.

Yet, was that not the reason that he had come?

"I often wonder if the men who crossed the channel with Constantine would rather have returned to their homes as well. Perhaps they died regretting that they'd ever left this island in the first place. I think if they had returned, we would be happy to see them now," he said burying his fears.

"If you seek a ghost, seek him elsewhere. You will find no peace here among the faithless."

"I do not come seeking ghosts. I come seeking horse and sword, and men to wield them!" Ambrosius shouted into the mist.

The black-armored veteran wheeled his horse and charged, knocking Ambrosius to the ground as he brought his lance down an inch from the younger man's face.

"You wish to know my truth. For honor and justice did I swear to war, for mercy I turned traitor, and for a life with my family, I gave up my crown. For this, me and mine are condemned to live out our days as oath breakers and deserters. I left my home once to defend the Roman Empire against the invaders and perhaps to see the idiot Emperor and his sycophants brought to justice for the evil they, out of vanity and greed, knowingly committed, and for the untold suffering, they in their arrogance unknowingly caused.

"In the end, however, I found myself fighting women and children to satisfy the greed and ambition of a power-hungry glutton. Thus, in the cause of justice, I turned on men, who I had marched and bled beside, in the defense of the enemy. For this, the whole of Britain scorns us!" Riothamus yelled before slumping his shoulders in resignation. "Leave and do not return. Not all are given such mercy," he said, gesturing to the skeletons hanging from the trees that stood testament to this fact.

As the horsemen turned to leave, Ambrosius called out, "I can hold your oaths fulfilled. I can pardon you for your sins against both this land and the empire."

"None but the Emperor and God can do that."

"I am Ambrosius Aurelianus, grandson of Emperor Constantine by his daughter, Princess Elen. I am going to fight the Saxons. Alone if I must. Join me! Fight for us. Defend this land and its people, as you once did and I will hold the oaths you made to my grandfather fulfilled. Win back your honor!"

Riothamus stopped but did not turn. "I should have known. You look like him. In the beginning, that is. In the end, he grew fat, and he grew cruel."

The older man stared off into the mist, as if looking back in time.

"The Empire was under attack. Goths and Huns were pushing into the west, driving the Vandal tribes before them. Most of the refugees were just men and women trying to get their families away from the chaos. Not all of them though. There were those among them who sought plunder and conquest.

"The reports we received were horrific. Villages pillaged, civilians slaughtered, innocents raped and murdered by the migrant caravans. As soon as they found themselves among rich towns and fat herds, even the meek among the refugees turned their hands to rape and plunder.'

"We were legionaries of Britain. The best of the frontier troops. We had the power to act. We had the duty to act!'

"After we killed our generals for their inaction, it was your grandfather who united us. We all believed in him, the legions, the auxiliaries, even the tribal armies. With that mighty force, we crossed the channel.'

"For three years, we drove the Vandals back. A successful campaign. In the end, their king and their warriors were dead. All who were left were the wounded, the women, and the children. As we closed in on the last of them, the barbarians sent a single boy to parlay with us. That's how few of them were left.

"He was the dead king's bastard son, and a braver lad I never saw. He asked for nothing but mercy for his people. Constantine had his leg broken in three places.'

"Your grandfather was eager to move against Rome. All he thought of in those days was taking the imperial throne. It was an obsession with him, a sickness.

"I remember the boy lying there, broken, crippled for life. As he hobbled away, he was spitting curses. Promising to dismantle Rome brick by brick.'

"I thought of my own son here in Britain. I wondered if he would be the same in that boy's place. Would he have been as defiant before the fat Roman general, while grown man laughed and beat him? I didn't know what my boy would do. I hadn't had the chance to know him. He had been four when I left."

Riothamus moved his hand to his temple. It was only then that Ambrosius realized that the man was crying.

"When he ordered me to attack the caravan, I refused. I had not left my family, nor marched hundreds of miles to wage war on women and children. Nor had my men. So, Constantine sent in the infantry. Mostly Franks but some Britons. He was good about making sure there was some mix in the units. It kept everyone loyal.'

"It wasn't enough to just stand by. I couldn't simply tell myself that I had not done the deed. It was not enough. I was an officer of the *Ala Petriana*, sworn to ride to the defense of the defenseless. I had the power to act. I had the duty to act. I rallied the cavalry under my charge, and we attacked our comrades. We routed them as we had so many other barbarian brigands. We saved many innocents to our eternal credit. We killed many of our own to our everlasting shame.'

"After the battle, many of those under my command went south with the Vandals to the warm lands of Spain. But I returned along with many who still had families here in Britain. Had we gone south with the Vandals, we would have been honored as champions and heroes. Instead, we are hated and shunned. It was the choice we made."

"Where is your son now?" Ambrosius asked.

A haunted look crossed the scarred warrior's face. "He died along with his mother. The sweating sickness, a month before I returned. So many died in that plague that there wasn't even anyone left who could recall in what pit they had been buried. Only that they had died."

Looking back to Ambrosius the grief that had looked like it would fell the aging king vanished, replaced by a cruel smile. "I hear the Saxons will pay a pretty sum for your head."

Ambrosius took a step forward, ignoring the threat. "I never met my grandfather, nor my uncles. I was born after they left these shores, and I have lived my life in the shadow of their ghosts. I don't fight for Constantine or because of who he was. I fight because of who I am. I am only a shepherd, but I am also the last descendant of Roman power on this island, the last of the bloodline of the Roman emperors. I have the power to act, and so I have the duty to act.'

"Vortigern of Kent is rotting in hell. Slain on his wedding night by his Saxon bride. Her brother Hengist has reduced Londinium to ruins and laid waste to the country Vortigern paid him to defend. The sons of Cole Hen of the Wall now squabble over the scraps of their father's kingdom in the North. I am the last hope there is of forming any unified resistance against the invaders, and because of this, I am a hunted man.

"I wish this burden did not fall on me, but it has!" Ambrosius shouted, surprising himself with his own determination. "Too many have died that I might live—my mother and father among them. I do not deserve their sacrifice, but I must do my best to honor it. You and your men are my last and best hope. You're Britain's last hope," he said, watching as new figures emerged out of the mist.

"I have brave men who fight for me, but I have no knights. No officers of war. Those with skill in arms, who would fight for the cause of justice, are dead. Those I might pay to fight, had I gold or silver, are in the employ of the Saxon Kings.'

"The barbarians drive us to the sea. The sea drives us upon the barbarians! We are either to be killed or drowned. Neither death is pleasant. No death before one's time is pleasant. Men should have the right to die in their beds, with loved ones at hand, and words of peace spoken to them. There on their deathbeds they should pass their lands and unbloodied swords to their sons. God did not make men and women to die like animals in a slaughterhouse.

"Riders of Britain! The *Ala Petriana* is again called to arms! Fight for me, and I will hold your oaths to my family and to the fallen empire fulfilled. Fight for what you were.

If nothing else, fight for yourselves and your families, for if I can find you, believe me, the Saxons will too. I have no gold to offer you, no land. I don't even have a sword, only this ax. I offer it to you. Refuse me, and you might as well use it to fulfill your threat. I would rather you take my head than the Saxons," Ambrosius said, kneeling down next to the massive hoof of Riothamus' charger.

The old Roman cavalier seemed to consider the ax for a moment. He drew his sword and dropped its blade down into the soft earth, next to Ambrosius' head.

"You will need a sword. You may take this one I have others," he said before turning to those with him. "I ride out with this man. For oath and honor! For wrath and justice! Will any ride with me?"

Ambrosius looked up as the fog cleared. Only then did he realize that the whole time he had been standing in the middle of a village.

Out of the hovels and dugouts, they came. Aging veterans, carrying blades and plate. Some meticulously maintained, so that they shined in the autumn sun. Others wore tarnished mail and carried rusted swords. There were younger men and women too. These were dressed in leather armor and carried spears and longbows.

Ambrosius stood stunned as they assembled in short order. Silently, but with drilled precision, they saddled their horses. Not one mount less splendid than the one Riothamus was mounted on. Only when they were all assembled in full war gear did they let out the cry that would be echoed across the island.

"FOR OATH AND HONOR! WRATH AND JUSTICE!"

The cavaliers of Ambrosius would come to be known as The Hundred Knights. Riothamus would be their commander, a king once again.

For three years, they would fight against the Saxon armies. The war was brutal, with victories and defeats. Yet, The Hundred Knights always placed the defense of the people above any gains and never did they target the innocent. Until, at last, came the day when Ambrosius Aurelianus would rally the full strength of the Britons to a small hill in the shadow of an old Roman ruin.

On that desperate hill, they would face the full force of the Saxon armies. Against all odds, the Britons would be victorious, driving the enemy back all the way to the ruined gates of Londinium.

In the wake of the Briton victory, peace would be made. Borders would be drawn, and tributes would be negotiated.

Riothamus would remarry. To a young Briton woman with a love of war stories. Together, they would have a son. However, before his son had sen five seasons pass Riothamus, would die in Gaul, in the city of Aballo, while attempting to secure a military alliance between the Britons and the Burgundian Franks.

His son, Lear, would instead be raised by his godfather, Ambrosius Aurelius.

Ambrosius never married. He fathered no children of his own. He built no castle, nor would he even have a hall nor home. He would never be crowned king.

The man who had spent his life fighting to preserve his people's freedom would die twenty years after the battle of Badon Hill in a stranger's bed. With him would be his knights and his pregnant younger sister, the fair Lady Pendragon. And as he lay dying, Ambrosius gave to Riothamus' son the same blade the young man's father had dropped at his head all those years before. And so would come the time of the Hard-Won Peace. The time of Lear, Lord of the Hundred Knights and High King of the Britons.

Chapter One

Gwenivier of Cameliard

Badon
June 8th, 543 AD

The King of Cameliard, had one fair daughter,
and none other child
and she was fairest of all flesh on earth,
Gwenivier, and in her his one delight.
For many a petty king ere Arthur came
Ruled in this isle, and ever waging war
Each upon other, wasted all the land;
And still from time to time the heathen host
Swarmed overseas, and harried what was left
And so there grew great tracts of wilderness
wherein the beast was ever more and more,
but man was less and less, till Arthur came.
For first Aurelius lived and fought and died,
and after him King Uther fought and died,
But either failed to make the kingdom one ...

... Arthur yet had done no deeds of arms
but heard the call, and came.

The Coming of Arthur
The Idylls of the King
Alfred Lord Tennyson 1859 AD

IT HAD BEEN THREE days since Gwenivier and the armies of Cameliard had left their ships, to join with the forces of Camelot.

For those three days, Gwenivier had watched Arthur ride ahead of her alongside the one-armed wizard Merlin. The grizzled druid never allowing the new king to stray more than a few feet from his side.

Gwenivier had never trusted Merlin. She did not have her father's blind faith in the priests of the old religion. Rather, Gwenivier worshiped the earth goddess, as her mother had taught her, in private ceremonies on hills, in oak groves, and by sacred springs. As far as she was concerned, the druids, with their pantheon of dark gods, were all scheming bastards.

Merlin certainly seemed to have an obvious vision for the role of the next queen of Camelot; a quiet figurehead who would sit by Arthur's side and do absolutely nothing. If Gwenivier had any say in the matter, the wizard would be very disappointed.

However, establishing herself as one of Arthur's inner circle was proving more difficult than she had expected.

She had offered advice on the campaign, only to be ignored.

She had volunteered to lead an advance scouting party. A proposal that had been rejected outright.

Even was she to simply try to ride up alongside Arthur, she soon found herself edged out by Merlin, Bedivere, and even her own father.

All too soon, they started to come across evidence of the Saxon advance. Burned-out farms and abandoned villages. However, they also saw the signs left by those who were already fighting the invaders.

At almost every crossroads there were Saxon heads piked on broken spears. Sword arms hacked off and hung from the trees. The message was obvious.

The Britons would fight.

To this end, someone, or Gwenivier suspected a few someones, were making quick work of picking off the enemy scouts and raiding parties. And Gwenivier had a good idea who those someones were.

Everywhere, there were signs of them. Cryptic runes carved in the trees. Camouflaged campsites that you would ride right past unless you knew what you were looking at. Heavy ruts in the tracks made by riders on large horses moving at speed. All of it pointed to the Rangers of Lloegyr.

She had pointed this out to Arthur and his captains, only to have her opinion dismissed out of hand. Her husband-to-be and the morons holding his leash had been quick to point out that the Rangers didn't come this far west. Even her father hadn't backed her up, and he knew the signs of the Rangers' work as well as she did. Yet, he too had accepted Merlin's theory that the bushwhacked Saxons had been picked off by local militia. As if a peasant band would be able to ghost multiple Saxon raiding parties without losing a man.

"The wondering rogues are not wanted in Camelot, and they know it. This is a country of order and kings," was all that Merlin would say.

It was true that the Rangers were outlaws and fugitives who operated almost exclusively in Saxon territory. Though

they might at times ally themselves with the kings and
lords of the borderlands, they held to no law but their
own. Still, the rangers were also one of the most effective
military forces in Britain, maintaining a constant watch on
the borders of the Briton lands.

True, Camelot might not want them, but the Rangers
wouldn't care. *Honor without Renown* was the oath and fate
of every Ranger. They didn't care for rewards or songs. They
would come simply to kill Saxons, avenge the dead, and if
possible protect the people.

The only one who acknowledged her opinion had been
Arthur's knight commander Lancelot. He'd been the one
to point out that there were those on whose behest the
Rangers would come west.

Even Gwenivier hadn't gone that far. The Bertilack lords
of Caer Celemion would never come to the aid of Camelot.
There was too much history there. Too much bad blood.

Or so she'd thought.

Then, her cousin, Gawain, had arrived with news that
George and his father were mustering the Briton forces
at Badon. The look on Merlin's face when he heard King
Urien's message had been priceless. Even now, as they
approached the Roman ruins of Aquae Sullis, the druid
looked as if he had bitten into something rotten. She might
have enjoyed that more had her own feelings not been such
a jumble.

It seemed that Owen, the chieftain of the Lloegyr Rangers,
had sent word across the West Country and the Old North.

Gwenivier knew well that this name was but an alias.
Owen was the name used by George Bertilack when he
warred beside the Rangers. A thin screen used to avoid
the actions of the partisans from coming back on Caer
Celelmion. Had Arthur not come to Cameliard himself,
George's messengers might have reached Gwenivier's

father's door first and saved her all the trouble of the current engagement.

Or maybe not. With his father's death, Arthur was now king of a rich and powerful kingdom. Since the loss of Cameliard's colonies in the Orkney islands, her father was now perpetually short of coin. An alliance with Camelot would solve many of her kingdom's problems.

Yet, like everyone, Gwenivier had a past. Her past even had a name. When he was the Prince of Caer Celemion, he was known as George. When he was in the wilds, he was known as Owen, or noble-born. However, neither of these titles fit the man George had become. Over the past few years he had changed. No longer was he the mild-mannered prince, or the unassuming ranger. No, since the Orkney's George had become dark, and brutal; the Black Knight born again.

It had been over a year since Gwenivier had last seen him. As she'd ridden on, silent and forgotten by the men, she had tried to tell herself that it didn't matter that George would be there at the end of the road.

After all, she was marrying Arthur. Despite the fact that her husband-to-be had barely spoken to her since she'd been informed of their impending nuptials.His proposal, or rather lack thereof, still set her teeth on edge.

She had walked in from a day of hunting with a string of birds and rabbits, and there had been Arthur, Merlin, and her father. Seeing Arthur, she had rushed to greet him, leaping into his arms like the maidens do in stories. For the past year, she had become something of a fixture at Camelot. Thus she had assumed he had taken the time to personally deliver an invitation to some festivity or another. She had looked forward to enjoying the hospitality of the Pendragon's Golden Hall.

However, to her surprise and horror, she was told that Arthur had not come with an invitation but a proposition.

She couldn't believe Arthur had gone to her father and arranged the marriage before so much as speaking with her.

In hindsight, she should have beat him black and blue right then and there.

However, she never got the chance, for as soon as Gwenivier had been informed of her imminent marriage, the conversation quickly moved from weddings to war. In short order, ships had been readied; warriors and levies summoned. Within a day, the warbands of Cameliard were sailing south ... and Gwenivier was as good as wed.

She had tried to appeal to her mother. But the queen had been too occupied with her own sobbing. She had dried her eyes only long enough to screech that it was Gwenivier's own fault for breaking off her engagement with George to "whore around" in Camelot with Arthur.

To say her mother had taken her breakup with the Prince of Caer Celemion badly was an understatement.

George's father Urien had grown up with Gwenivier's parents. That is, before he had gone south to carve out his own kingdom in the forests of Caer Celemion. Gwenivier had long suspected that her mother's feelings for Urien might be something more than that of childhood friends and allies. The queen's determination to play matchmaker between her and George had always seemed more personal than political.

It wasn't that she didn't like George. He was nice, charming, capable; but he was George. He was her friend, and her feelings for him were hardly romantic. She wouldn't go as far as to call him her brother, since that would be disgusting... but still, choosing George felt like settling. That is, until she'd needed him and his knights.

Cameliard's wealth came from their maritime colonies. Wheat and silver from northern Ireland. Fish and pearls from the Haberdines. However, none of it compared to the wealth that they had received from the Orkneys. For only on the remote northern islands could one find walruses. Slow and ugly as the creatures were, their tusks were worth more than their weight in silver. Control of the ivory trade had made her father one of the wealthiest kings in the islands.

This wealth however had brought enemies. Hungry for plunder, the Viking Geats had sailed out from their frozen lairs to seize the wealth of the Orkneys for themselves. Her father had naturally sought to retake the islands.

Gwenivier's people had faced invaders before. It was they who had drawn the line in blood where the Romans would build their wall. Camliard's army was formidable. However, they lacked the heavy infantry and shock cavalry required for fighting on open ground. Unlike Briton knights of the south, who rode heavy Sarmatian-bred mounts, the small Celtic ponies of Camliard were too weak and small to break apart the dense shield walls of the Geats.

Despite her father's wealth and influence, it had been no easy thing to find allies willing to send their heavy horse across the water. After all, these armored knights were, in many cases, the only thing holding the Saxons at bay. Camelot might have had horsemen to spare, but they were no close friend to Cameliard in those days. And Urien of Haustdesert made it clear that neither for love nor treasure, would he risk his own kingdom's security by sending his horsemen to the Orkneys. This said, he had agreed to have his riders patrol the borders of Cameliard in Leodegrance's absence. An honorable compromise but hardly what her father had hoped for.

For Gwenivier the campaign had been her chance for fame, adventure, and reputation. She had been trained to ride and wield a blade. She could drive a chariot with reckless speed that few men would dare. However, since she was a woman, her father had decided she would be left at home.

Gwenivier, however, had not been thwarted. Urien might not be willing to risk his army, but not all the defenders of Caer Celemion answered to the Green King.

Having been supplied mounts and weapons by King Lear during his reign, the Rangers sported strong horsemen and skilled archers. Many of the partisans still remained loyal to the memory of the former High King. They had even gone as far as to declare his grandson their chieftain.

Therefore, when George of Caer Celemion came to Cameliard, the Rangers came with him.

It had been all to easy for Gwenivier to lead the half-drunk prince out of her father's hall and into the glens near the fortress.

"Will the Rangers be staying with you while you're here?" she'd asked, already knowing the answer.

"Most likely. The Rangers are laying low this season. The Saxons are fighting amongst themselves again, and Cedric is threatening to take his frustrations out on civilians. Worse, he also seems to have come into some treasure. He's placed a price on the Rangers. Fifteen pieces of silver for every Ranger's sword arm. If we operate with that sort of heat, all we will do is bring down death on the common folk," George said.

"I hear he'll pay double for one Ranger. He wants both the hands of the chieftain Owen. They say he can fight with either hand, so Cedric wants them both. Thirty pieces of silver, how biblical," she said, placing her hand against his.

"Would you like me to teach you how to do it?" he asked, smirking.

"Please, no one can fight like you. Anyways, we don't have time," she said coyly.

"We have all summer," he replied, leaning forward until his face was inches from hers.

"I won't be here. I'm going with my father to the Orkneys," she said, pulling away.

"What? I assumed your father would leave you in command?"

"Stay at home and take in the harvest? While others win glory and renown?" she snarled.

It had been a lie. However, if she could secure George's, and more importantly his Rangers, assistance in the campaign, she had every expectation that her father would agree to let her join him. Her father would have taken her thirteen-year-old cousin to war if the girl could have secured the service of a troop of armored heavy horses.

Looking at the stricken disappointment on his face, it was obvious that George had expected to spend his time in Cameliard with her. No doubt playing lord and lady in her father's hall.

He would patrol the borders, battling the enemies of their kingdoms. All while she would manage the home and hearth. No doubt, while her mother sat around knitting and picking out names for her future grandchildren. When her father returned, she and George would have been married.

She would grow old and boring; forgotten before she was even dead.

It was what her parents wanted. It was what George had wanted. However, Gwenivier refused for that to be her fate.

She remembered how she had leaned into him. Pressing herself against his side, before purring in his ear, "You could come with me."

At this, George stood up. A dark look crossed his face as he spoke, "Is that why you brought me out here? You want me to go against my father's orders and bring the riders of Haustdesert to the Orkneys with you? Even if I would, they wouldn't do it. My father's orders are clear. Our forces are to remain on this island. That way, they can return south to defend our own lands if need be."

"I'm not asking George of Haustdesert for his da's army. I'm asking Owen for the Rangers of Lloegyr."

"The Rangers are not mine to command," George answered sharply.

"You are their chieftain."

"A title bestowed on me out of respect for my grandfather, and to honor the partisan's alliance with Haustdesert."

"Maybe in the beginning, but you've since earned the title. That's why so many followed you here," Gwenivier said with a flattering smile.

"A chieftain is still not a king. I have no right to ask them to fight your father's war."

"Then, don't ask them. If you came with me to the Orkneys, many of them would choose to follow you of their own free will."

"It's not their fight."

"What do you think the Geats will do once they secure the northern islands? Do you think they will be content there? Of course not! They will come south and join Cedric. You think the Saxons are bad? The Northmen have warriors who aren't even human anymore. They corrupt themselves with dark spells and potions until they become nothing but demons in human shells. You can help turn them back now or fight them later when they sail south. That is your choice," she said, leaning up against him, before softening her tone. "Come on! It will be fun. You and me, taking the fight to the invaders."

"Lovers on a rampage?" George asked hopefully.

"To ruin or glory," she whispered before kissing him.

Three days later, George and sixteen Rangers boarded the ships that sailed north. Gwenivier had been with them.

Only later would she realize what she had done. The Geats were cruel and brutal, worshiping dark deities of fire, blood, and shadow. Those who fought them on their terms grew dark as well. With little more than a smile and a sweet promise, Gwenivier had led George right into the maws of hell, where only monsters survive.

Perhaps it would be kind to say that George had been a reluctant monster, but he had become one nonetheless. Gwenivier could not shake the feeling that both man and monster had come to hate her for bringing him to that place.

As the momentum of the war turned against them, the Cambrians' and Britons' only hope for survival, let alone victory, had become reckless brutality.

In the South, the Rangers had dealt justice with the hope of fair peace. However, In the Orkneys there was no justice to be had and no peace to be hoped for. Two years they spent trapped on that island, set upon by the forces of the Northmen. In the end, there had been monsters on both sides.

That war had changed George, and not for the better. True, there were others to blame. Certainly, Grendel bore his share of responsibility for what George had become.

She shivered as she remembered the giant they had found, chained to the oars when they'd seized the enemy fleet. Grendel's skin had been nothing but scars bound tight over slabs of muscle. His lips, nose, and face had been cut away so that he looked more like a living skull than a man. However, the former slave, knew the Northmen well. He knew their myths and beliefs, and he knew how they fought. George had struck an instant bond with the man. That is if there had still been a man under all the scars and hate.

How many days had she watched as George and that troll-man plotted and planned their brutal stratagems?

Long had the Britons practiced psychological warfare against their enemies, as the Celts of old had done against the Romans. In Caer Celmion Urien had marked out his borders with the skulls of his dead enemies, and his men were famous for painting their faces with glowing goblin-green moss. However, in his time George would adopt even darker tactics.

He took to skinning the skulls of those he killed, and hung the scalps from his bridle as his great grandfather had. As the campaign progressed, men began calling him the Black Knight, or sometimes the Angel of Death, as he wore two human skulls impaled on the shoulder spikes of his armor.

George had refused to commit his troops to pitched battle. Choosing instead to find ways to draw out their lines and deny the invaders the use of their shield walls.

Together with Grendel, he would sneak into the enemy camps at night to slit the throats of the guards. Silently tieing ropes around the ankles of sleeping men, before using horses to drag his screaming victims off into the night. He would hamstring these prisoners like bait goats, drawing the man's friends and brothers away from the safety of their war camps and fellows. Easy pickings for the Pictish ambushers.

Each morning, the Geats would wake to find their dead hanging from the trees, their heads and sword arms hacked off. This was done to show that they had died without steel to hand. For the dark gods of the Vikings only granted paradise to those who died in combat.

Such tactics were effective, but they did not please her father or uncles. She could recall the nights they had raged at George, accusing him of everything short of cowardice. They had dreamed of wiping the Geats back into the sea in a single decisive battle. But in time, even they would admit the folly of this. Regrettably, only after her uncle Lot had lost half his men in such a foolhardy confrontation.

For Gwenivier's part, she had learned the thrill of the fight and had reveled in the rush. But there was no glory or acclaim to be won in that war. The adventure soon lost its appeal, and she came to miss soft beds, warm halls, and the company of her ladies.

The campaign ended in disaster. Ten longships had come from the Danish stronghold of Heorot to reinforce the decimated Geats.

There had been nothing that they could do against such numbers other than evacuate. Those who had survived the campaign piled into leaking longboats and sailed for the coasts of Britain. Grendel had not come with them. He and the mute, blind girl that the troll called "mother," had taken a skiff east to sate their thirst for vengeance in the Northmans' homeland.

Of the Rangers who had followed George, when he sailed with Gwenivier, none returned but George himself.

She and the prince had parted badly. Gwenivier would admit that she was not without blame in that.

George always had a hard edge. She had known him capable of dark things, but until the Orkneys, she had never been afraid of him. Those islands had taught him to hate and there was no one more worthy of his hate than the girl who, for want of renown and adventure, had dragged him to hell.

Now, as she rode up the track, she saw him. His black armor was blood-stained, and he still wore the skulls on his shoulder guards and the scalps on his bridle. However, the face was not that of the man who had left the Orkneys with her. No, the man before her had the same easy smile of the George she had always known. The monster was gone, or it was at least dormant for the moment. Looking at him now, all she could see was the boy who had once sat with her on the clover, as he whispered sweet nothings in her ear.

"He always had to make things difficult, didn't he?" she mumbled to herself. Clenching her fists as she looked over to where Arthur was now waving to the cheering soldiers.

Chapter Two

Galahad of Corbenic

Badon
July 8th 543 AD

When Gwenivier beheld Galahad, she said,
"Truly, I dare well say that Sir Lancelot begat
him, for never have two men more resembled
each other in likeness. Therefore, it is no
wonder that Sir Galahad is of such great
prowess."

Sir Thomas Malory, 1485 AD
Le Morte D'Arthur

THE SOUND OF CHEERING men outside roused Galahad from
his prayers.

It troubled him that he found relief in that. Prayers had
once been easy for him.

George had left already. Tristan having sought him out during the sermon.

Galahad had considered leaving with them, but instead, he had remained.

Had it been important Tristan would have asked him to join them. He hadn't. Therefore, Galahad stayed, trying to decide exactly what he should be praying for. A task that was not as easy as it had once been. For he had discovered that the world was a far more complex place, than he had once believed.

Not that long ago, yet a lifetime past, Galahad had been serving at an abbey on the coast of Armorica. The same abbey where his mother had died giving birth to him. The same abbey he had grown up in, and the same abbey part of him had always expected to grow old and die in.

He could barely remember what that life had been like. Now he was a warrior. A knight. A captain in the Outriders. It was the life that God had thrust on him.

Who was he to question it?

Thus, on hearing the commotion, though the monk he had been bid him remain, the warrior he was hurriedly crossed himself and rushed for the door.

"What happened?" Galahad asked, grabbing one of the Outriders under his command.

"It's Camelot. Arthur has come!" the man answered, a look of relief showing plainly on his face. As if he had been a man dying of thirst and had just received a glass of water.

Galahad quickly made his way over to where Tristan and George were standing. Unlike the rest of the jubilant camp, the princes of Kernow and Caer Celemion both seemed to have mixed feelings about Arthur's arrival.

It wasn't hard to understand George's reaction. Caer Celemion and Camelot had been rivals for almost as long as the two kingdoms had existed.

As for Tristan ... Galahad glanced over to where Iseult was standing.

Tristan was here for his own reasons.

There had been a time when the affair between Tristan and the queen had bothered Galahad. He had made no secret of his concerns, both worldly and ecclesiastical.

He had lost track of how many nights he spent in prayer, sorting through his feelings about his friend's adultery. However, when Tristan had told Galahad his plan to elope with the Irish Queen of Kernow, Galahad had agreed to do what he could to help.

In the end, he found that he couldn't condemn them. Tristan and Iseult loved each other, mind, body, and soul. Even a blind man could see it.

How could God condemn a man for falling in love?

Galahad didn't know. He had never been in love. He had spent all his younger days, studying scripture. There was a time he could have recited the gospels from memory. However, now he could summon but one line to mind.

When I was a child, I spoke as a child, I understood as a child, I thought as a child: but when I became a man, I put away childish things. Corinthians 13:11.

Had he remained in the monastery, Galahad might have always remained a child, and as a child, he would have blindly condemned those he now called friends for who they were. *But who was he to condemn them?*

Judge not lest thee be judged! Matthew 7:1

Had Galahad not killed men? Did he not covet the love that Tristan and Iseult shared? Or for that matter, simply the love, and respect shared between George and his father, Urien?

Galahad, for his own part, to be sure did not honor, nor even respect, his own father, and the feeling was mutual. It was a sin he could not bring himself to repent for.

Let he that is without sin amongst you, cast the first stone.
John 8:7

Yet, despite his sins, Galahad found that he did not regret becoming the man life had made him.

The boy who'd left that monastery only a few years ago would never have dreamed of coming to befriend and respect a pagan such as Tristan.

Nor could that boy have looked beyond George's grizzly battle trophies, to see the crucifix behind them. No, before he would have seen only a savage, and never known George for the righteous and pious man he in fact was.

It was true George was a savage. He would be the first to admit it. He thrived on trouble and turmoil. However, it wasn't out of pride, or morbid eccentricity, that he mounted the skulls on his armor and hung scalps from his bridle. Rather, it was done to frighten those he fought and give hope to those he defended.

At his core, George was a good man, principled, righteous, and decisive.

Even so, it had surprised Galahad when the Prince of Caer Celemion had joined him at mass rather than attend to his men, horses, and plans. However, none of his men had so much as blinked when he had done so.

In the church, George had knelt down, reciting Latin prayers that he knew as well as any monk, before eventually drifting off to sleep in the pew.

There was a time Galahad would have seen that as disrespect. However, for days now, he had seen George doze only in snatches. Yet, in that church, in those prayers, in that holy place, the Black Knight had found peace enough to let his soul relax and shed its burdens. The man Galahad had become did not begrudge George his rest. For he could see it for what it was; the truest mark of the man's faith.

However, as he stood outside the church, watching the vanguard of Camelot approach Galahad could feel his own peace slip from his grasp, replaced by righteous anger, wrath, pride and envy. For there, riding next to the newly crowned king, was his father, Lancelot.

He clenched his fists at his sides, trying and failing to calm his temper. Galahad had been in Camelot for nearly two years and in that time he had spoken to his father on but a handful of occasions. None of those meetings had been pleasant experiences.

For his entire life he had heard stories about his father. He had lost count of how many pilgrims, refugees, and peddlers he had paid to recount him the tales of the First Knight of Camelot. Stories he now knew to be mostly lies.

It was those lies that had brought Galahad to Britain. The foolish urge of a sixteen-year-old boy, bored with life in a monastery.

The monks had not been eager for him to leave. However, there were conflicts brewing between the lords of Armorica, the church, and the Frankish Merovingian kings. The bishop hoped that Galahad might convince his father, to renounce the Arian heresies and return to reclaim his ancestral lands. Thus providing a buffer against Frankish expansion.

Crossing the channel, Galahad had fantasized about how that meeting would go. How his father would embrace him, renounce his heretical beliefs, and the two of them would return across the channel together, to reclaim their land.

He had been a fool.

Arriving in Camelot, Galahad found that his father had little desire or inclination to reclaim his titles. He had even less interest in being a father. Rather, Lancelot had made it quite clear that if he'd had his way, Galahad would have been drowned at birth, like an unwanted puppy. He had even gone as far as barring Galahad from the court of Camelot, lest the presence of his bastard son embarrass him.

Galahad had refused to return to Frankia in failure. Part of that was embarrassment. Part of it was fear. Growing up, every time he had failed to recite his prayers correctly or recall his scriptures with absolute accuracy, he had been caned. The first time a nun novice had smiled at him, he had been flogged. When he'd been caught kissing that same girl, a month later, the nuns had made him flog himself. He had not been eager to discover what penance they would demand of him for this failure.

Instead, he begged lodgings in a church cloister outside of Camelot. That was where Tristan had found him.

"You are Galahad, the son of Lancelot du Lac?" the Kernish prince had asked him one day as he had been on his way to prayers.

"Not according to him," Galahad had answered morosely. "But yes, he is my father."

"Can you ride, wield a shield, and blade?"

"Yes." He answered, honestly. As a boy two of the brothers at the monastery, a pair of former bandits who had found religion, had taken it upon themselves to train him in the methods of combat.

"You are bloodied?" Tristan had asked.

"I've killed men, if that's what you're asking. Two years ago, pirates laid siege to the monastery. I served in the defense," he answered, kneeling down in the pew and reciting the psalms.

"He teacheth my hands to war, so that a bow of steel is broken by mine arms.

Thou hast given me the shield of thy salvation: and thy right hand hath holden me up-"

"I am Tristan of Kernow," He said. "There's a group of Irish raiders who are troubling the monasteries along the coast. Most of my men are followers of the old faith. I need a Christian to ride with us. Someone who can deal with the monks without the customary hour of them bemoaning us our heathen ways. What say you?"

"I... I don't know what use I would be to you. I have no armor. Just a staff and dagger? "

"We can get you a shield and gear. Can you use a bow?"

"A sling. I'm good with a sling," Galahad had offered.

"That will work," Tristan said nodding. "A sling can be more fearsome than a bow in the hands of someone who knows how to use it. Let's go see the armorer."

At the time, Galahad had thought it charity. However, he had been too desperate to be proud.

The lord armorer, Caius, hearing who he was, had offered Galahad a shield with the insignia of house *Du Lac*. However, his father had arrived to voice his outrage at the idea of a bastard being issued his livery.

Tristan had objected, arguing that bastard or not, Galahad was entitled to carry the insignia of his father's house. However, Galahad got the impression that the argument had less to do with him and more to do with the two captains' mutual dislike for one another.

It had been Galahad who ended the dispute. "My lords, there is no need to argue on my behalf," he said, picking up a plain, whitewashed shield, and walking over to the armor's bench. Dipping a large paintbrush deep into a bucket of crimson paint, he had drawn two thick, intersecting lines across the white laminate.

"If my father here on Earth feels shamed by my carrying his name and mark, then I shall bear the mark of my father in heaven," he'd said defiantly. Then, fearing that a lifetime of tears might choose that moment to escape, he had rushed from the room.

Galahad had worried that without the prestige of his father's name and crest, Tristan would no longer desire his service. However, Tristan had been genuine in his desire to have a Christian knight ride with his primarily pagan troop.

He had needed someone who would be accepted by the bishops and abbots of the parishes along the western coastline. A warrior monk bearing a red cross on his shield had suited this role quite well.

The Archbishop Dubricius especially had taken a liking to him. Through his patronage, Galahad had been able to equip and support himself and his men-at-arms in the manner of a landed knight. This, in addition to some luck, had allowed him to rise quickly through the ranks of the Outriders.

As Arthur's procession approached, Galahad nodded to the archbishop riding next to Arthur. It seemed that the bishop was in competition with the high druid Merlin to see who could ride closest to the young king. However, if either got any closer, all three would be forced to share a saddle.

Galahad quickly moved up next to where Tristan, George, and King Urien were standing.

He smiled as Lancelot, glared down at him. Galahad felt a sick feeling of pride at that. The rare occasions where he could force his father to acknowledge him always felt like a victory to Galahad. No one else noticed. For all eyes were on Arthur.

As the procession stopped Sir Bedivere shouted, "Presenting the Overlord of the lands of Camelot and the Dumnonii and Rightwise High King of all Britons. Arthur Constantine Pendragon."

"May God and His Son, Our Savior, Jesus Christ, look on our King with favor this day. Amen." Archbishop Dubricius said, shooting a victorious glance at the very put-out-looking High Druid Merlin.

The druid looked ready to say something, but George stepped forward putting an end to any further heraldry.

"Arthur, I am glad to see you. We've been scouting the area ..." his voice trailed off as his eyes landed on the red-haired figure coming up beside Arthur. "Gwenivier! I'm so happy to see you! I sent word to Cameliard, but I feared it wouldn't make it on time-"

This time, it was Merlin who stepped forward to speak.

"The forces of Cameliard have not come on Haustdesert's behest. Princess Gwenivier is to be married to High King Arthur tomorrow, to honor this coming battle. Thus shall the gods of land, sky, blood, and water grant us victory over our enemies," he said, glaring back at the bishop.

However, the ecclesiastical pissing match, between the bishop and the druid, seemed to be lost on George. A dark look came over his face as he turned to Arthur. "I will let you get settled. Congratulations on your upcoming wedding, my lady," George said, nodding to Gwenivier before turning and walking away.

"What the hell was that about?" Galahad asked, to no one in particular.

"You don't know?" Iseult asked.

"Know what?" Galahad was confused.

"George and Gwen were engaged to be married. Like since they were children. She broke it off a year ago after George trounced Arthur in a duel and took Morgana from Camelot. I figured everyone had heard the story by now," Iseult explained.

"You should join us in the tavern more often. Listen to a bard now and then. Get drunk. Have a laugh," Tristan quipped.

Galahad looked up to where his father, Lancelot, was helping the Princess of Cameliard down from her horse. He noted how the knight commander's hand lingered on the curve of the future queen's back a moment longer than was strictly appropriate.

He found himself with the sudden urge to beat his head against a wall.

"Why bother with bards and jesters? After all, God seems to have a better sense of humor than anyone," the monk mumbled as he picked up his shield and headed back to camp.

Chapter Three

King Alba of Saline

Leptis Magna
July 8th 543 AD

Whenever those states which have been accustomed to live under their own laws and in freedom have been acquired, there are three courses for those who wish to hold them: the first is to ruin them, the next is to reside there in person, the third is to permit them to live under their own laws, drawing a tribute and establishing within it an oligarchy which will keep it friendly to you. In truth there is no safe way to retain such nations other than by ruining them,

and he who becomes master of a city
accustomed to freedom and does not destroy it,
may expect to be destroyed by it.

Niccolò Machiavelli 1532 AD
The Prince

The trek north had been hard on Alba.

There had been a time when he could have crossed the desert without even feeling fatigued by the end. Now, however, it seemed like every muscle and bone in his body ached. The constant pain making it hard for Alba to keep his mind off the pipe and bag of opium that sat in his satchel. Still, he willed himself to ignore the demands his mind and body now made.

He had not seen his daughter in five years and he would meet her with a clear mind. During the journey north, he'd been haunted by visions of the demon that now held his city in bondage. The beast that demanded his one last, and most precious treasure. To so much as think about the horror that resided under that blackened dome, had him fumbling for his opium pipe, and the sweet release it offered.

However, Kahina had told him she was under the weather. His head pounding, he had shouted and demanded that she produce his daughter. However, the witch woman had refused saying only that it was a feminine issue. This had left him with no recourse, and so the king had been left to sulk with his thoughts.

He realized that he could not deal the threat of the dragon directly. If he stood any chance of thwarting the Cult and their demon, he needed to clear the board. He could not fight the monster, the Cult, and the Vandals.

The blonde-haired girl was proof of a connection between the three. If he was to resist them, he would need to understand the nature of that relationship. He hoped that he could accomplish that here. Here he could meet with his former allies, Kaboan and Pudentius, and perhaps secure their aid. To what end he was unsure.

A thousand doubts gnawed at him. The dragon had known of Alba's plans to neutralize the Vandal threat and it had not cared. If the Vandals were the dragon's masters or even his tools, why not stop Alba from pitting the Romans against them?

Unless it somehow served the beast's ends for Alba to do so. But why ... the Cult thrived off fear. They traded in the currency of war. If he could neutralize the Vandal threat, then the Cult's power over his people would be diminished.

However, was it enough? If he rid the desert of the Vandals, would not others quickly fill the power vacuum? Ierna certainly seemed in a position to do so.

It was pointless.

Every time he tried to puzzle out some solution he always came to that same conclusion. One could not fight a god. Even if he could convince them of the truth, and he doubted he could, what aid could his allies realistically provide?

Pudentius served his imperial masters, he could do nothing without their blessing. As for Kaboan, for Sabra's sake the desert warlord might offer soldiers and support. Or maybe not. The dragon's voice was as clear in Alba's mind as when he'd heard it in the temple.

She is his soldier, and he will sacrifice her to achieve his goals.

Alba knew the truth of the statement. Kaboan was a good man, but he had always been a warrior to the core. He would sacrifice any piece on the board if it meant victory—even the queen. The beasts final whispered warning still echoed in his mind.

No. He could not trust Kaboan.

All Alba could do it seemed was wish for it all to be just a bad dream. Inevitably though, he would feel the aches in his weakened joints. That pain bringing him back to reality.

He could try to buy as much time as he could, but his time was running out. Yet, Alba still could not shake the feeling that he was missing something.

Too tired to consider strategy, and too sore to care for fear, he walked over to where Ierna was dismounting.

"Why?" Alba demanded.

"Why what, my lord?" Ierna said with the obsequious tone the man always used when addressing the king.

"Save your flattery. I am not your lord! You have never served me," Alba snapped.

"Yes, the dread god told me he had spoken with you. You should be honored. Few alive have had the privilege of seeing his full splendor," Ierna said.

"I ask again. Why? Why bother to negotiate with Sergius or any of the Byzantine lords? What's the point of fighting off the Vandal remnant? Why bother with this charade."

"Are the Vandals not a threat to Saline?" the desert mystic asked.

"I would say the demon living in that monstrosity you call a temple is the greater threat."

"Gurzil is no threat to Saline. On the contrary, he wishes only greatness for your city and our people."

"Then, why doesn't he simply destroy the Vandals?"

Ierna paused for a moment, giving an indifferent shrug. "You must trust in Gurzil."

Trust me ... It was the mantra of every liar ever to walk the earth.

"I don't," Alba said, glaring at the high priest.

Ierna spun on the king, the obsequious mask he had always worn before was gone, replaced by a disgusted scowl. "Who are you to question a god? Would you have him wipe your ass for you? The power of Gurzil is not unlimited. We must all do our part to secure the coming empire, and you will play your part, or you and your people will suffer the consequences. Keep to your assigned role, and the Lord Gurzil might allow you to keep your daughter for a little while longer. Who knows, she might even outlive you."

Alba looked at the man before him, seeing him for who he was for the first time. Even after Sabra had fled the city, Ierna had always acted the loyal servant, even when they had both known it was a fiction. With one hand, Ierna would take the legacy of his house and the freedom of his people. Yet with the other, he offered flattery and vice.

Apparently, the time of flattery was gone. Surprisingly, Alba felt the loss of it keenly. His last shred of royal dignity ripped away with a look and an unkind word.

"Come, you have business with the Byzantines," Ierna said, glancing over Alba's shoulder to where the purple banners were fast approaching.

There had been a change in the high priest over the past few days, ever since the night Ierna and his cultists had left the camp with no explanation. Since then, the desert mystic had seemed to lash out at everyone around him. Something had not gone to Ierna's plan. Yet, Alba could not determine if that was a good thing or not.

There were pieces moving on the board that the king could not see, and it seemed the only way he would reveal them was to keep playing the game.

He wished his wife were still alive. She had been the planner, the plotter, the chess master. He had no doubt that, was she still here, the queen could have come up with a plan.

He couldn't shake the feeling in the back of his mind, that feeling he used to have when he would play chess with his wife. She always won, and he never learned how. He would make a move. The one intelligent move left to him. Then, once his hand left the piece, she would make hers, and he would always find himself in checkmate.

He tried to put the pieces together. The Vandals, the Byzantines, the wars, the famine, the Cult, somehow it was all connected. Somehow, all of it was tied to the dragon.

But that was impossible. *How could one being wield such power?*

Alba now lacked both the skill and the will for this game.

His head was pounding, and his insides churned. He tried to focus. The pipe in his bag beckoned to him. Offering the sweet peace of oblivion. He pushed such thoughts aside.

Walking over to where Kaboan was meeting with the Byzantine delegation, he listened as the Amazigh warlord and Tribue Pudentius reviewed the security arrangements for the meeting.

"Eighty negotiators, attendants, and guards should be more than enough," Pudentius said.

"You have twice that many soldiers in the palace," Kaboan countered.

"To be fair, it is our palace, and we have serious doubts about some of your companions," the Byzantine tribune said, glaring at Ierna as the priest came up behind Alba.

"You're the ones who need our grain," one of the Amazigh nobles snapped.

"We need each other," Pudentius muttered before turning to Alba. "My Lord, Sergius will swear to your safe conduct on the gospels as is customary, and your people can remain camped here. It will be far more comfortable to conduct negotiations over dinner and wine, do you not agree?"

"Agreed," Alba said with a nod.

"I would add one condition," Pudentius said before the delegation could disperse. "Given the nature of these negotiations, it would be preferable if the priests of the Temple of Gurzil do not attend the banquet."

"That is unacceptable!" Ierna spat.

"It's a simple request," the tribune countered.

"Your lord would swear by his gospels, but we are barred from having our priests present!" said a man Alba recognized as Prince Stastiga. He was the son of Mastigas, a warlord who controlled the regions north of Saline and a well-known supporter of the Cult of Gurzil.

"Enough. We agree, but we have conditions of our own," Alba said, smirking as Ierna sputtered in indignation behind him. "You have a number of Vandal auxiliaries in your garrison forces, many of whom we have cause to believe are agents for the outlaw Gunthuris. We would ask, given the nature of our grievances, that they not be present."

"How can you tell which ones are the Vandals? The pale-skinned bastards all look alike," Stastiga sneered.

"The ones who speak German and are covered with tattoos are the Vandals," Kaboan said, glaring at the surly prince. "And, Pudentius, don't try anything cute. I know it wasn't you who sent that slave girl to pump me for intelligence, but if I see any more Vandal servants with vegetable dye covering their ink, I will take it personally."

"I'll make sure it's understood. So, we have terms?"

"We have terms," Alba said, nodding to the other lords.

"Then, I will inform the *Dux*, and we will await your arrival," he said, looking over the king's shoulder before adding. "And, My Lady, I hope we will have the pleasure of your company."

"I wasn't sure I would be welcome," said a smooth feminine voice behind him.

At the sound, Alba wanted to turn and look. However, he couldn't find the courage.

"You were specifically asked for. I believe my lord might wish to apologize for his outburst at the hunt."

"Then, I will attend. I wouldn't want to miss that," the feminine voice laughed.

"I will inform the Dux. My Lords... Princess," he said, nodding respectfully.

As the delegation dispersed, Ierna moved towards Alba, obviously wishing to voice some objection, but Kaboan silenced the priest with a glare.

Only after everyone else had left did Alba finally work up the courage to turn around.

And there she was, the very image of her mother, dressed in red silk, her long braids falling behind her back.

"Sabra," he said in a whisper, afraid anything more might cause the image before him to disappear.

Chapter Four

Sabra of the Lauathai, Crown Princess of Saline

Leptis Magna
July 8th 543 AD

In the province of Libya, there was a city called Saline. And by this city was a lake, wherein was a dragon which threatened to envenom all the country if not appeased ... So it happened that many of the land were then delivered unto the dragon, until the lot fell upon the king's daughter, whereof the king was sorry, and said unto the people: "For the love of the gods take my gold and silver and all that I have, but let me have my daughter." And they said "How sir! you have made and ordained the law, and our children be now dead, and you would do the

*contrary. Your daughter shall be given, or else
we shall burn you and your house." When the
king saw he might do no more, he began to
weep, and said to his daughter, "Now I shall
never see you married."*

*The Golden Legend
Compiled by Jacobus de Voragine, Archbishop
of Genoa, 1275 AD*

SABRA'S HEAD WAS POUNDING. As she walked out of the tent,
she winced against the pain that shot through her with every
step she took. However, she'd hidden too long.

It had been five years since she'd seen her father, and she
refused to miss this chance.

It took her a moment to recognize him. He had looked so
old and gray when he had been speaking with the tribune.
He was not like she remembered him. Yet still, there was no
mistaking him.

As she approached, Kaboan turned to the other nobles.
"My fellow lords and princes, we should prepare for tonight,"
he said, ushering the nobles away, leaving father and
daughter alone for the first time in years.

"Sabra?" he asked, turning to face her.

"Yes, *Baab*," she said, choking back a sob.

"By the gods. You're all grown up. You look so much like
your mother," he said, and tears leaked out of the corners of
his eyes as he fell to his knees. "I'm so sorry," he said as she
ran forward to him.

She couldn't imagine how frail he had become. It looked
like it would take only a solid breeze to knock him over.

"It's ok," she said, her voice thick in her mouth. "I'm here now."

"Look how beautiful you are," he said, hugging her close. "It's really you? It's not some trick?"

"Yes, it's me," she said, tears welling in her eyes.

"I have something for you." He pulled out a linen-wrapped parcel, opening it to reveal a beaded white silk dress.

"It was your mother's." he said.

Sabra was stunned. It was a beautiful dress. However, it did seem a little odd for her father to give her what was obviously a wedding dress.

"I always hoped to see you wear it. Perhaps to the banquet," he said, reaching out to her.

As he did so, Sabra saw the red flash of silk in his sleeve.

"Is that mother's scarf?" she asked.

"Yes," he said, pulling it out and placing it around her neck. "I've kept it with me ever since the day you left Saline."

Her father's hands moved to the necklace hanging around her shoulders. "This is interesting. Where did you get it?"

"It was a gift," she said, not sure what else to say.

She didn't understand the necklace herself. It was the same one the prince had given her in the dream world. However, she could not, for the life of her, understand how it now sat around her neck. She had meant to ask Kahina about it, but hadn't yet found the time.

"Quite the gift," he said, touching the chain of gold, diamonds, and amber. There was a question to that statement, but she ignored it.

It just seemed surreal. Here she hadn't seen her father for five years, and he was asking about a necklace. A necklace that by all rights should not even exist.

"Have you converted to the Christian faith?" he asked, running his fingers down to the cross pendant.

"No, it's just a necklace. I pray to the idols mother gave me, when I came of age. I worship neither the Christian God nor the demon Gurzil." she answered sharply.

"Times change, daughter. Gods change with them."

"No, it's men who change. You made a deal with the devil."

"I am more aware of that than you know," he said, a haunted look coming over his face.

"Then, resist it," Sabra said, reaching out to touch her father's arm.

When had he become so thin?

"You are so much like I was when I was your age," he said, touching her face proudly. "But I fear this enemy is beyond our strength."

His eyes moved back to the necklace. "An interesting piece. I have not seen its like for a long time."

"You have seen something like this before?" she asked, her breath catching.

"Not as impressive as that, no. But the manner of twisting and molding the gold to look like rope and knots ... it's a style found in the islands of Britannia in the Far North. Legends say that the islands are made of metal. The people who live there are known to be masters of war. Lions of men."

"You have met them?" she asked, her heart quickening.

"Only stories. The Britons were among those who fought the Vandal tribes after they invaded Gaul and Hispana. Vandal parents still frighten their children with stories of monsters that attack out of the mist and sneak into camps to slit the throats of sleeping men. 'Eat your vegetables, or the Britons will come for you.' It has been a long time since merchants came here from that far north. Some claim those islands have sunk beneath the seas. Others say that the last descendants of the old Roman emperors still rule there, besieged by the barbarian tribes." He pointed to the jeweled chain. "This has come a very long way."

Sabra stood there stock-still. The knight from her dreams was a Briton. Hearing it, she was sure of it. She had heard the Vandal stories too. Lions of men. Warriors who would appear from the mist, and attacked in darkness.

The dragon's taunt echoed in her mind. *He fights monsters because he is one.*

Perhaps she needed a monster to fight a monster. *Was that why the dragon feared the Briton prince?*

Then again, if her father was right, then the prince was far away. In a land beset by its own monsters.

"A far-away island of fog and war. A harsh land that breeds the savage," she whispered to herself, remembering the dragon's words.

But then, she too came from a land of war and darkness. A land of evil men and blood-drenched sands.

She looked at the necklace. Perhaps the prince was not her hero, nor her monster. Maybe he came to her dreams so that she might see that she could be her own hero. Her own monster.

"We could fight it," she said quietly, almost to herself.

"What?" her father asked.

"The dragon, we could fight it. Together, we could gather the free tribes and defeat it."

"What do you know about the dragon?" the king asked, panic catching in his voice.

"It doesn't matter what I know. I know that it is afraid, and if it's afraid, that means it can be defeated. It can be killed. We can fight it."

"I have considered this course and found it hopeless." He said, lowering his eyes. "You cannot fight a god."

"But he's not a god. Gods don't feel fear," Sabra countered.

"The beast Gurzil fears nothing. Believe me, whatever he is. He feels no fear, no pity, and no remorse. He is immortal."

"But ..."

"No buts, we are not here for the dragon. We have business with the Romans. We must deal with them first ... that is why we are here. To see that our people are protected. Then, we can determine what to do about Gurzil."

"The Vandals, the Byzantines, the Cult, Gurzil, they are all connected. Can't you see that?"

"We will strike a bargain with the Byzantines and rid ourselves of the Vandal bandits. That will buy us time to deal with the dragon," he said. Yet, something in his eyes told her he was unconvinced. He was resigned to his doom. He just wasn't ready to admit it yet.

"You're a coward," she hissed. "You don't strike bargains with monsters."

"You're young. To the young compromise seems like surrender, and delay feels like defeat. However, there is a difference. As a ruler, you have to make hard choices. Kings and queens are privileged in many ways, but that is because in the end, we must be prepared to sacrifice that which we love most."

"Like you sacrificed me." Sabra said, tears wetting her eyes.

"I did not sacrifice you! That is why I am now a king in name only! The dragon cannot be defeated, but he can be survived. Our people will survive. I have seen to that."

"Thanks for the dress," Sabra hissed, as she stood up to walk away. "Kaboan will listen to me. He believes in me. I am his soldier."

"Yes, I see that," Alba said quietly to himself as he watched her move across the sands. "You are most definitely his soldier. That's why in the end, he will sacrifice you for his cause."

Tears rolled down Alba's cheeks, but no one was left to see the old king crying in the desert.

He had no one. No queen. No guards. No soldiers. No attendants. He was alone. A king no more.

"What can I do? I cannot save you. I wish your mother had lived. She would have known what to do. It is sad that I will never see you married. What a queen you would have made. But now, the dragon will take you, and there is nothing I can do."

Sabra did not hear him, but when she finally decided to look back he had already pulled out his pipe.

Chapter Five

Morgana an Spyry

Haustdesert Castle
July 8th, 543 AD

They be of foolish fashion, O Sir King. The
fashion of that old knight-errantry. Who ride
abroad and do but what they will ... Such
as have no law nor king ... Being strong
fools, and never a whit more wise. The fourth
always rideth armed in black, a man-beast
of boundless savagery. He names himself the
Night and oftener Death and wears a helmet
mounted with a skull

Alfred Lord Tennyson 1859 AD
The Idylls of the King

MORGANA LAY ON GEORGE'S bed with her face pushed into a pillow. The room smelled of horse, saddle leather, smoke, and weapons' grease. She would hardly call it a pleasant smell, yet it was his smell. Even though it was only a year and a half since she had met the Prince of Caer Celemion, it felt like she had always known that smell.

She first laid eyes on George at her mother's funeral feast.

After nineteen years of being a prisoner, her mother, had finally decided she'd had enough of Uther's cruelty. Ending her life with a cold razor in a warm bath.

In truth, the feast was not to honor her mother's passing. Rather, it was that she had chosen to take her life two days before the Spring Equinox celebration of Ostara. However, there were those who wished to honor the late queen and pay their respects. They were happy to lie to themselves and act as if the feast was in her honor, and Uther was happy to indulge their delusions.

Facing what had only been bad choices, Morgana had chosen a somewhat reactionary response. She had distilled a bottle of poison and hidden it in her dress. Her plan being to poison the wine at the feast.

If she had been successful within a day, most of the inner court of Camelot would have been dead. It was a terrible plan, almost certainly doomed to fail. However, her other choices required either submission or direct suicide.

She couldn't remember how, but during the feast, she had made it to the wine jugs. She was about to tip the toxin in and seal her fate when the Green Lords of Caer Celemion arrived.

Morgana had, of course, heard of Urien Bertilack and his son, George. One could not live in Camelot and not hear of them. Warriors who painted their faces with glowing goblin green. Men who moved by night and attacked out of the mist.

To listen to her stepfather, Uther, talk about them, the woodsmen of the forests of Caer Celemion were worse than Saxons.

Urien had reportedly come from the kingdom of Cameliard in the North, half a decade before Morgana had even been born. Back then, he had been no more than the leader of a group of cattle bandits, operating out of the forests in the border region, raiding both Saxon and Briton lands alike. That was until Creoda and Cedric had made the mistake of landing their Saxon army on his doorstep.

The way she had heard the bard tell the story, Creoda and his Saxon army landed south of Caer Celemion, believing the lawless border region would put up little resistance.

When he landed Urien sent the Saxon king a message asking him to meet him at a nearby river ford. Believing the outlaw wanted to ally himself with them, Creoda and his best men had gone to meet him. Expecting to parlay, they didn't even bother to dawn armor before leaving. However, Urien had not been interested in an alliance. Rather, with only a handful of horsemen and archers, the outlaws from the North held the Saxons at Itchen ford. Yet, this desperate defense of the crossing had only been a diversion. For while Urien and his best fighters held the ford, the rest of his men had cut around the Saxon lines to burn their undefended fleet.

Seeing the smoke from their burning ships, the invaders broke ranks. However, as they rushed back to defend their fleet they had been ambushed by Lord Maleagant and the Cavaliers of Gore. In the end, with their king dead and fleet destroyed the surviving Saxons had been forced to flee overland into Kent.

In recognition of his service to the Briton cause, King Lear had granted Urien Bertilack hereditary title to the lands of the Caer Celemion and made him the Warden of

Haustdesert. The former outlaw would even marry the High King's youngest daughter.

Morgana liked the story, and she especially enjoyed the bright shade of red her stepfather had turned when he heard it. It was a pity the bard had been so caught up in his tale that he totally failed to read the room.

Uther beat the minstrel half to death with his own lute before having his Saxon executioner, Bors, chop the man's head off.

It was sad. He played well.

Uther's list of grievances against the woodsman was extensive. Top of the list, however, was the fact that Urien had sided with Lear against him when he tried to usurp the title of High King. Uther had claimed victory after the war was over. However, the Pendragon king had never been able to establish a solid hold over the whole of Lear's former dominion.

Since then, Camelot and Caer Celemion remained bitter rivals. Therefore, the last thing she expected was to see Urien and George Bertilack come waltzing into the great hall like they owned the place.

Disappointingly, they had forgone their iconic, glowing green warpaint. Instead, Urien had worn a simple, quilted tunic. While George and the two men with them wore tattered grey Ranger cloaks with branches of evergreen and mistletoe woven into the rough burlap fabric. They wore no gems, chains, or ornaments on their garb, only a simple silver star broach that held their cloaks around their necks.

The group looked altogether normal. They could have been anyone.

That said, their entrance wasn't completely uneventful. For they announced their arrival by throwing two squealing guards into the hall like sacks of flour.

"So, this is the great hall of Camelot," Urien had called out as he stepped over the brutalized guards as he entered the hall. "You know, I could have sworn I remember it being bigger."

"What are you doing here, Urien? I do not recall extending you an invitation to my Ostara feast. What business do you have bringing wandering ruf-" He stopped, and grit his teeth. Morgana's stepfather held the Rangers of the Lloegyr in contempt. However, many of his nobles and vassals were more sympathetic to the partisans.

"What brings the Rangers of Lloegyr to my hall?" Uther said, collecting himself.

"We have come to pay our respects to the late Queen Igraine, who was my mother's good friend, and to give our condolences to her son, Prince Arthur, and, of course, to her daughter, the Lady Morgana, now lawful Queen of the Dumnonii. I am George Bertilack at your service, my lady," he said, stepping forward and bowing to her.

That was how she met George Bertilack. The Black Knight of Haustdesert, Prince of Caer Celemion, Chieftain of the Lloegyr, Champion of the Orkneys, King Lear's last living descendant ... He had almost as many titles as she did.

Of course, mentioning Lear, Urien, George, his mother, or even wearing the color green in Uther's presence, were all excellent ways to meet the executioner's ax.

As far as Uther was concerned, he was the rightful High King. The fact few outside of Camelot agreed with him on that point annoyed him to no end.

Morgana had been at Camelot long enough to sour herself on the concepts of chivalry and handsome knights in shining armor. However, the man bowing to her was not in polished plate. He was genuine in his sympathy, and she had to admit there was something rather appealing about the boy in green.

He was young, yet old enough to have a full beard, that he wore cut close to his face. He was attractive, though hardly in the same league as the likes of Lancelot or even her half-brother Arthur.

However, at the time, George's hazel eyes and rugged good looks, had not been among her major concerns. For at that moment all the eyes of Camelot were on her. That is to say, on the girl holding a vial containing enough concentrated aconite to fell a herd of horses. Not knowing what else to do she put the bottle in her pocket before giving a quick curtsy.

"Thank you for your kind words ..." she said but fumbled over what to call him ... lord ... prince ... She didn't know, so she just stood there, like an idiot trying to figure out what he meant when he called her Queen of the Dumnonii.

Her father, Gorlois, had been King of the Dumnonii by his marriage to her mother. It was only at that point that Morgana had realized that with her mother dead Uther might well have planned on marrying her. It certainly would have helped strengthen his claim over the Dumnonii territories. That thought alone made her seriously consider downing the entire bottle of poison herself that very instant.

"Thank you for your words," Uther snarled. "But we buried my wife yesterday. You can leave now."

"Well, if we aren't standing on traditions of hospitality, then I'll just present to you the will, and we can finish our business here," Urien replied.

"What will?" Uther asked as he snatched up the parchment.

"The will of the Lady Igraine," Urien answered. "It was delivered to me two weeks past bearing her seal. It states that in the event of her death, guardianship of her daughter, Morgana, passes to the Wardens of the Green Woods, the

Bertilacks of Haustdesert. To be enforced by the defenders of the Britons, the Rangers of the Lloegyr."

"What is this? Some plot? You have your son name my stepdaughter, Queen of Dumnonii? A title she has no right to? Now, you come here to steal her away so that you have the pretext to annex my kingdom?" Uther stood, his face turning red.

Morgana stood stock still. *They had come to take her away*.

For a moment, her heart flew with the thought of leaving the court, but the ice-cold reality gripped her.

They wanted to take her away!

But she couldn't leave Camelot, not without her ... Her mind rebelled, refusing to register the next thought ... She just couldn't leave Camelot. Her mother had known the reasons for it all too well.

In hindsight, she could think of a dozen things she should have done that day. Things she should have said. Instead, she just stood there.

"I have come to honor the last wishes of the honorable Igraine," Urien answered, picking up an apple from the table and taking a bite. "And perhaps remedy a wrong I should have righted twenty years ago! I have come in peace, bearing a branch of holly," he said, tossing Uther his half-eaten apple as he held up the green branch above his head. "We come with no host of arms, leaving both our armor and tools of war with our mounts. We wish no quarrel. I have come in peace, on the holy night of Ostara, to honor the wishes of the dead. May the banshee queen strike dead any who raise hands or arms to oppose me in this endeavor."

Uther stood up, stomped down the hall, and swung open the great doors of the hall. "I don't hear any banshees, do you?" he shouted, looking out over the courtyard to where George's horse was tethered.

"Now that is a nice horse," Uther said, pointing to the giant white mare. "One thing I'll give that mad, old bastard Lear, he had good taste in horseflesh. Best horsemen ever to step foot in Britain, save for my oath man Caius, Butcher of Cent. Though perhaps past his prime he is still the hardest of my hard men."

"I was never Lear's equal, not even at my best. I was only ever worthy of being a pawn to be used against your grandfather's enemies," Caius said gruffly, nodding to George.

Uther turned red as a murmur of agreement went up amongst some of the knights of the court. Caius, like a number of the older lords in Uther's court, had served in the Host of High King Lear. He had only sworn fealty to the pendragons in order to protect his family and hold onto his lands following the High King's abdication after The War of Eleven Kings. Yet Uther was proud of these men's forced fealty, believing it somehow transferred the authority of the former high king unto himself.

Sensing the mood of the room shifting in a dangerous direction, Uther decided on a diffrent tact. "Tell you what. Since it is Ostara, I'll let you both leave here, without my stepdaughter, but with your lives. Provided that you make my son a gift of that horse."

"Over my dead body!" George shouted,

"That is the idea, boy." Uther chuckled.

George's hand had moved to the blade at his belt, but Urien stopped him. Only Morgana was close enough to hear what the grizzled, elder Bertilack had whispered to his son. "Remember what I told you on the road. Whatever happens, you get yourself and your men out of here alive."

George hesitated before nodding slightly.

"Why don't they joust for it," Urien offered with a smirk.

"What!" Uther shouted, his face turning red.

"Our sons can settle this in the old way. My son has a lance and armor on his saddle, and your son is also reported to be skilled with horse and lance. The first to yield takes the loser's horse. That way, we will have a mount for the lady to ride when we leave here. Unless, of course, your son isn't up for it. You could always choose a stand-in. Perhaps Caius since you say he is your best on horse?"

"Sixty winters is a little old for one to engage in such sport. Though even was I younger I would still never fight the son of Cordelia," Caius answered, taking a long swig from his cup.

"In that case. How about your Frank, Lancelot? Rumor is he has some skill," Urien Bertilack said, pointing at the handsome mercenary.

"No. I accept. I will fight," Morgana's half-brother shouted, standing up.

"You will do no such thing," Uther snarled. "Arthur, this is a matter of state."

"Father, these men have insulted us in our own hall. I will meet their challenge."

"My king, the prince is correct," Eldol said, standing up. "These two young men are princes; they will be kings and neighbors one day. Arthur has accepted George's challenge on fair terms. He must honor it."

"Well, we must postpone this fight until your son has appropriate seconds to assist him," Uther argued, pointing to George.

"No need," Urien said. "He needs but two attendants. He has three including myself."

"We have civilized rules here woodsman," Uther hissed. "Only the son of a king can serve as second in a duel between princes. And you, Urien, are no son of a true-born king."

"True, my father was a woodcutter. I have never been ashamed of that. However, may I introduce Mynyddog, third son of Mwynfawr of Gododdin and Caradog, the son of King Braith of Cymry."

"Gododdin is my sworn vassal," Uther bellowed.

"Yet I serve the Rangers of the Lloegyr. Therefore, my allegiance is to my chieftain and the cause of the Britons," Mynyddog shot back.

Watching Uther's face turn that wonderful shade of red, Morgana had to resist the urge to jump up and down and clap.

It was so perfectly done. In that moment, Uther's own paranoia was defeating him. She knew that her stepfather would have liked nothing more than to order his knights to cut the four men, before him, down where they stood. But he couldn't!

The Bertilacks were making it very clear that if there would be war between the kingdoms of the Britons, the first battle would be fought right there in the middle of Camelot. Uther couldn't risk that fight. Not unless he was sure all the assembled nobles would be on his side, and how could he be sure of that when his champion was refusing to fight, and the son of his most powerful vassal state was standing there next to his sworn enemy?

It was all fluff, and showmanship. In the end, everything could be explained or denied. If Uther was to ask any of the men present, they would all claim that they would be the first to draw steel at the King's command. If he went to Braith demanding he explain his son's actions, the king of Gododdin could simply apologize and claim his son was nothing more than a young hothead.

But was that the truth? He would have no choice other than to accept them all at their word. Still he would have to wonder.

In his head Uther was seeing a full on rebellion!

"So, they ride today," Urien roared. "We still have a few hours of light left. Let us honor the goddess with some sport! What say you Camelot?"

No one was going to deny a chance to see such a contest, and soon, all the assembled lords and knights were banging their cups and knives on the table in agreement.

As soon as the Bertilack lords had left the hall, Uther had loudly demanded that everyone clear the room.

Most did so eagerly. Some obviously wishing to put as much distance between themselves and the angry king as possible. While others were hoping to secure good seats for the upcoming joust. Morgana, on the other hand had simply wanted to get away from the insanity that now seemed keen to consume her.

However, before she made it to the stairs Uther stopped her. So, she sat alone and forgotten in the corner with a bottle of lethal poison in her pocket, while Uther, Arthur, Lancelot, Merlin, and Bors did what they always did. They argued.

"You're a fool, boy. Do you know whose challenge you just accepted?" Uther shouted.

"Some border Ranger with delusions of adequacy. He's nothing but a thug," Arthur said, pouring himself a goblet of wine, but Uther smacked it away.

"That boy is no mere Ranger. He is the grandson of King Lear, which wouldn't matter so much if the man had lain down and died after abdicating like he was supposed to. But no! The mad, old bastard had to stick around for over a decade, hiding out in a woodland church while grooming his grandson to take his place. You heard those fools. Even as an old man, Lear was one of the best horsemen ever to stand on British soil, and by every account, that boy out there is better than he was."

"By whose account!?" Arthur scoffed.

This time, it was Merlin who spoke. "King Lot of the Orkneys, King Leodegrance of Cameliard, his daughter Gwenivier, the Dane Lords of Heorot, the Saxons of Wessex, the Rangers of the Lloegyr, several popular bards, the Faye court of Avalon, the gods themselves. Should I keep going?" Merlin asked in the condescending tone that only the old high druid could get away with.

"Question," Lancelot asked. "For those of us who weren't born on this damp, little island, who exactly is this Lear, *un connard*? I have never really gotten a solid answer on that."

"No one. A mad man," Uther snarled, knocking another wine goblet across the room.

"Lear un Riothamus was the last duly elected High King of the Britons," Merlin answered. "The only son of the man who led the Alani-Sarmatian *foederati* back when the island was still under Roman control."

"Who cares who his grandfather was! Urien, the boy's father, is nothing but a base-born bandit," Uther bellowed.

"King Lear's royal historians said otherwise. They insisted he was in fact a distant cousin of Vortigern, and a direct descendent of Cole Hen." Merlin argued.

"And since when do druids put faith in the written word? That royal lineage is nothing but lies, made up so Lear could justify giving a cattle reaver title to an entire kingdom."

"King Vortigern of Kent. You mean the idiot who flung the doors of the island open for the Saxon brothers, Hengist and Horsa? The one everyone on this island curses to the deep hells every time they stub their toe? Why would we be worried about the people siding with his kin?" Lancelot said, taking a swig of wine.

"There are those who believe that Uther made a similar error five years ago when he allowed you and your Frankish rabble to settle in sacred Britain," Merlin hissed.

"My Frankish rabble, as you call them, is all that stands between you and Saxon axes, old man," Lancelot growled. "Would you prefer us to leave?"

"You can't leave. You're Arian. You step foot in Frankia, and the Merovingians will burn you at the stake for heresy," Bors replied idly, while sharpening his ax.

"And what will the Saxons do if they got hold of you? Should we take a trip to the other side and find out?" Lancelot shot back.

"I don't think I'd enjoy that," Bors said soberly.

"Enough. Vortigern might be infamous among the common people, but Lear was not Vortigern. Ambrosius Aurelianus himself left the high kingship to him," Merlin said in an obvious attempt to put an end to the pointless posturing.

"He left it to Lear's troop of a hundred armored horsemen. The Pendragons are the rightful heirs to the throne of Constantine. I am Ambrosius' nephew. I am his blood!" Uther screamed.

Not even Merlin was dumb enough to point out that Uther hadn't even been born when Lear was crowned. The succession traditions in Briton were more screwed up than most places. However, Morgana was pretty sure that there was no kingdom on Earth where people believed in leaving crowns to unborn fetuses.

"Where was his hall?" Bors asked.

"Hall? Lear never had a hall!" Uther yelled. "He started building one in the ruins of the old Roman temple, but he never finished it. Rather he preferred to travel around the country with his knights, demanding hospitality from whatever petty kings or lords were unlucky enough to lie in their path," Uther spat in disgust. "He was nothing more than a madman leaching off nobles who were too terrified of his personal guard to do anything about it. In the end, even his own daughters realized he had to be stopped."

"Two of his daughters. Princess Cordelia sided with her father," Merlin corrected before looking over to Uther. "Only Goneril and Regan fought against him, and a certain young Pendragon lord was all too happy to assist them in their plots."

"You try my patience, Merlin. That slut Cordelia was no princess. Her father disowned her. Only that low-born peasant out there was willing to marry her. No one expected they would fight for Lear. That asshole Urien turned what was supposed to be a simple matter of deposing a mad king into a full-blown civil war."

"That might be how the nobles see it," Merlin countered. "The common people remember it differently. Lear and his knights kept the Saxons, Picts, and Irish at bay. Moreover, he kept the Briton lords leashed. He gave the Britons thirty years of peace. No other king has managed to do that since the Romans."

"That scruffy horsefucker. You're saying the people would rather have him as High King?" Arthur yelled.

Merlin turned towards his protege, "What I am saying, is that George and Urien Bertilack are not men to be fucked with."

"Well, in that case, they're here now. Why don't we just kill them?" Lancelot offered.

"Bit late for that," Bors said flatly.

"What was that, Saxon?" Lancelot said. "When the king needs an executioner's advice on matters of court politics, he will ask."

"And when I need a *forligerwif* to tell me my business, I will ask!" Bors said quietly. "If the plan was to kill them, you should have done it when they were here in the hall.

Now, they are out there in the courtyard; armed, armored, on horse, and inside the castle."

"The Saxon's right," Merlin said. "Right now, four of the most seasoned and skilled warriors in Britain are out there, ready and willing to fight."

"They will be no trouble. We will use my men," Lancelot replied.

"Your men are currently in the front row of the lists waiting to see the day's unexpected sport. Do you think no one will notice if you pull them away? Lords, knights, and commoners from all over Britain are gathered outside. Can we be absolutely sure all of them will support you if you attempt to assassinate George and Urien Bertilack on the challenge field?" Merlin asked Uther. "Or is it more likely someone will scream 'Long live the Lear,' and the entire affair will descend into a bloodbath? A bloodbath that will likely end, with you, Uther, hanging as raven bait from your own gatehouse. For decades to come, bards will compose funny songs about the treacherous King Uther who lost his whole kingdom to four men in a single afternoon."

"How dare you speak to the king in this manner? Who do you think you are?" Lancelot yelled.

"Shut up. He's right," Uther said, looking at the chessboard that he kept by his throne. "It's check. There's nothing to do but make the move left open to us."

"Father, I'm sorry. It was all a trap, wasn't it? I... I didn't see it," Arthur babbled.

"No, you walked right into it. As did I. Well, you wanted this fight. Go get ready. Lancelot, see to him," Uther said, waving Arthur away before turning to Morgana. "Go change your dress. Black doesn't suit you. Not for a joust. Something white, I should think."

Morgana got up and carefully moved towards the door. She knew Uther well enough to be afraid at those moments when he attempted to appear kind or tender.

"And have the ladies do your hair." He yelled, knocking over his chessboard to send the stone pieces scattering across the room. "Make sure you look your best for the damn forest lords!"

Morgana had fled to her rooms, and quickly put on her best white woolen dress. However, when she went to get her mother's gold torque and pearl earrings, her ladies stopped her.

"Uther said not to wear any jewels, and asked us to braid a sprig of mistletoe in your hair," Enid said placing the jewelry box back in the dresser as, Tega and Diyvi came barging into her room.

Enid was arguably the kindest of the three girls. However, it seemed everything that she heard made it to Uther's ears. Morgana couldn't blame her for that. Her father had launched a failed coup against Uther a few years prior, and Enid had been a "guest" of Camelot ever since. However, the girl was far too clever about her spying to be considered an innocent.

"She looks like the virgins that the druids of old used to sacrifice to the great dragon," Tega quipped and giggled as Enid braided Morgana's hair.

"Quiet! Don't even say such things," Dyvi said, crossing herself. "I think she looks beautiful. Like she's going off to get married."

Dyvi was a pretty peasant girl who Uther had his henchmen snatch after seeing her in the market. Pretty blondes, after all, were not something one came across every day. Morgana might have pitied the golden-haired dim-wit if she wasn't such a pious, little bitch. For, at the mere mention of magic or the old ways, Dyvi would dissolve into a bumbling mess. Praying and crossing herself, as if the Hordes of Hell themselves were coming for her. And, the pagan Tega never missed a chance to bait her.

"Really, the mention of the dragon requires you to cross yourself, but you're ok with the idea of marrying one of the border savages? The woodsmen of Caer Celemion, I hear they're worse than Picts," Tega said with a mocking shudder.

"Well, you would know, wouldn't you?" Dyvi muttered.

"What's that supposed to mean?" Tega hissed.

"You pagans are all the same, aren't you? All devil and dragon worshipers. With your spells, potions, and orgies," Dyvi said, glaring at Morgana's collection of herbs and glass bottles.

Morgana and Tega were both pagans. However, that's where any common ground between them ended. The spiteful, red-haired witch was Merlin's creature, and Morgana didn't trust her as far as she could throw her.

Tega smiled at the blonde-haired Welsh girl, like a ferret circling a rabbit. "Oh, don't worry, blondie, no one's going to invite you to any orgies. They wouldn't dare touch a single golden hair on your pretty, little head. Uther wants to keep those lovely curls of yours all to himself."

Dyvi's eyes went wide, wet with tears. "Burn in hell! Pagan slut!"

"Well, even in hell, my boobs will still be bigger than yours," Tega said, sticking out her chest to showcase her melon-sized breasts.

"All the better to fuck the devil with!" Dyvi hissed.

"Well, as long as he's a good lay."

Leaving her room, Morgana tried her best to outpace the chattering magpies who had been assigned to spy on her.

As she stepped outside, she was stunned to see the castle packed with spectators. In the time it had taken Morgana to do her hair, the entire castle courtyard had been transformed into a festival. A great bonfire even burned in the center of the square.

Morgana looked over to where Arthur was being helped up onto his horse. He was dressed in full chainmail with a thick boiled leather cuirass. His gold inlaid helmet was polished to a mirror shine and, in his hand was a heavy kite shield emblazoned with the red dragon ensign of Camelot.

It was Dyvi's appalled gasp that her drew her away from the humorous spectacle of watching her half-brother being mounted onto his warhorse. Looking over she saw the girl had bowed her head and was muttering an endless string of prayers. It took only a moment to see what had her so distressed for, across the field, the Black Knight, had arrived.

George wore a set of black laminar armor and a heavy Roman-styled helmet. Both looked like they were left over from the invasion of Julius Caesar. However, while the metal was dented and scratched, his gear appeared well maintained. This, however, was secondary to the fact that he had about thirty or so human scalps hanging from his horse's bridle. Along with two bleached human skulls mounted on the iron spikes of his shoulder guards. The black knight in front of her no longer seemed the sincere and noble prince who had spoken to her before. Gone was the pleasant boy in green. Now fully armored, George's appearance seemed to say "Abandon all hope. Surrender now, or I will cut you down and feast on your soul."

It was intimidating. It was frightening. It was also hot... It was very, very hot. Given the way Tega was all but panting at him, despite her earlier comments, Morgana was not the only one who thought so.

She had to admit he had looked more comfortable in his armor than Arthur did. Nor did it take three squires to get George into his saddle. Rather, he simply gave a quick click of his tongue and tapped his horse's leg. The crowd gasped and clapped when, tame as a trained puppy, the monstrous mare bowed down to its knees to let George swing his leg over the saddle.

Morgana smiled as she watched her stepfather turn that wonderful shade of crimson he always did whenever the world wasn't working in the way he wished.

"Cheap tricks, my lord," Lancelot said comfortingly.

Uther glared at the Frankish knight as Morgana and her attendants took their seats in the stands below. As George rode up, she saw he was wearing a brand of mistletoe woven through the armor around his neck.

"My lady," he said, bowing his head with a smile.

She smiled back and made sure to play with her braid so he would see the mistletoe woven in. For a moment, she let herself remember back to the long-ago happy days when her father had been alive. Back when she'd been a proper princess, and knights had smiled at her all the time.

She hoped he would say something more. Instead, he just stood there looking rather lost and awkward, as her maids giggled behind her. She turned to tell the bitches to cut it out. However, before she got the chance, George spun his horse and rode off to take his position on the jousting line.

When both men were in position, Uther's herald, Bedivere, called out. "This duel has been called to settle a matter of honor. Each contestant will be allowed three lances and three shields. After these arms are spent, they may continue to fight with steel alone until one has yielded or one is dead."

"Ready, bucket head?" Arthur taunted from across the field.

George gave only a respectful nod in answer. As the flag dropped, Arthur reared his horse and buried his spurs to bring it to a charge. George, on the other hand, gave no thought to style. Bringing his mare to a full gallop down the track with no more than a hard tap of his heels.

"He's using an underhanded grip. Alani style. Gaining power on the strike in exchange for mobility and accuracy," Lancelot said. "Odd. The Rangers typically favor an overhand stance."

"Arthur will destroy him," Uther said confidently.

Morgana bit her lip, unsure of who she should be rooting for. She wanted nothing more than to see Arthur put in the dirt. But she couldn't leave Camelot! *Not without* ... These thoughts, however, had been interrupted by the clash of metal on metal.

Arthur was attempting a quick victory, trying to maneuver his lance around George's shield to strike his head. George deflected his opponent's lance with his buckler, while simultaneously breaking Arthur's larger shield in half with the precision with which a woodsman splits a log.

She heard Lancelot stand behind her. "That's impossible."

"Any idiot can split a shield," Uther countered.

"He used an active defense and attacked simultaneously with an underhanded grip. No one fights like that," Lancelot said.

"His grandfather Lear did. The Old King could fight with either hand. He often used both spear and sword at the same time," Caius replied from the seat below them.

"He's ambidextrous! Why did no one mention that before?" Lancelot snarled.

"Never seen the boy fight before," the old knight said, his eyes never leaving the field, as Arthur slowed down to grab a fresh lance from one of his attendants. George, however, didn't slow. Instead, he wheeled his horse in a teeth-shatteringly tight turn and came charging back down the track.

"Shit!" Lancelot exclaimed. "Get moving you idiot! This isn't the practice field," the Frankish captain yelled, and pushing past Morgana, he leaped down to the muddy field.

Arthur began his charge too late, leaving no time to build up his own momentum. George spilt Arthur's second shield as easily as he had the first but broke his lance in the process. For a moment, it seemed Arthur was losing control of his horse, but he still managed to stay in his saddle.

By this point, Lancelot reached the young prince and, with a whirlwind of speed, changed up Arthur's stance, moving his lance to an underhanded grip similar to George's. However, George had no intention of waiting for Arthur to finish his last-minute jousting clinic. Discarding his broken lance, he pulled a cavalry mace from his saddle and once again beat a fast charge down the track.

Lancelot quickly smacked the flanks of Arthur's horse to get the beast moving. However, unsteady and using an unfamiliar grip, Arthur completely missed his target. Dropping his lance, Arthur drew his sword. George, however, ducked away from the blade and spun to strike Arthur across the middle with his iron flail.

Arthur was pushed back, out of his saddle, landing hard on his horse's kidneys. In response to this unexpected indignity, the massive beast bucked and snorted, throwing Arthur into the mud.

Her brother's squires rushed forward. One grabbing his horse while Lancelot and the others surrounded the prince.

George ignored all this, grabbing his spare lance, before riding up to the downed Arthur.

There was a loud metallic CRACK as George's horse stepped on Arthur's fallen sword, snapping the blade in two with its iron-shod hooves.

"Does he yield?" George asked coldly, his lance pointed at the fallen prince.

"He yields," Lancelot said with a nod, and George casually took the bridle of Arthur's warhorse and hitched it to the pommel of his own saddle.

Morgana couldn't help but smile at seeing Arthur with his gold-inlaid armor all covered in shit and mud.

Then the bitches started screaming.

In retrospect, she should have expected it. Uther always had a plan. He never lost. He simply changed the game. She looked back just in time to see her stepfather give a slight nod to Tega and Enid.

"I saw her! I saw her!" Enid shrieked, jumping up and pointing at Morgana. "She spelled Prince Arthur's horse! I saw her!"

"She's in league with the dark fairy devils from the woods! Look, she wears their totem in her hair!" Tega screamed. "The witch tried to kill Prince Arthur!"

The entire crowd suddenly all turned back towards them as Dyvi, right on cue, fainted. Morgana barely had time to register what was happening before Uther bellowed, "Seize her! She spelled my son's horse! The witch tried to kill my son!"

The castle residents, their bloodlust whetted from the joust, now saw an opportunity for even more sport.

"Burn the witch! Burn the witch!" they began to chant gleefully.

Morgana would admit that she'd hardly been the most popular girl in Camelot. She could be a bit prickly and cold at times.

Ok, fine, she'd been a raving bitch!

Still, she had known these people since she was a little girl. For a moment, her brain refused to register that these people actually planned to burn her alive.

That reality came crashing home all too soon as hard, angry hands dragged her off the bleachers straight towards the roaring bonfire, that had already been so conveniently lit on the other side of the courtyard. Say what you will about Uther, you had to admire the man's attention to detail.

She attempted to rip free of the mob that bore her towards the flames, but what chance did one woman have against an angry mob?

Then, everything was pandemonium. Suddenly, she was dropped to the dirt, as the crowd ran for cover.

Looking up, she saw George on his white warhorse scattering the crowd. Extending his hand, he screamed, "Take my hand. Come on, let's go."

Thinking back, the entire experience of being rescued had ended up being far less romantic than it could have been.

George was sweating and stinking from the joust. His horse was attacking anything that came in kicking or biting range, including her. And instead of gently lifting her onto his saddle, like the knights did in the stories, George had roughly dragged her up onto the back of his horse like she was a piece of meat!

There was no poetry, no kind words, no kiss, not even a warning that she might want to hold on! No, he just turned and started barreling towards the gate, where his father and the other two Rangers were already making themselves busy beating the guards to pieces.

Morgana barely managed to hold on as they galloped out of Camelot, riding hard across the hilly farmland surrounding the castle. Only when Camelot was a speck on the horizon did they stop.

"Well, that didn't go to plan," Urien said.

"Sure, it did," George said with a laugh. "We are alive, free, and we even saved the princess. I'd say it worked out perfectly."

"You're seriously enjoying this?" Morgana asked.

"I like it when I win. Are you hurt?" he'd asked.

"No. I'm fine," she said. Her mind spinning. In the heat of the escape, she hadn't really thought about it. However, at that point she was acutely aware that she had no idea what these men actually wanted.

She thought about the dagger that still sat in her boot, but knew it would be useless against armored men.

George turned to his father. "We should move her to the spare horse," he said.

It took a moment for Morgana to realize what horse he was talking about. A new flash of panic came over her as she looked at the massive warhorse that had previously belonged to her half-brother.

Llamrei, as the warhorse was called, was a *Gwaed* stallion and stood nearly as tall as George's enormous mount. It was rumored that such horses were the product of breeding the giant Scythian horses of the East with unicorns of the legendary island of Avalon.

As the story was told by the bards, when Sarmatian mercenaries first came to the island of Britain in the service of Rome, one of their chiefs had a fair young daughter. Her purity and innocence drew the unicorns out of Avalon.

One by one, the princess had brought the best of her people's mares to breed with the great, horned stallions. These sirings would produce the giant horses of Britain. Warrior mounts strong enough to bear both armor and rider at speed. Brave enough to willingly charge through a line of shields and spears.

For years, the great horses had been the key to the Briton defense against the Saxons. The Britons called them *Gwaeds*, or The Bloods, and it was often argued that the bloodline of a Briton nobleman didn't matter, half as much, as the breeding of his horse.

In Morgana's opinion, the Saxons' name for the foul-tempered creatures was far more fitting. They called them *Heleoh*, or hell-steeds!

Sitting on one of the mammoth beasts was frightening enough with its master holding the reins. The idea of riding one herself was almost as terrifying as being burned at the stake.

Self-poisoning, burning alive, trampled under a two-ton war horse! What wonderful manners of death she had been presented with that day.

"I can't ride. I don't know how," she said at last.

"What?" George exclaimed, as if being able to ride a horse was a skill people were expected to be born with.

"I never learned. What of it! My father gave me a pony for my fifth birthday, and the damn thing bit me. Then, for most of my life, I was a virtual and, at times literal, prisoner in Camelot. For obvious reasons, they don't teach prisoners to ride horses. So, I never learned."

"It's too late anyway. We're out of time," Urien said, looking down the valley at the line of mounted Frankish knights coming in their direction. "We go to plan B. Split up."

"Hold onto me," George said, wrapping her hands firmly around his waist.

It was a surprisingly intimate thing to do with a man she barely knew. However, not even two seconds later, she was holding on for dear life, and intimacy was the last thing on her mind.

No one had bothered to tell her that Plan B was a heart-stopping gallop across Sarum plain, with the knights of Camelot right on their heels. As the horse bounced up and down Morgana's light wool stockings had been torn to shreds as they rubbed against the rough leather of the saddle. This left her bare thighs to take the brunt of the punishment.

The whole time, however, George was grinning as if this was the most fun he had ever had. Worse was that the damn horse seemed to agree with him. For her, the whole affair was torture. Had she any inkling of what she'd have to endure on that ride, she might have just said, "fuck it," and let them burn her. Eventually, she couldn't take it anymore.

"I need to stop!" she screamed, after finally losing all feeling in her legs.

"Not much farther. We're nearly there," he said, pointing to the massive circle of stones standing up on the plain.

She had heard of the great druid henge before, but she had never actually seen it. As they rode into the stone circle, George leaped from the saddle, before helping her down.

"What are we doing here?" she asked, as George sat down calmly. He had seemed oblivious to the enemy knights rapidly closing in on their position.

"We are going to negotiate. What else?" he answered, pulling out an apple and taking a bite.

"Here?" she said, looking at the circle of stones.

"The Henge is holy ground. No one sheds blood here, not unless they are stupid enough to want the attention of the *Aes Sídhe*," George replied.

"Arthur is Christian, as are most of the knights following us. You do know that, right? They don't give a shit about the old ways," Morgana countered.

"I'm a Christian as well. What's your point? Anyone who has spent time in these mists knows there are things out here that move unseen, things that are to be respected. To not believe in them is sort of like not believing in wolves. Sure, you can tell yourself that their howls are just the wind, but that doesn't stop them from eating you," George said. He pulled out a flask and took a long sip before offering it to her.

"So, now what?" Morgana asked with no small amount of venom, as she downed the bottle in a few large gulps. Her desperate need to dull her senses blinding her to the burning spirit as it moved down her throat.

"What do you mean? I told you we negotiate."

"I mean, what do you plan to do with me? Provided we survive whatever this is. Will I get held for ransom? Locked away in a dungeon? Or will it be marriage by rape in the nearest chapel, before being dragged back to the castle, to be raped again each night for the next twenty years?"

"I don't hold with rape!" George said darkly.

"Then, pray tell, what is your plan here?" Morgana said. "Why drag me from my home?"

"Drag you? I just rescued you from a blood-thirsty mob that wanted to burn you alive!" George said, somewhat put out.

"Only because you forced Uther's hand. I didn't need your help. I had everything under control," she said, her hand finding the bottle of poison in her pocket.

"A little gratitude might be in order. I'm risking my life here," he said.

"And who asked you to?" she snarled, angry and frightened.

"Your mother," he countered, grabbing her arm. As he did so, her hand came out of her pocket, sending the bottle tumbling down to break on the rocks.

"What is that?" he asked, reaching down, but stopped before touching it. Standing bolt upright his hand went to the blade at his hip. "That's wolfsbane!"

"It's perfume," Morgana lied.

"Like hell it is, I know what wolfsbane smells like. The Picts use it for hunting bears. No woman wears wolfsbane perfume. Not one who plans to live more than a few hours anyway," George snapped.

"Fine. If you must know, before you came barging in uninvited and unwanted, I had planned to poison the wine. If it weren't for you, half the castle would have been dead by now, and all would have been right with the world!" she shrieked.

"That's the worst plan I've ever heard," George said. "Lemmings have better plans than that!"

"Really, and this plan of yours is so brilliant? Admit it; you don't even have a plan. You're just making it up as you go along. Relying on dumb luck and your fancy horse tricks."

"I have plans and backup plans, princess!" George objected. "So far, my plans have worked out just fine, and don't change the subject. We are still on the question of why you were carrying around a big bottle of bear poison!"

"You're right, but what you really should be asking is whether or not it's a good idea to force a marriage on a woman who has skill with such lethal elixers," she snapped.

George sighed. "I have no intention of forcing you to do anything, my lady. Nor do I have any plans to marry you at this point. Right now, that would be an open declaration of war with Camelot. Which happens to be something that I am working quite hard to avoid."

"All evidence to the contrary. Why are you doing this? What do you have to gain other than war?" she asked.

"My father is doing this because he regrets not helping your mother twenty years ago after Uther killed Gorlois. My reasons are more complicated."

"Then, do explain quickly. I don't think we have very long to live," Morgana said, looking at the horsemen heading in their direction.

"For about twenty years now, the Briton kingdoms have been at peace. The Saxons stay in the East. Uther and my father hate each other, but neither will risk open war. It's a bad peace, but it's peace. Now Cedric is massing an army in

Kent. There will be a war and that will change everything. Especially since both me and Arthur have legitimate claims to the High Kingship.'

"Uther forced your mother to marry him over the objections of both the church and the other Briton lords. Keeping both of you at Camelot was a symbol of his strength. Proof that he was strong enough that he need not give a shit about anyone else's opinion. Your mother's will gives us the pretext to take you from Uther. By doing so, I correct an injustice and show that the Pendragons are not as powerful as many might presume."

"So, I'm a pawn in your bid for your grandfather's throne? You do realize Uther considers himself to be High King. He will destroy you for even considering this course of action."

"If Camelot had the power to destroy Caer Celemion, then Uther would have done it already. He tried and failed back in the civil war. That attempt ended in nothing but a pointless bloodbath. The best of the Briton warrior's dead, no clear winner, my grandfather deposed, and no one strong or respected enough to take his place.'

"I have no plans to become High King. I have no interest in wading through the amount of Briton blood that would require. I simply don't want Arthur to be High King if it can be avoided. Caer Celemion is the last Briton kingdom in the East. If we swear to a High King, then our lands are an easy carrot to hand to the Saxons when it comes to negotiations. Our survival requires our independence," George said with a sigh.

"But you must know this stunt gives him cause for war. Trust me, Uther won't give me up easily."

"Please, this bullshit isn't enough to make a case for war." George chuckled. "All we did was make the Pendragons look like the bullies everyone knows they are. As for snatching you, had we taken your mother when she was alive, then the other Briton lords would have backed Uther. She was his wife. Right or wrong, there are rules to this game. But, a grown stepdaughter, rescued from execution by a prince, who holds a legitimate will naming me your guardian ... no one will rise for this fight. It's the stuff of cheap fiction, up there with Paris eloping with Helen and stealing away to Troy. It's too ridiculous. All I have to do is play the next five minutes correctly, and all will be well."

Standing up, he yelled to the approaching horsemen, "Prince Arthur of Camelot, let's talk!"

"Send out my sister," Arthur yelled back.

"I don't think she wants to come out," George replied. "Come on, Arthur, for all our differences, we're both Britons, Christians, descendants of Romans ... etcetera. etcetera. Let's discuss this like civilized men."

"You're no Roman, your father is a Pict, and your mother was a half-breed Sarmatian whore," Arthur shouted back.

"Grow up. This isn't a cattle raid. Let's have a real talk without bringing our mothers into it," George said, standing up.

"How do I know you won't kill me?"

"Paranoia isn't becoming, Wart," Morgana replied, using the nickname she had bestowed on her half-brother when they were children.

"Don't call me that!" Arthur shouted back.

"If my plan was to kill Arthur Pendragon today, I would have pinned you to the dirt back in Camelot," George said, then added, "Come on, let's talk. I'll even give you back your horse."

Arthur walked into the stone circle, snatching the reins to Llamrei. "You violated the peace between our kingdoms."

"It is a bad peace. It has been a bad peace, since before you and I were born. But bad peace is better than good war."

"What now? You plan on marrying my sister?" Arthur asked, pointing to Morgana.

"You can speak to me directly, you know," she snapped.

"If I thought it would bring peace, I would be down on one knee in a moment," George said. "After all, there are worse fates than marrying a pretty girl. But given how your lot just tried to roast her as a witch, I do not think a bride will bring peace. More likely to have the opposite effect at the moment, and a war camp makes for a poor honeymoon location."

"Then, why bother taking her?" Arthur demanded.

"Because it was what your mother wanted," George answered. "Arthur, this argument was settled on the field. Honor that."

"She spelled my horse."

"Don't be a baby. We all know that's not true," George replied.

Arthur looked down, obviously embarrassed.

George dropped the point of his lance down in the turf. "Listen, the Saxons are gathering an army. Now is not the time to fight a civil war. Our fathers' feuds need not be ours."

"No, they don't. We have our own feuds now," Arthur countered, walking out of the stone circle. "My men won't violate the sanctity of the stones, Merlin would never let me hear the end of it, but we both know you can't stay in here forever."

"So, what do we do now?" Morgana asked as Arthur rejoined Lancelot and his knights.

"I don't know. What could two attractive people on a beautifull spring night possibly do to pass the time?" George asked, with a wolfish smile.

"Really? Isn't there some Pictish princess your supposed to be marrying?" She had asked.

"It's complicated." George, said leaning forward.

"Seriously, with my brother, and his boys right there? Yeah, that's not happening," Morgana said, smiling despite herself.

Standing up she resisted the urge to rub her sore thighs, worried that might give George the wrong idea.

"Can't blame me for trying. Probably for the best. After all, It's been a long day." He chuckled, before yelling, "Lords of lost lands, LET FLY!"

Suddenly, dark-hooded archers and spearmen, their faces painted with glowing green moss, leaped out from hidden foxholes dug around the circle. Arrows whistled through the air towards the mass of unsuspecting horsemen. Then came the sound of hoofbeats as a troop of green-clad riders, in Haustdesert livery, charged over the hills towards them.

"Reculer! Reculer!" Lancelot yelled, wheeling his horse to beat a rapid retreat, Arthur close at his heels.

"Run, Wart, run!" George called out behind them as Morgana gave George a stern look.

"What? I told you I had a plan. I'm just glad Arthur saw sense, it's too early in the morning for killing princes," he said, looking over to where the first rays of the sun had just started showing above the horizon. As he walked forward to join his men, he turned back to her, shooting her an almost goofy smile, before asking, "Are you coming, my lady?"

Morgana had been at Castle Haustdesert ever since. Free, honored, a Briton princess once more, and now ... she thought about the room that had been prepared for her upstairs. The large bed, the warm carved wood, the beautiful yellow dress of silk, and lace ... She tried to put it out of her mind as she looked down at the lock of dark hair in her hand.

It was one of the few items she'd had with her when she left Camelot. The only one that was truly precious to her.

That lock of hair was all she had of the one thing in the world that truly mattered.

And she had left him behind in Camelot.

Chapter Six

Iseult la Blonde, Queen of Kernow

Cairisford
July 8th 543 AD

The Consul's brow was sad, and the Consul's speech was low,
And darkly looked he at the wall, and darkly at the foe.
"Their van will be upon us before the bridge goes down;
And if they once might win the bridge, what hope to save the town?"
Then out spoke brave Horatius, the Captain of the Gate:
"To every man upon this earth, death cometh soon or late;
And how can man die better than facing fearful

odds ...
Hew down the bridge, Sir Consul, with all the
speed ye may!
I, with two more to help me, will hold the foe in
play ...
But now no sound of laughter was heard
among the foes.
A wild and wrathful clamor from all the
vanguard rose.
Six spears' lengths from the entrance halted
that deep array,
And for a space no man came forth to win the
narrow way ...
Was none who would be foremost to lead such
dire attack:
But those behind cried "Forward!" and those
before cried "Back!"

Horatius at the Bridge
Thomas Babington McAulay 1922 AD

As MORNING CAME, KING Arthur's forces started to fortify their camp. It was no more than a trench, peppered with wooden stakes. Nothing that would halt a proper army, but such defenses might prevent a blitz attack or night raid. Yet crude as it was, such construction was still back-breaking work. Especially as Lancelot and the other captains demanded that their men work in armor, brutally berating anyone who attempted to shuck their leather or mail for the sake of comfort.

It was old Roman military doctrine, and Iseult could see the logic to it. If the enemy attacked while they were setting up camp, none of the soldiers would have a chance to don armor before finding themself in the fight. Outnumbered as they were, if a man was not ready to fight when the attack finally came he would be a liability to the rest.

However, the Rangers and Outriders were all known as named and chosen men, and in times of war tradition stated that chosen men did labor only under arms. Therefore, while the army dug and prepared, George and Tristan set to their own work.

George wanted to continue scouting out the area. However, given that he and Tristan both seemed confident in their opinion of where the army would cross, Iseult suspected the scouting mission was little more than an excuse for the two men to be rid of the war camp for a time.

Tristan had requested she remain with the rest of the army, but Iseult had steadfastly refused.

For as long as she lived, the islands had been at war, and in those wars, many of those she loved had died. Cousins, uncles, friends ... her brother. They had all ridden out, promising to see her again, only to break those oaths. They had fallen to arrow, spear, and sword.

Bards still told their stories. Tales of the victorious dead. In the end, however, that was what they were, tales and stories.

She remembered her cousin Peredur and how nice he had always been to her growing up. George had said he had fought to the last. She had heard likewise from several people who had been at Caer Greu. They claimed that he and his squire had held the rear guard alone against the armies of the Angle King Eda to buy his people time to flee south when it was apparent that they could no longer hold the fortress. However, just as many insisted that Peredur had been a coward who had cut and run and been stabbed in the back, attempting to flee the stronghold during the siege.

She had no doubt that George would gladly tell her of her cousin's death. From what he had said before, his account would likely refute the slander of his enemies. However, Iseult had spent enough time around men of war to know what would be said.

The story George would tell was likely be the facts as well as they could be known in the press of combat. He would fill the blank spaces with what he believed she would wish to hear. Then at last, there would be the accounts of valor that were as likely to be his own, as they were to be her cousins. The humble sacrifice of their own glory that men of war would offer up to the fallen. All of this would combine to be George's truth. But it would be his truth... not hers.

Just as the Tristian's account of her brother, Morholt's, death was his truth. It was not her brother's, and not her own.

That was why she had not returned to Kernow as Tristan's message had insisted.

Rather, on hearing of the treachery at the druid henge of Sarum, along with the size and intention of the Saxon force, she had ridden with all speed to reach Tristan before the fighting began.

She had seen the aftermath of such battles. The coming confrontation would be the brutal harvest of war. On whatever field it was to be fought, the Morrigan would dole out death at random. The mass collision of mettle and men being no skirmish nor duel of skill. Cowards would cut down heroes, and peasants would bring down lords. There would be no logic to it, no reason, just death.

She was not sure if she could bear Tristan's death. However, for him to fall, with her never knowing the truth for herself... That, she would not endure.

No. If it was Tristan's doom to die in this battle, then she would be there fighting by his side.

As they approached the bridge of Cairisford, there came the sound of the village bell, singing out clear and desperate over the downs.

The riders with her sped their mounts. Iseult pressed her thighs against her horse to push the light pony to keep pace with the group.

As they reached the top of the hill, they saw the Saxon horsemen on their small, shaggy mounts as they closed in on the town.

The villagers were already moving wagons and tables to set up rough barricades. Then in a last futile effort to make the barrier more imposing, they piled hay and straw on top and set it alight.

"Scouts," Tristan observed. "The vanguard won't be far behind."

"If we can turn them here, we might be able to slow the enemy's advance," George said before looking to Tristan. "Are you with me?"

"To death or glory," Tristan said with a nod.

The Saxon raiders had already reached the village by the time they joined the fray.

Most of the enemy having dismounted to fight on foot. For the Saxon horsemen were not like their Briton counterparts. Where the Briton and Celtic knights typically fought as if they and their mounts were of one body and mind, the Saxon cavaliers saw their horses as little more than a means of moving quickly over distance. If they had to do any real fighting, they would dismount. Their horses being trained to hold position nearby in case they were needed.

Yet, despite this training, the meek Germanic ponies still scattered as the warhorses of the Britons charged through them, kicking and biting as they went.

From her place in the rear ranks, Iseult saw the Saxon warriors fall below the spears of the Briton cavalry.

However, just as she thought, they might have won an easy victory. Five Saxons with heavy axes rushed the Briton flank.

She watched with horror as one of them brought his great pole ax up to cleave both horse and rider in two with one swing.

"Horse cutters!" Tristan yelled. "Archers, bring them down!"

Notching an arrow, Iseult rushed forward. Drawing back her bow, she loosed an arrow at one of the Saxon axman. However, the man's mail and padding prevented a killing shot.

Before she could follow up the attack, the axman had closed the distance to her. She heard her horse scream, as the brute buried his ax into her chestnut pony's neck. Blood soaked her golden hair as the poor beast died beneath her, pinning her leg under it as it fell to the hard turf.

The Saxon jumped onto the dead horse and raised his ax. But before he could bring it down to finish her, two heavy arrows struck him in the back. He fell over dead, making a sick gurgling sound as his punctured lungs filled with blood.

Looking up, she saw three Rangers crouched on the roof of one of the houses, fists of arrows stuck in the thatch beside them. The experienced partisan snipers choosing to forgo horse archery. Instead, leaping from their mounts to the rooftops, they now took their shots from the more stable high ground.

"Iseult!" Tristan called as he rushed forward to pull her free of the dead horse.

Rising, she snatched up her bow, loosing an arrow into the throat of a charging Saxon.

This arrow proved more effective than her first, catching the attacker in the throat. A sick exhilaration came over her as she saw the man choking on the ground as he clutched his bloody neck.

Then, as soon as it had started, it was over. The enemy either dead or fleeing.

She looked over to where George was leaning over the pommel of his saddle. Both horse and rider breathing heavily from the exertions of battle. It was not him who spoke first but rather Galahad.

"People of Cairspont!" the warrior monk shouted. "You have fought bravely, but the army that comes against you is no Saxon raiding party. Rather, it is a legion, thousands strong. Take only yourself and your loved ones, leave everything else behind, and head north with all speed. There, a Briton army is waiting."

Some of the villagers stood up and seemed ready to argue. However, before they could voice any objection, the sound of drums beat out over the hills.

"Mommy, what about dolly?" Iseult heard a little girl cry as her mother herded both her and a teenage boy up the hill, following the other villagers as they fled north with all haste.

"They won't make it. The Saxons are too close behind," George said, listening to the drums.

"What if we destroy the bridge?" Galahad asked.

"I doubt we have time. Even if we did, this river is three feet deep here at most. They will walk right across it."

Iseult looked up over to the end of the valley to the dam that formed the small lake they had passed on the way there.

"What about the dam?" she said, pointing to the wall of stone and timber that held back the river, letting only a trickle of water release over a small spillway.

"Wash out the crossing. It might work." Tristan agreed.

"It won't stop them long," George answered.

"But it might stop them long enough," Galahad argued.

"Then, let's get to it," George said, grabbing two discarded Saxon pole axes from the battlefield and passing one to Gwaine.

Swiftly, they rode to the dam at the top of the hill and began hacking at the sodden timbers of the structure.

"Griflet! Cassady!" one of the village women cried out in distress.

"My Lady!" she said, spotting Iseult and rushing up to her. "My Lady, I can't find my children."

Before she could speak, a horrified gasp went up among the villagers as the mass of the Saxon vangusrd crested the hilltop above the valley. And there below them, before the advancing Saxon force in the center of the village, was a little curly-haired girl, clutching a small rag doll. Not far up up the track, a boy no older than thirteen was running towards her, bearing a javelin that was easily twice his size as he rushed to his sister's defense.

"BREAK THE DAM!" George yelled, dropping the ax he had been carrying before leaping onto the back of his warhorse.

Tristan and Gawain stood still as stones watching him as he charge back down the valley. Picking up the ax Iseult pressed it to Tristan's chest. "Break the dam," she said.

"But my lady ..." Gawain babbled as he looked at the ax in his own hand.

"He will make it!" she said more to herself than to the men, who, in compliance, began to hack at the timbers that held up the sodden wall of stone and wood.

Reaching the girl, George scooped her up onto his saddle, spinning his horse around to rush back to where the boy now stood dumbstruck before the bridge.

Dropping from his saddle, George snatched the spear from the boy, before lifting him up to place him in behind his sister. Yanking the stirrup straps up to their full height so that the boy's feet would reach them, he smacked his horses flank to send it flying up the hill.

"What's he doing?" Gawain shouted in alarm as George turned to face the rapidly closing Saxon force.

"He knows he can't carry both of the children together, at least not at speed. He plans to hold the bridge," Iseult said soberly. Watching as the leader of the Saxon advanced force stepped forward.

"I am Cynric! In the name of my father, Cedric Bretwalda, King of the West Saxons and Dread Lord of this island, I order you to stand aside! Stand down and your life will be spared."

"I move for no man," George shouted back.

"What is this bridge to you? You are George of Haustdesert, these lands give fealty to Camelot. What are you even doing here?" Cynric shouted.

"None of your bloody business! No one is crossing this bridge."

The Saxons of the vanguard laughed, but not one stepped forward.

"But I must cross this bridge. I have people to kill on the other side," the Saxon prince said, laughing.

"Anyone who steps foot on this bridge will die. My oath to God," George replied darkly to the jeers of the Saxon vanguard.

"The Pendagons are your enemy as much as they are ours. You have proved yourself a worthy fighter in these past days. Join with us and take your share of the plunder!" Cynric called out, but George only stood in mute defiance.

"You make me sad," The Saxon sighed. "Bring me his head!"

Grabbing up the spear the boy had been carrying, George rushed forward and buried it in the chest of the first Saxon to reach the bridge. He did not pause to dislodge the weapon.

Instead, grabbing up his attacker's ax he hurled it into the face of the man behind him. Thus, he continued in a rapid and relentless dance of death. Taking the weapons from his fallen enemies to slay their fellows as he built a wall of corpses and iron before him.

As his horse reached the overlook where they were demolishing the dam, the boy lost his stirrup and fell to the muddy ground before his sobbing mother. Grabbing the horse by the bridle, Iseult lifted the girl down before snatching up her bow and leaping onto the mare's back.

"What are you doing?" Tristan yelled, looking to where she was struggling to gain control of the giant warhorse.

"It's no use!" Gawain shouted. "She will obey no one but George."

The Saxon advance had stalled. None it seemed were eager to face the Black Knight in the narrow corridor of the bridge. Yet sooner or later, she knew his luck would run out. Eventually, one of the enemy would get lucky with the thrust of a sword or throw of a javelin. She refused to let the story of this battle end in martyrdom.

"*Deirfiúr síochána. Tá tú ag teastáil uaim,*" Iseult whispered urgently to the mare in Irish.

The horse settled, but no sooner did Iseult feel the mare steady than she buried her heels into the animal's sides and set off galloping back down the track towards the river.

Behind her, she heard the snap and groan of timbers as the dam began to buckle.

"Not yet! Hold the dam," Tristan shouted as he, Galahad, and Gawain jammed the hacked beams against the foundation of the sluice to keep it upright.

However, Iseult focused only on the path before her, knocking three arrows into her bow as she rushed towards the bridge.

"George, get down," she yelled as she reached the bridge. As George dropped to his knees, she loosed her fan of arrows at the enemy, forcing the Saxons at the front to duck behind their shields.

"Come on!" she shouted, but George was already moving.

"Take your feet out of the stirrups!" he yelled, as grabbed the horse's mane and brough his heavy, steel-shod boot, down on Iseult's soft leather riding shoes as he crammed them into the stirrup.

She tried to move herself back in the saddle so that George could hoist himself up onto the massive warhorse. However, before he could, the Saxons rushed forward to attack their vulnerable adversary.

"ĐU DÊAĐCWYLMENDE MÎN FÆDER, FORDÊMAN WÎTE DÊADIAN!" A red-faced Saxon at the front yelled, tears and spittle wetting his face as he charged forward. It was then that Tristan appeared. Rushing forward he blocked the attacker's path. His agile Celtic pony danced left and right as the Kernish hero struck out with spear and hammer.

Once in the saddle, George wasted no time. Taking up the reins he wheeled his horse and made for the high ground. Tristan following close at their heels, as the crash of thunder signaled the start of a storm.

No sooner had they made it to the ridgeline than Iseult saw Galahad and Gawain release the dam they had, against all endurance, held firm.

The Saxon vanguard scrambled to retreat as a wall of water, stone, and timber rushed towards them, propelled forward by the vengeful force of the now freed river.

"*And the Lord said unto Moses 'raise your hands over the sea and make the water fall ...'*" Galahad said, as he came up behind them.

"Yes, and then God said run like hell! This won't hold them long, a few hours at most. Get the children and wounded on horses, and let's move out," he shouted. His eyes were fixed on the Saxons that now gathered on the far on the bank, as they attempted to help those who had been caught in the torrent make it to shore. King Cedric made his way to the bank, he and his son, glaring at George on the other side.

Standing in the rain, Iseult felt the adrenaline of the battle fade quickly as the warm water rinsed the blood and sweat from her milk white skin. However, looking over to where George and Tristan were organizing the wounded and the refugees, she found the rush of combat replaced by an overwhelming feeling of lust.

Settling herself into the saddle behind Tristan, a bolt of desire came over her, hot and demanding. The smell of his sweat causing her body to insist that she comply with its primal imperative.

She wondered how long it would take to get back to the war camp.

Could she wait that long? Perhaps the two of them could ride ahead, divert off the track and find a glen... a soft patch of grass, or maybe just up against a tree...

Her breath came out ragged against Tristan's neck as she imagined him pressing her against the firm bark, rough hands on her hips as he-

"Don't ever do anything like that again," Tristan said sternly, interrupting her fantasy.

Refusing to let go of the anticipatory glow, she rubbed her cheek against the coarse stubble of Tristan's beard before whispering. "If I hadn't done it, then you would have."

They rode on in silence for a moment before Tristan spoke again. "He was magnificent, wasn't he? I've never seen anyone fight like that. If ..." he began but looked away.

"If what?" Iseult asked, nuzzling his ear with the bridge of her nose.

"If he had fought in the tournament for your hand, he would have beaten me. He would have won. You would be his."

"I think you underestimate your own prowess. He might have bested you, or maybe he wouldn't have. It doesn't matter. That wasn't the will of the gods. It was you who won me."

"I won you for my uncle," Tristan said soberly.

"It was you who won me! You are the only one I want," she purred, running her hand across his hip to his crotch. Sliding it under his belt, she smiled as he went instantly hard in her hand.

Chapter Seven

Pudentius, Tribune of Leptis Magna

Leptis Magna
July 8th 543 AD

"Here shall stand the angels who have connected themselves with women, and their spirits assuming many different forms shall defile mankind and shall lead them astray into sacrificing to demons ... and the women also of these angels who went astray shall become sirens."

Archangel Uriel
Book of Enoch Chapter XIX

PUDENTIUS WAS SMILING AS he walked down the halls of the Dux's palace.

So far, everything was going surprisingly well. He had been worried, especially after Kaboan had left the palace before speaking to him. Despite Sergius' insistence to the contrary, he'd been justifiably worried that the idiot had said or done something to the Amazigh king that might have soured the deal.

They needed this deal. The soldiers hadn't been paid in over two months and the grumbling was already starting. With the war going poorly in Italy, most of the funds and military supplies were being diverted to Belisarius and his army fighting in Rome and the southern Alps. Saline's offer of grain had come like an unexpected summer's rain. Without the grain from Saline, it would be a very long and hungry summer. Hungry soldiers who hadn't been paid were trouble.

So far, however, all was going to plan. Better than planned, in fact. Alba had arrived with the grain caravan on time and agreed to camp most of his retinue outside the city. He'd even agreed to Pudentius' request that the king not be accompanied by Ierna or any Cult soldiers.

He hadn't expected the king to accept that last condition. The few reports he had received from the oasis state indicated that the Cult was in undisputed control of the area, with the Alba firmly under their thumb. However, if the king was willing to meet without Ierna, it was possible the monarch did not know the full extent of the Cult's crimes.

Pudentius had known Alba a long time. He was a good man. If he was ignorant of the Cult's involvement in the recent troubles, then it might be possible to drive a wedge between the throne of Saline and the temple. Or perhaps he was aware, and was hoping to secure the resources to expel them.

It would have to be carefully done since Gunthuris' Vandal mercenaries and possibly even renegade Byzantine soldiers were certainly both responsible for their share of the pillaging. However, he could rein those factions in later. He just needed time. If he could lay all the recent sins at the temple's door... that just might buy him the time to bring some sanity back to the region.

Pudentius' hopes, however, faded as he entered the Dux's apartments and found Sergius naked, sprawled out on his bed surrounded by his whores.

"Sire! Why aren't you ready yet?" Pudentius gasped.

"Ready for what?" Sergius moaned.

"King Alba's delegation from Saline is due to arrive any minute! ... The grain shipment!"

"Oh, I am in no condition," the *Dux* whined.

"You!" Pudentius said, grabbing the most clothed of the women. "Fetch some water and bread. Now!"

"Please, Pudentius, no. I have every faith that you can handle this matter," he said, burying his head in a pillow.

"You are the Imperial *Dux*. They have come to speak with you. At the very least, you will need to count out the payment once it's agreed to."

"Yes, about that ... the gold for the grain is gone," Sergius said, lifting his head slightly.

Pudentius' world stopped. "What do you mean gone? We just received a gold shipment from Belisarius only a few days ago! The dowery on his niece." It was the single good thing Pudentius expected to come from that marriage.

"Yes, well, that had to go to make the arrangements for the wedding, payments to certain parties, cost of a ship to bring her here. You served with Belisarius' *bucellarii*. You know how it is."

Oh yes, Pudentius knew how it was, all too well.

His experience serving as one of the general's bodyguards was why he harbored deep reservations about having any of that witch Antonia's kin in his proximity, let alone one that was "favored" among the demonic leeches that controlled the imperial court.

However, having a full treasury had done wonders to alleviate other anxieties. He had hoped to solve many potentially life-ending problems with that treasure chest of gold.

Now, it was apparently gone!

"Why didn't you send to Solomon for the money?"

"Please, you know how loath my uncle is to part with even a single copper. Using the dowry was more expedient," he said, laying back down on the bed.

"Get up!" Pudentius snarled.

"Oh, go away. I have a headache, and I can't tell you how much I don't want to meet with the Moors. If I smell camel, I swear I will blow chunks ... Talk to the Vandal chief *Gunbouris* or whatever his name is."

"Gunthuris," Pudentius corrected him. The Vandal pirate had slunk back into the port two nights ago. "I left orders that he and his men were to remain at the docks."

"Yes, well, I rescinded that order. The Vandals will be handling security at the palace," Sergius moaned.

"That's my men's job!" Pudentius yelled.

"Yes, but I don't trust your men. They're very good at drilling, eating three square meals a day, and bitching about their pay. Have I left anything out? Oh yes ... plotting mutiny, they seem to be very good at that. You don't think I've heard what they say about me?" Sergius sneered. "Speak with the Vandals. They have the whole matter in hand."

"King Alba is here because the Vandals have been raiding his lands," Pudentius cried.

Sergius sat back down on the bed, "my sources tell me that the raiding has, in fact, been the work of a cult centered in the city of Saline. King Alba and his priests are pillaging his own kingdom and blaming it on the Vandals. We aren't here to get mixed up in petty, local squabbles. Nor, will I be played for a fool by a bunch of camel herders!"

Pudentius' head was starting to hurt. He was too old for this. "What sources? You have no sources! Unless it's the Vandals themselves telling you this."

"The Vandals buy our slaves, they bring gold, and they have respect for the proper order of things. What do the Moors bring to the table?"

"GRAIN! They bring GRAIN! You can't eat gold," Pudentius yelled. "Not to mention, they happen to be the people of the province you are supposed to serve."

"Please! You sound like a peasant."

Pudentius put his hand over his face. "I need to give the Lauathai something. Even if it's only partial payment."

"You can give them that," Sergius said, pointing to a wooden and bronze chest.

Pudentius breathed a sigh of relief. However, when he opened the chest and saw its contents, that relief turned to panic.

Inside the chest was a thin circlet crown, what looked like a shoe that someone had coated in silver plate, a white cloak, a few broaches, and some other pieces of cheap jewelry.

It was all second-rate junk. The whole chest could have been bought for half a purse in the markets of Carthage. The most valuable item in there was a molded rod gilded with gold, though it was obvious that it was nothing but gold leaf wrapped around a carved piece of scrub pine.

"What is this?" Pudentius yelled as he slammed the lid shut.

"Payment for the grain."

"Get up and get dressed now!" Pudentius said, grabbing Sergius roughly. "King Alba and his people might have been willing to excuse being snubbed if we had the gold. But once they realize that you plan to buy them off with a box of junk, I suspect they will be rather insistent on seeing you."

"It won't matter. Like I said, the Vandals have everything in hand. Talk to Gunthuris," Sergius said, laying back down.

"Listen, you!" Pudentius said, hurling the lazy, young noble across the room. "Get up. Get dressed. Get out there, and do your job. And tell your Vandal friends to keep the fuck out of sight!"

"Or what?"

"Or I will come back and hang you from your ankles and beat the gold out of your hide!" Pudentius bellowed before turning to the collection of concubines who were now cowering in the corner. "You lot, get him cleaned up, dressed, and out that door in the next ten minutes. Otherwise, I will personally throw you all into the barracks, and once the men are done with you, I'll invite his Vandal friends in to take their turn. Then I ship any of you who are breathing after that, off to the darkest Persian hellhole I can find!"

Pudentius stalked down the hall, trying to think of what he was going to tell the Lauathai. *Sorry ... the kid's an idiot ... Where is the gold? Um, he sent your gold to Constantinople so the empress could ... who knows, roll in it ... throw yet another massive orgy ... buy herself an even bigger hat.*

Of course, he knew Sergius must have some gold hidden away. He was sorely tempted to follow up on his threat and beat the soft-headed noble until he gave it up. But that would likely lead to other problems, and he had enough of those.

He could figure out how to pay Alba and Kaboan later. The more immediate problem was that he apparently had a fortress full of both Moors and Vandals. If they ended up in the same room, his lack of funds would be the least of his problems.

All he had to do was to keep them away from each other for a few hours. How hard could that be?

As if in answer, a blonde-haired woman turned the corner in front of him, carrying a plate of food towards the courtyard where the Moors were waiting. Her thin, dark tunic barely concealed the fylfot tattooed on the back of her shoulder.

"Stop!" he screamed, catching up to her.

Where the hell had she come from?

He would have known if they had a noble-born, Vandal slave girl working in the palace.

Sergius must have bought her without telling me. He thought to himself, but then it really didn't matter. What mattered was that the Moors didn't see her.

"Go back to the kitchen," he ordered.

"But ..." the girl objected.

"Look, you must be new, but the Lauathai delegation is in there ... the last thing I need is for you and all your tattooed blondeness to walk into that courtyard," he said, looking at the serving platter the girl was holding. "Actually, do me a favor. There is a group of Vandal mercenaries someplace around here. Go find them. Tell them to stay out of sight. Bring them some food... just keep them entertained."

"Fuck it, I don't have time for this," she said, dropping the platter as she spun on him. She had him pinned to the wall, her hand on his crotch, before he could react. In that moment, Pudentius' world went white in a mixture of pleasure and pain. Then, in this fog, he heard the Vandal witch's voice echo in his mind.

Take your blade from its sheath and draw it across your throat.

His reason told him to resist, but his body still moved to comply.

He could hear the click of armor as two of the garrison guards approached. Pudentius tried to cry out, but all that came was a grunting moan.

He heard them stop and turn away. "Thought it was hands off the *Dux's* whores," one of the soldiers grumbled.

"Command has its perks," the other answered as they walked away.

"Alone at last," the blonde witch purred.

Pudentius snarled as an unwelcome rush of pleasure pulsed through his body, as cold steel touched his throat. However, this was not his first witch.

Mustering all his willpower, he pulled the blade back from his neck.

A sinister smile crossed the woman's face.

"Oh, that's different, you're resisting!" she whispered with glee. "Another has had you before me. Well not like me, but someone else has been in this brain before. Good, virgins are overrated." She said pouring more of her magic into him.

"So, who was she? Was she pretty, or some old hag? ... Oh, come on. If you tell me, I promise to make it quick. Then again, maybe you'd prefer it slow?... for me. You can do it. Just cut your throat, it's so easy," she whispered, watching him struggle against her power before he finally managed to open his hands and drop the dagger to the floor. The witch looked down at the clattering steel.

"Really, you're going to hurt my feelings," she said.

"Burn in hell," he gasped as she poured more magic into him.

The witch smiled, seeing through his blatant posturing.

"She must have been powerful, this witch. Only a few in this world have such power. Can I guess who she was?"

"Fuck you," he snarled.

"Oh, if only we had the time. It would be a life-changing event, I promise you. Come now, my master knows many things. I know all about the creatures that rule your empire."

"You're a lying bitch," he hissed, forcing his will to resist as the woman's magic ripped through his mind.

"Sticks and stones will break my bones, but my magic can melt your brain and drive you insane! But you know that. This witch, she didn't just have you once, did she? No, she had you in her clutches over and over and over again. Did you go to her, or were you just the loyal soldier, following the orders of your betters?"

Pudentius felt his will slip with the stab of guilt that knotted in his guts.

She was right. He had gone to her. He had betrayed his general, his lord, and friend. The fact Antonia could barely be considered human did not ease his guilt. Nor did the fact that he had only been one of many.

She had still been the wife of his general ... the best man he had ever served under.

"Oh, so ashamed. The first time she came to you, but you couldn't get enough, and you went to her. Her power made you stronger, smarter... harder," Una whispered as a painful tension tightened across his loins.

The general's wife liked to get her hooks into the young officers. The handsome ones, but also the up-and-comers, people who might be useful to her one day. He grimaced, remembering the times Antonia had come to him, as she had others.

Once she had you in her grasp, you were hers. Some tried to escape. They hid in monasteries and foreign courts, only to be forcibly dragged back into her web, or vanishing into the dark ether.

Nor was Antonia the only such creature lurking in the imperial court. If you wanted to live, you played the coven's game their way. Fail to keep the witches happy, and there were no executions, no bodies. One day you were there. The next, you were gone, bunks empty, names erased from the rosters as if they had never been.

This witch was different though. Her magic felt older and fouler.

"Oh, poor little Roman. Are you remembering the glory years? Back when you were the clever young officer who conquered Libya. How the mighty have fallen. From honored hero to babysitting the whoring fool. You know, I could offer you the same power you once had. My master would be pleased to have one such as you in his service. He might even help you exact vengeance on those who wronged you. All that you desire could be yours."

Pudentius felt her power strike the back of his brain like a brick.

"I've survived worse than you," Pudentius said, gritting his teeth. "You're nothing but a whore!"

"Oh, that hurts," she purred sweetly, pouring more magic into his mind.

"Wait, do you think you're the good guy?" She chuckled. "You do, don't you? The loyal imperial officer, sending little slave girls to 'entertain' mercenary pirates. If I had been just some normal slave, what do you think would have happened? Do you think they would have said, 'Thank you, for the food miss... Have a nice night?' We both know that's not what would have happened. Did you care, or maybe ... did it excite you. Does it make you hard thinking about what those pirates would have done to me, over and over again?".

"I've survived worse than you," the tribune cried, tears rolling down his cheeks. With a final force of will he felt the magical tether that held him snap. His mind free he fell to his knees panting.

"I am Pudentius, Tribune of the Imperial Army. Officer to Military Maximus Belisarius. Do you think you could best me? Worse than you have tried? The empress herself had me locked in her fucking dungeon for over a year, no sun, no light at all, with only rats, flies, and demons for company. I survived her, and I didn't run and hide in some fucking monastery afterwards like others did. I resisted her. Just like I resisted that bitch, Antonia. You ... You are nothing," he said, picking up his knife.

But before he could attack, Unahild picked up the serving platter she had been carrying and brought it down hard on the tribunes head.

Pudentius took a step forward before collapsing on the flagstones.

"Nighty night. I would say until we meet again, but I don't think you are long for this world. And I'm not nothing! Nor am I some whore succubus. I'm the dragon's fucking mistress." she hissed, looking towards the hall to where the delegation of Moors had just entered.

Chapter Eight

Gwenivier of Cameliard

Aquae Sulis
July 8th 543 AD

Afterwards, a boy-child was born ... a comfort sent by God to that nation. He knew the long times and troubles they'd come through without a leader; so the Lord of life, the glorious Almighty, made this man renowned ... A young prince must be prudent like that, giving freely while his father still lives, so that afterwards in age when fighting starts, steadfast companions will stand by him and hold the line.

*Behavior that's admired is the path to power
among people everywhere.*

*Beowulf
Unknown 640 AD
Recorded in the Nowell Codex 975 AD*

Gwenivier had spent the day, sitting next to the freshly crowned King Arthur and watching as the parade of Briton princes and warlords went through the motions of jerking off and sucking off her groom-to-be.

This, of course, wasn't what they were actually doing. That might have been worth watching, and it would certainly have taken less time.

Rather, they came in, one by one, to wax on poetically about the virtues of the new king of Camelot. Old men and boy princes, robber barons and noblemen, all the same pointless, boring shit.

As a prince, Arthur had never been shy about sharing the wealth and favor of his father's court. Now, Uther and most of his senior lords were dead, their corpses in the care of the ravens of Sarum plain. The surviving strong men of the island were eager to see what boons they might earn from the new king.

Thus, they came to talk and talk and talk, about absolutely nothing. At times, Gwenivier found herself desperately wishing that the Saxons would hurry up and get there before she died of boredom.

No sooner would one group leave than the next would arrive. Each man eager to see if they would be the lucky bastard who would get the new king to bust-his-nut right in their mouth.

Wasn't there a war that needed fighting?

Obviously not since she had now spent twenty minutes listening to Sir Kay as he talked about Arthur's childhood. Half that time so far dedicated to Arthur's first boar hunt.

"I tell you it was the biggest boar I'd ever seen. I remember how you told the hunt's master that you wanted to keep the blood and guts. You had it all in bucket. I couldn't believe it when you told me what you planned to do with it." Kay said.

"Well, I had to tell you. I needed someone to help me balance it on top of the door."

"takes us like two hours to lug that bucket back to the castle. But finally we get the bucket balanced on the top of the door and then... we wait. In comes Morgana, and down goes the bucket. The whole thing empties out on her head! Right there in front of the whole court. Oh, I remember how my father laughed," Kay said, his voice suddenly sad.

"Lord Ector will be avenged. We will avenge all of those who fell at the Henge," Arthur said.

He was always saying that "he will be avenged ... we will avenge them all ..." Thirty-three times Arthur had said it, just in that one day. Gwenivier had counted. Every time, he said it exactly the same way.

"Yes, we will avenge them." Kay replied, tears in his eyes, as he placed his hand on Arthur's shoulder. "This, brother, will be the moment we draw swords together."

"To victory!" Arthur said, raising his horn.

Another toast? She had lost count of how many toasts he had done. Yet, Arthur showed no signs of intoxication. He must have some sort of iron stomach, she thought. *Unless the mead he was drinking wasn't mead? His horn didn't smell of alcohol. Was he swapping the mead in his drinking horn out for water?*

That was actually quite clever.

"I did always wonder though," Arthur said after downing his horn. "Why she stabbed you with the fork and not me. I mean, she was so angry at you."

"Well ..." Kay said, cocking his head to the side.

"Oh, dear god. Were you sleeping with her," Arthur said.

"Well, not after that." Kay laughed.

"She got you pretty good in the arm, there was blood everywhere."

"Nothing but a flesh wound. Barely left a scar," Kay replied.

"I remember, my father locked her in a crow cage for three days for attacking you. The whole time she was still covered in boar's blood. By the end, she smelled so bad people wouldn't even go near her to throw rotting fruit. Even the dogs stayed away, that's how bad the stench was," Arthur said as he and Kay both bent over laughing.

Gwenivier didn't laugh. She didn't like Morgana, but she liked feeling sorry for the witch even less. Mercifully, Merlin arrived and cut Sir Kay's epic tale short. It was the first time that Gwenivier had ever been happy to see the druid.

"King Brandegoris," he announced, bowing.

Gwenivier stood up. This was, at least, a lord she knew. He controlled a border kingdom in the Old North, a good man. However, he was not known to be a friend of Camelot, he being one of the eleven kings who fought for Lear during the civil war.

"Prince Arthur, My Lady Gwenivier," Brandegoris said with a curt nod.

"King Arthur!" Merlin corrected sharply.

"Uther is dead then?" he asked.

It was the archbishop who stepped forward this time. "Yes, sadly, King Uther has been treacherously slain. But through the grace of God, he has left his son, Arthur, to succeed him and lead the Britons, in this dark hour," he said, crossing himself before casting a smug look at a pinch-faced Merlin.

Gwenivier rolled her eyes. *Did the two of them ever get bored of the constant need to one-up one another?*

Surprisingly, both men seemed desperate to keep some sort of balance between the old ways and the Christian faith. Yet, at the same time, both were determined to see that the scales would end tilted slightly in favor of their preferred religious views.

"He looks more like Gorlois than Uther," Brandegoris said coldly, pointing to Arthur.

"I assure you, my lord, he is Uther's seed, conceived after Gorlois's death and born after his lawful marriage to Queen Igraine," Merlin said with a bow.

"If you say so. It is of no consequence to me who rules Camelot," the northern lord replied.

"If you were not aware of my ascension, how did you know to come?" Arthur asked.

"I received a message from Prince George. I am much indebted to the Rangers and to Haustdesert for their assistance in the defense of my borders. My men and I have ridden hard to honor this debt. However, I do not see him present here," he added, looking around the tent.

"I suspect he is with his men outside," Arthur said, gritting his teeth.

"I saw neither the Prince of Caer Celemion nor any of the Rangers when I came in."

"I am sure they are simply seeing to some minor matter elsewhere," Arthur said, shooting a pointed look to Lancelot.

With a quick nod, the Frankish knight quietly exited the tent. However, no sooner had he left than the sound of cheering men came from the camp outside.

Arthur jumped up, making for the front of the tent, and scowled as he opened the flap.

Coming up behind him, Gwenivier, quickly saw what had him so displeased. Riding up the track were Tristan and George, followed by a contingent of mounted Rangers and Outriders.

Every man and horse were covered in the blood and mud of battle, and several had the heads of Saxon housecarls piked on their lances.

"What happened?" Lancelot asked, grabbing a squire in the red dragon livery of Camelot.

"The Saxon army sacked Cairispoint. Word is that George of Haustdesert held the crossing single-handedly against the Saxon vanguard, while Gawain and Galahad destroyed the dam to wipe out the ford!" the man said brightly.

The Frankish knight spun around, looking over to where his son was walking beside his horse. The mount he was leading bore two mud-caked children, a terrified girl and a young boy who looked to be half in shock.

"Is George alright?" Gwenivier asked instinctively.

"Apparently, he and Iseult managed to get away from the river before the dam gave way," the squire answered hesitantly, having realized that the knight commander was not as pleased by this victory as everyone else.

Gwenivier looked to where George had dismounted to help the woman, who had been riding behind him, down from his saddle. As he set her down on the ground, the woman's left leg gave out, and she tilted hard to one side. George immediately knelt down to examine her bandaged ankle.

The woman's big brown eyes gleamed with tears as the two children who had been riding behind Galahad rushed up to her. Standing, George patted the bedraggled young boy on the head, leaving the young mother with her children as he followed Tristan to the command tent.

Uncharitable and murderous thoughts came to Gwenivier's mind as she looked at the woman. She was older than Gwenivier. Older than George for that matter. However, she had perfect, dairy maid white skin and sleek, caramel-blonde hair.

Gwenivier pulled on her tangled, red curls and cursed her freckled complexion as she watched George and Tristan stride up to Arthur.

"My King, My Lady, the crossing of Cairispoint is destroyed," Tristan said with a nod. "It will take the Saxons at least another day to reach us now."

She saw Bors tense next to her as George dropped a gigantic, bearded pole axe at the young king's feet. "Horse axes. Cedric came prepared."

"We lost two men, and three horses, to them. However, we have victory, our people are safe and we bought our side some time," Galahad said soberly.

"And who ordered this attack?!" Merlin shouted.

"Yes, don't you realize that by blocking their advance, you might well have set the Saxon wolves on innocent Christian souls!" Bishop Dubricius snapped.

"Or blocked reinforcements from reaching us," Merlin hissed.

If Gwenivier had thought the bishop's and the druid's constant backbiting was annoying, watching them agree with each other was downright creepy.

Didn't they realize that victories were good things? As much as one might want to, you can't pour hate on the knights who save little kids and annoyingly pretty young widows. Not without pissing everyone off.

The pair were so preoccupied with ingratiating themselves to Arthur that they were utterly oblivious to the fact that they were alienating the whole of the army in the process.

Gwenivier ignored the glaring high druid and aghast archbishop as she walked up to stand between the two battle-worn princes. "We thank you, noble princes, for your bravery in thwarting our foes and your quick action in the defense of the people of Camelot. By your skills, you have not only harmed our foes but bought us precious time with which to prepare our forces. We also thank all the noble Rangers and brave Outriders who ser ... who fight beside you," she said, recovering herself.

She remembered that neither the Rangers nor the Outriders saw themselves as serving their commanders. They were free men who swore no oath and fought only on behest of their own conscience and sense of honor. They fought alongside their captains, not for them.

"We all owe you a debt, for your actions this day and for the great pains you take to safeguard the free people of this island. Far too often, you go without thanks. But not today. For today, we thank you and honor you," she said, smiling smugly as soldiers and knights raised weapons and cheered.

However, looking back at Arthur, she saw the king was not smiling. Rather, his eyes were focused on her hand. Realizing that it was now resting on George's arm, she quickly pulled it back.

"My Lords of Kernow and Caer Celemion, we are much in your debt," Arthur said curtly before turning back to his tent. "Compliments to you and your men on a most skillful ... skirmish."

Both George and Tristan moved to follow after him. However, as they reached the tent, Arthur turned to his hulking Saxon bodyguard. "Please, let Captains Tristan and George know that I will send for them when I once again require their skills."

The large Saxon turned back to George and Tristan and their glaring companies of grim, battle-worn men.

"We heard him," Tristan said. "Come on, George, time to break out the beer."

Chapter Nine

Unahild of the Hasdingi, Priestess of Gurzil

Leptis Magna
July 9th 543 AD

*If they seek to know some secret ... They learn
it in dreams from the devil, by reason of an
open, not a tacit, pact entered into with him.
And this pact, again, is not a symbolic one,
accomplished by the sacrifice of some animal,
or some act of sacrilege, or by embracing the
worship of some strange cult; but it is an actual
offering of themselves, body and soul, to the
devil, by a sacrilegiously uttered and inwardly
purposed abnegation of the faith.*

And not content with this, they even kill or offer
to devils, their own and others' children.

The Malleus Maleficarum
Heinrich Kramer 1486 AD

Una was done playing spy games. She'd gone the whole disguise route when she tried to seduce the Berber Chieftain Kaboan, only to end up half-drowned for her efforts.

She had considered using her magic against the African warrior, but he had never given her a chance.

This time, she'd taken the Moor's advice and gone as herself. However, that had worked out no better, as she'd ended up snagged by the fortress tribune. It was fortunate that he hadn't pegged her as an infiltrator at the start. Had he done so, she might not have been able to get the drop on the veteran officer.

But in the end, it had all worked out ...

Leaving the Roman in an unconscious heap, she turned and placed the cheese back on the serving plate before entering the hall.

Sergius was there, though he must have come the other way around since he hadn't passed her. The Lauathai delegation were already pressing their demands. However, Sergius was paying far more attention to the various serving girls than the angry men seated around the table.

Then Una saw *Her*.

The princess Sabra was seated between the desert chieftain Kaboan and the King of Saline.

She was younger than Una with beautiful, clear dark skin, long braided hair, and a toned, slender form.

"We have honored our agreements with the empire, yet our lands are still being plundered and our people enslaved," one of the nobles yelled.

"These are lawless times," Sergius said, stuffing his mouth with suckling pig.

"Lawless? What are we paying for, if not for your protection?" Kaboan yelled.

"You have your own cavalry," Sergius replied with a yawn.

"And we use them, but your navy is supposed to patrol the coasts! Yet, our people are still being loaded onto ships to be sold as slaves. How do you explain that?"

"There have been problems with pirates. They are being dealt with, but these things take time."

"Many of those ships bear imperial colors! Our people are being sold in your slave markets! How is that not something you have control of?" Sabra yelled.

"Are you sure they are your people? I mean how can you tell? You all look so much alike," Sergius said, standing up. "Anyways, I'm afraid that is all the time I have today."

"We aren't finished," King Alba said. "We have an agreement with the Emperor ..."

"And it will be honored. I have already taken steps to secure additional forces. They will oversee the affairs of justice in this district. I'm sure they will be more than happy to address your concerns," he said, clapping his hands together.

At the signal, Gunthuris and his men walked into the hall. No sooner had the Vandals appeared than the Lauathai delegation exploded in cries of outrage.

"What is the meaning of this?" Kaboan shouted.

"That man is a thug and a killer?" another delegate cried.

"He is the very one responsible for the banditry," Sabra shouted. All around were shouts of agreement.

"Gentlemen," Sergius said, standing up. "I have every confidence in Gunthuris and his auxiliaries. I can see you have concerns and matters to discuss. I wish I could remain. Sadly, I have other matters I must attend to. My deputy should arrive soon to present you with gifts that I'm sure will show the esteem the emperor has for the tribes of Libya. In the meantime, feel free to discuss matters amongst yourselves," Sergius said, taking two of the prettiest servant girls by the arm as he went to leave.

"This is unacceptable," King Alba said grabbing Sergius by the arm.

"Get your filthy hands off me! How dare you touch me!" Sergius yelled.

Una watched as Gunthuris gave a slight nod to one of his men. Without a word, the Vandal officer walked over and, grabbing the Moorish king by the shoulder, drove his sword through the man's back.

"*Baab*!" the princess cried out, leaping to her feet.

Horror and panic seized the delegation. In that moment of hesitation and indecision, the Vandals descended on them in a brutal blitz. Cutting the Moors down like animals in a carney house. Some of the delegates attempted to defend themselves, but the unarmed Moors stood no chance against armored spearmen.

Blood and gore pooled in the hall as slaves and servant girls fled, with more than a few dying in the chaos.

Una, however, was blind to all of this. For she was focused on but one target.

Princess Sabra was among those to attempt a defense. She charged forward, screaming as she stabbed the man who had killed her father in the eye with a dinner knife. Her immediate vengeance sated, she knelt down next to the fallen king's side. The old man whispered something to his daughter before bleeding out.

It was at that moment, when Sabra was raw and vulnerable, that Una chose to strike.

Lunging forward, Una drove the princess to the floor. Pulling out her dagger, she attempted to plunge the blade into Sabra's chest. Hoping that one good thrust was all it would take to end the dragon's obsession.

Yet, despite her grief, Sabra managed to deflect what should have been a killing blow. The knife instead, slicing deep into the Libyan princess's leg.

"Why are you doing this?" Sabra asked, gritting her teeth against the pain as she grappled with Una for the knife.

"They're doing this to start a war. For all the normal reasons: slaves, plunder, rape, vanity, and opportunity. Me, I came for you bitch!"

"What?"

"He told them not to harm you. But I will not be replaced. Not by you. Not by anyone. The master belongs to me, and you will not have him. You don't deserve him," Una whispered.

"The master? By the gods, you serve the dragon!" Sabra gasped, panic in her eyes.

Pulling her hand free of Sabra's grasp, Una raised her knife and plunged it into the princess's side. However, before she could bring the blade up into the woman's vital organs to finish the job, Gunthuris grabbed Una by the shoulder and ripped the blade from her hand.

"What are you doing? She was not to be harmed," he bellowed, staring at the bleeding princess.

Una did not get the chance to answer as the massive muscular form of Kaboan came charging toward them wielding a bronze dinner platter as a shield. The desert warlord slammed into the pair like a battering ram, sending them both sprawling across the room.

Una recovered herself just in time to see him, pick up the wounded princess before leaping off the balcony.

"Shit! We can't let any of them escape!" Gunthuris bellowed, before he grabbing Una by her ice blonde hair. "What the hell were you playing at?" he snarled.

"I was just killing a Moor bitch," she answered, with a coy smile. "Isn't that why we are here? Run a game on the idiot and his greedy uncle. Kill the Moors ... start a war. Then, once the Africans and Romans kill each other, the cultists take the desert, and we take the coast. Isn't that the master plan?" Una hissed, gesturing to the blood-soaked room as the Vandal corsairs cut down the last of the Lauathai and started helping themselves to trophies and plunder.

"The princess was not to be harmed! Your Horned God made that clear," Gunthuris growled.

"She doesn't deserve him!" Una sobbed. "What makes her so special?"

Gunthuris fired a hard hook to her head. "Stupid bitch! How dare you risk my destiny!" he yelled as she fell to the warm, bloodstained tiles.

"You will return to your master, and you will tell him exactly what you have done. I will not be held accountable for this," Gunthuris yelled before turning to his second in command. "Ulitheus, secure the gates, and tear this city apart. Find that Moor bastard and bring me the princess. She had better be alive!"

"Is it over?" Sergius whimpered from his hiding space under the table.

"Yes, my lord, thank god you are unhurt," Gunthuris said, helping him up as he wiped the sand and dust off the man's tunic.

"You were right. That man tried to attack me," Sergius said. "If you and your men hadn't come to warn me ... If you hadn't been here—"

"I am only glad that we arrived in time. However, it seems some of the enemy might have escaped," Gunthuris said smoothly, helping the Dux up as the man slipped on the blood and gore. "Don't worry. We will find them."

Chapter Ten

Gwenivier of Cameliard

Aquae Sulis
July 8th 543 AD

For it has always been a custom with our
nation, as it is at present, to be impotent in
repelling foreign foes, but bold and invincible
in raising civil strife ...
For Britain has kings, but they are tyrants;
she has lords, but unrighteous ones; generally
engaged in plunder and rape, always
preying on the innocent; whenever they exert
themselves to avenge or protect, it is sure to be
in favor of robbers and criminals; they have an
abundance of wives, yet they are addicted to
fornication and adultery; they are ever ready
to take oaths, and as often perjure themselves...
they make war, but their wars are against their

countrymen ... they rigorously prosecute thieves
throughout the country, but those who sit at
table with them are robbers ... they give alms
plentifully, but in contrast to this is a whole pile
of crimes which they have committed; they sit
on the seat of justice, but rarely seek for the rule
of right judgement; they despise the innocent
and the humble, and seize every occasion to
exalt utmost the bloody-minded; the proud, the
murderers, the adulterers, and the enemies of
God.
Those who ought to be utterly destroyed and
their names forgotten.

Gildas Sapiens, 542 AD
De Excidio et Conquest Britanniae

As THE DAY TURNED to night, men continued to filter in from the countryside. Sometimes, it was two or three veteran warriors who would arrive escorted by one or two Rangers. Other times, it was a lord, often with a small platoon of men at arms, who had come answering Arthur's call.

The army was growing, and that was good. However, every lord, consul, and knight who came to pledge sword and fealty to Arthur only served to underline the fact that her husband-to-be had not even tried to pay court to her once since their engagement.

Gwenivier's anger and fury over this only grew, with every knight and noble who arrived. Eventually, she took to pacing around the tent like a captive she-wolf. Still no one payed her any mind.

She understood that there was work to be done. A battle to plan, lords to muster, and troops to rally ... but couldn't Arthur have at least found a few minutes to pick her flowers or something?

Even when the campaign in the Orkneys was going badly, George had still always found time for her. This thought alone brought on a new flash of anger and resentment. For George's current behavior was hardly helping matters.

She looked over to where the Prince of Caer Celemion stood crouched over a table of maps and game pieces. Around him were grim-faced men from all over Britain; border lords, partisans, reavers, and brigands. They were Britons, Irishman, Geals, and Picts, but there were Saxons, Angles, Jutes, and mercenaries from even more distant lands. They were few in number, yet they were one and all legends in their own time. All coming out of some form of debt or allegiance to either Haustdesert or the Rangers.

However, as the sun started to dip below the horizon, a very stark divide was forming between the camps. Even the red dragon standards of Camelot now seemed to snap in the wind at the glowering green bear ensigns of Haustdesert.

It was stupid! Just more evidence that people should listen to her!

Had Arthur bothered to ask her opinion earlier, she would have counseled him to immediately take George and Tristan into his confidence as captains. They were, after all, among the best warriors in Britain. If Arthur had just acknowledged them for who they were at the start and listened to their reports on the enemy army, they would have gladly deferred to Arthur as commander of the larger force.

But noooo!

The assortment of Christian bishops, pagan druids, and general assholes who held her betrothed's leash believed a

Queen should be seen and not heard. As a result, Arthur had utterly mishandled the situation.

Her husband-to-be seemed to believe that the men who followed George did so because he was the grandson of King Lear. He was wrong! The men who fought beside George would walk through fire for him because they knew the Prince of Caer Celemion would be the first into the inferno.

She would admit Arthur had his talents as well. He was charismatic, a born politician. He looked and sounded the part of a king, in a way George never could. Simply if George was the man with the plan than Arthur was the man with the speech.

If only they could work together!

Instead, Arthur had stupidly acted like a jealous child and sent George away. Then, he'd done exactly what Uther would have done and hid in his tent with his flatterers and sycophants.

Worse, he thought he was being clever by putting George and the Rangers in their place.

One only needed to look over to where George was sitting to see how badly that had backfired. George was in his place all right. In the middle of a host of the most seasoned warriors in all of the islands.

Neither George nor Arthur seemed to have the slightest inclination of making the first move towards coalition.

This was not how she had imagined she would spend the night before her wedding.

Her mother and sister had remained back in Cameliard, along with her friends and ladies. There was no one to wash her hair in the sacred waters. No one to set the table for the goddess and sit vigil with her. Instead, she was stuck sitting next to Arthur as nothing but a silent figurehead.

However, standing outside the tent was no better. At least, inside the tent, she had some purpose. Outside, all she could do was stand there like an idiot watching from afar as George plotted war.

There was a time she would have been part of George's councils and plans. But those days were done. Even if she wasn't marrying Arthur in the morning, she imagined that in his heart George still blamed her for the men he had lost in the Orkneys. Even if he had moved past their deaths, she knew he would never forgive her the fact that he hadn't died with them.

For her part it was George's behavior after the war was over she couldn't forgive.

She'd understood his need to blame someone for the senseless death of those under his command. She would have understood had he drown the pain in whores or maybe found peace with some pretty dairymaid for a time. It would have hurt, but she could have moved past it. They had been friends, lovers at times, but first friends, and as friends, Gwenivier could have forgiven George a great deal.

But not her ... not Morgana! She couldn't forgive him for that

Worse he had made a spectacle of the whole affair. Even commissioning bards and minstrels to sing about how he'd thrown down the gauntlet against Arthur, besting him in single combat. All before single-handedly defeating the army of Camelot and riding off with the helpless damsel.

Not that he need bother to pay a single copper to have a bard sing the tale. No, the story sold itself. The brave Prince of Caer Celemion, rescuing the Daughter of Gorlois and Igraine from her wicked stepfather, Uther ... It had been the talk of every court in the islands.

She would admit. It was a great story. It had action, political intrigue, a witch-bitch in distress. It was everyone's favorite joke, and she was the punchline. Gwenivier, the sword maid, jilted for the pretty princess! It was a tale as old as time. Or she had no doubt it soon would be!

"I hear he bested Arthur in single combat before he saved her from being burned at the stake. How romantic," maids would gush.

"I hear the witch slipped him a love potion. Not that she would need to, she's quite beautiful," rival ladies would sneer.

Even when she went hunting, the wind and the birds were talking about it. There were too many bloody songbirds flittering through the trees singing, "Morgana, Morgana," and never enough rocks to sling at them all!

Then came the straw that broke the oxen's back.

She had been helping in the kitchens, when one of the maids, a pleasant girl from the South, who Gwenivier had considered a friend, had come to her. "You shouldn't listen to the gossip about George, my lady," She said. "I'm sure there's an explanation. After all, he is so honorable. They say no lady could ever hope for a truer friend."

"Who says? How many other women has my betrothed rescued from certain death?" Gwenivier asked sharply.

"Well, me and my sister ... a few others ... I don't know an exact number. But I know he hasn't slept with all of them," she'd answered with a coy smile.

Oh, if her mother hadn't been there to stop her, she would have ripped the slut's pretty, blue eyes out of her perfectly symmetrical skull!

In hindsight, Gwenivier was sure Molly was right. There was no way George had slept with every shepherdess, princess, and woodcutter's daughter he rescued from wolves, rapey Saxons, and the other assorted terrors of Britain.

No, he was a busy guy, after all. People to kill, kingdoms to overthrow, sheep to steal ... Not enough time in the day to fuck every damsel in distress. However, she and George had been betrothed! It was understood! It was known! Therefore, the only woman George should have been allowed to save was her, and only her!

All the other damsels could just find their own knights to rescue them. Or they could just get robbed, raped, murdered, eaten ... whatever. If they didn't have protectors of their own, that was not Gwenivier's problem! She was a princess, and she shouldn't have to share her prince with anyone!

Drunk on jealousy, she had gotten on her horse and ridden straight for Haustdesert. Of course when she arrived, just to add insult to injury, she had been greeted by "The Lady Morgana."

Not even a month after being whisked away from firey death, the silken-haired, skinny witch-bitch had been made lady of the fucking castle!

Damsel in distress, her ass!

No, as far as Gwenivier was concerned, Morgana was a spider. And that moron George had let himself get trapped in her web.

She could still remember how the bitch had met her at the gate."Princess Gwenivier, it's so good to meet you," she had said pleasantly. However, from the way she subtly arched her back to showcase her full perky breasts, along with the predatory smirk she had given Gwenivier, the witch might as well have just come out and said, *Hi, I plan to fuck your boyfriend in ways you've never even thought of. We can still be friends right?*

Gwenivier had marched right past the witch-bitch and into the hall to find her bastard betrothed just sitting there like he'd done nothing wrong!

Looking back on it, she would admit that tossing an ax at George's head might have been a slight overreaction.

In hindsight, she should have thrown it at Morgana! She could still see the spider as she stood smirking in the doorway while Gwenivier shrieked and ranted.

Nevertheless, Gwenivier had gotten her own back. After leaving Haustdesert, she had ridden straight to Camelot. On her arrival at the Golden Hall, she had told Uther that she had come on a diplomatic mission. "To ensure that the actions of the forest lords do not result in any conflict between the Picts and Pendragons."

She had thought it quite clever at the time.

Uther had been quite obliging when she had asked to have a message delivered to her father insisting that he dissolve any understanding between her and George, official or otherwise.

The recent events had left the Pendragons eager to strike a blow against George and Urien. Robbing them of their alliance with Camliard was a significant blow. Moreover, it was hardly like her father could refuse, under the circumstances. After all, she was a guest in Camelot. There was the implied possibility that if he refused to cut ties with Caer Celemion, Uther could take her hostage and force her father's hand.

Not that she had been in any real danger. She was turned out to be to good a diplomat. During the weeks she had been a guest of Camelot, she had "diplomacied" Prince Arthur's brains out. Making up for any lack of experience she might have had with pure enthusiasm.

However, that hadn't been all about George. After all, Arthur was tall, handsome, rich, and not without his charms. But if she were honest, she probably wouldn't have gone to bed with him, but for the fact that she knew it would piss George off when he found out.

Part of her had hoped that the Prince of Caer Celemion would come riding in to challenge Arthur to get her back.

Not that she would have taken him back, but it would have been nice to see him charge in on his white horse, sword drawn, and banner flying.

He hadn't. Rather, four weeks after she had arrived in Camelot, her father finally came to collect her. He had come alone, driving an ox cart of all things. No one even recognized him, even after gwenivier identified him they still didn't believe it. After all what sort of king drove a wagon.

The wagon it turned out had carried the great Round Table of Hall Haustdesert. A "peace offering" from Caer Celemion. The great table was a marvel, a masterpiece of oak and stone. It had been the treasure of the forest kingdom.

With it, Urien sent a message. *If it's too big for your hall, you can send it back.*

Refusing to be shamed by the forest lords, Uther, had immediately installed the great table in his banquet hall. However, he had not fully considered the implications of a round table.

Its arrival threw the entire court into chaos.

Who was first? Who was last? Was status simply determined by whoever's seat was closest to the king, or were those sitting at the Round Table all considered equal as was the custom in Haustdesert?

The entire chain of command and patronage, on which the Pendragons had built their empire, crumbled as the result of a single piece of furniture.

In the end, the damn thing had started a full on brawl, one that came within inches of sparking an actual civil war. She suspected that this had been Urien's intention when he'd sent "the table."

Gwenivier, however, had not been witness to the resolution of this chaos. Instead, as soon as the brawling started, her father had dragged her out of Camelot and back to Cameliard.

He had refused to say a word to her their entire journey home. Of course, this had been preferable to her mother's far more vocal reaction.

After that, Gwenivier had hardly expected to end up marrying Arthur as a result of her rebellious foray into diplomacy.

Yet, tomorrow morning, she and Arthur would be married. A ceremony to bring the luck and blessings of the war gods on the battle that would follow.

She looked over again to where George and his Rangers were holding council. To her surprise, George's dark, hooded eyes stared right back at her.

Apparently, coming to some decision, George moved away from the other men. Gwenivier's heart thumped hard in her chest as she imagined for a moment that he was coming to speak with her.

He didn't.

Instead, he walked over to his horse and pulled a black cloth from his saddle. Unfurling an old, war-torn standard, he hung it on a lance and drove it into the ground.

Gwenivier's confusion quickly turned to anger as she looked up to see eleven white stars set on a tattered, black banner. It was the Banner of The Eleven Kings. The battle standard of the coalition that had fought for High King Lear under the command of Urien Bertilack after Uther Pendragon and the Lear princesses Goneril and Regan had attempted to usurp the High King's power and claim dominion over the Britons.

Gwenivier ground her teeth as concerned, angry murmurs issued forth from both camps. Those murmurs barely covering the sounds of blades being loosened in their sheaths.

"By the fucking Morrigan, what does he think he's playing at?" she swore, stamping over towards where George was once again issuing orders to his men.

But before she made it three steps, a smooth, cultured voice stopped her. "Shouldn't do that, Princess."

Turning, she saw Lancelot leaning against the side of a decrepit cow shed.

"Do what?" she snarled, instantly regretting her temper.

Of all the people she was angry at, Lancelot was not one of them. Over the past few days, Lancelot had been one of the only people who had treated her like a human being. Everyone else treated her like she was nothing more than a political bargaining chip, or an annoyance. That is, if they deigned to acknowledge her existence at all.

She watched as the well-groomed Frankish knight popped a cherry into his mouth. "You're going to go tell George he should go talk to Arthur. You shouldn't. It will get sorted out soon enough."

"By whom... Merlin?" she spat.

"Maybe," Lancelot said, spitting out the cherry pit and flashing her a predatory smile.

"Really look around, Lancelot. We are supposed to be on the same side. So, why are both camps doing everything but setting up fortifications between each other?"

Lancelot shrugged. "It's always tense the night before a large battle."

"This isn't pre-battle stress. Do you notice something about these two camps?" Gwenivier asked in an exasperated tone.

"Yes, Arthur's is bigger," Lancelot said calmly.

Lancelot was, of course, right. Even with the reinforcements trickling in throughout the night, the men who now sat in their private camp away from the main town still numbered only a hundred or so men. Camelot and her allies numbered nearly three times that.

However, the men with George were Rangers who had lived as fugitives and wanderers in enemy lands their entire lives. That or they were border lords who, against all odds, had managed to hold out against the invaders.

The knights of Camelot seemed like boys when compared to these hard, grim-faced men. It was true that the warriors of Camelot were well trained, and many were also seasoned veterans. However, they had lived off good lands and peace for too long. They had grown accustomed to comfortable beds and fresh bread.

"The men over there are all idiots who came to kiss Arthur's ass now that Uther's dead," Gwenivier said, pointing at the line waiting in front of Arthur's tent. "Fodder," she said, before turning towards George and his Rangers. "Vanguard."

"Arthur still has more men and horses. Math matters in war."

"So does unity. Many of these men have spent more time fighting each other in the past twenty years than they have fighting Saxons. How long before someone does something stupid and the two camps start killing each other?"

"Something stupid ... Like, say the future queen of Camelot walking over there, to tell her angry former lover that he needs to go speak to her husband-to-be?" Lancelot smirked. "You're right. I can't see that potentially going wrong in any way."

"He was not my lover," Gewenivier retorted.

"You were engaged. You fucked. Let's not quibble about labels, princess."

"I'm getting married in the morning, you ass."

"My point exactly," Lancelot said, grinning.

"Fine, then you go tell George to grow up and come talk to Arthur." *Lancelot and his mercenaries, at least, wouldn't look out of place in that company.*

"Now that would be the definition of 'doing something stupid,' Princess." Lancelot laughed, white teeth gleaming in the moonlight.

"Oh, is the mighty Lancelot afraid of the Black Knight?" Gwenivier snapped.

"Princess, when the border lords of Caer Celemion would raid Uther's cattle, who do you think he sent to steal them back? When the Rangers would sneak into Camelot to hide out, who do you think had to go toss them back over the border so the Saxons wouldn't cross over to look for them? I doubt anyone over there wants to talk to me," Lancelot said, glancing over to where George, Tristan, and Galahad were moving stone game pieces around a map.

"It's fine. George can be scary when he wants to be. It's nothing to be ashamed of," Gwenivier smirked.

"Please, he's skilled. I'll give him that. But he's not that good. He's the kind of clever *plouc* who performs wonders with amateurs," Lancelot scoffed.

"I've seen George take fortresses with twenty men," she snapped, surprising herself with how quickly she came to George's defense.

"Twenty hard men with climbing spikes, scaling a cliff face at night, is exactly the work of amateurs."

"Oh, and how would a professional go about it?"

"A professional sets a siege. He starves his enemy out, uses fire, engines, arrows, and illness to wear his adversary down. A professional lets hunger, disease and despair do his fighting for him."

"While he sits in a field on his ass," Gwenivier quipped.

"Exactly. Only a professional soldier can sit around in full armor for weeks on end. Do you think men willingly sleep and labor in their harness and mail, always ready for battle? They don't. Nothing takes more discipline than waiting in an open field for months until the enemy decides to come out. Peasant fyrds and militias, they get antsy. They either give up and go home or they attack early.'

"Clever strategies work well with talented amateurs. When all goes to plan, it's spectacular. However, such high rewards come with high risk, and when the clever tactics fail, everyone dies," Lancelot said, looking at her sternly with piercing hazel eyes.

Gwenivier's breath caught in her throat as she thought of the Rangers she'd watched slaughtered in the Orkneys during that last disastrous battle.

"Then, why won't you talk to George and Tristan about their plans? Lend your professional insight." Gwenivier asked, swallowing.

"That would be going over my king's head. Which would likely end up with my neck meeting the executioner's ax. While I'm sure Bors would truly enjoy that, I'm just going to have to disappoint him."

"Arthur would never execute you. You're his first knight, his friend."

"Kings don't have friends. They have followers, allies, and foes. Those foolish enough to believe they can befriend kings are the first into the head basket."

"Arthur would never kill you," Gwenivier shot back.

"Maybe not. Still, I'd have to worry about Merlin poisoning or cursing me, for interfering with his master plan," Lancelot said, stepping up next to her.

Gwenivier pondered this for a moment.

"Merlin does seem to have some master plan, doesn't he?" she said, looking back at Arthur's tent.

"Yes, he does. Just, as far as I can tell, no one knows what it is. But whatever it is, I'm not about to mess with it. Few men in this world frighten me. That druid is one of them," he said, leaning forward to whisper in her ear. "Leave the princes, priests, and druids to their politics. George and Arthur know they can't ignore each other all night. For now, Arthur is doing what he does best, as is the Prince from Caer Celemion. Both tasks need to be done, so let them to it. Until they come to an agreement otherwise, the lords of the Castles Haustdesert and Camelot are enemies. Get involved at this point, and it's treason ..." he said, leaning forward, Gwenivier becoming suddenly very aware of how close he was as he whispered in her ear, "I for one, can think of several more pleasurable ways of committing treason."

Gwenivier felt a tingle move up her spine as his hot breath tickled her earlobe before moving down her neck.

"You forget yourself, Lancelot. I am to be your queen," she said, jumping back and turning to leave.

"But what is a queen of the Britons without a dowry," he said with a cruel, knowing chuckle.

"What do you mean?" she said, stopping dead in her tracks.

Lancelot smirked in victory.

"What do you know?" she demanded.

"Didn't you hear Arthur is marrying you in exchange for your father's troops and support here? No gold, no land, not even a cow."

"But I'm a princess," Gwenivier said, stricken.

She couldn't believe it. Her father was seriously sending her off with no dowry? That money and land were her security in the event something happened to her husband. More than that, it was money and resources that she would need to build up her own power base in her new home. A queen without a dowry was like a lame mare, good for nothing but breeding!

"I know dowries, such a foolish Roman custom. In Frankia, husbands pay bride prices," Lancelot said coolly.

"Sounds very Frankish. Buying and selling women like horses and cows. Who needs wives when you can buy whores?" Gwenivier snapped.

"I don't know about that. But I imagine most men would gladly give all they had for a woman like you," he said, cocking his head down as he leaned in towards her.

"You can't afford me," she said, swallowing thickly as Lancelot's wolfish eyes locked with hers.

She bid her heart to slow back to a steady pace as she worked up her will to walk away. However, before she could, Iseult ran up behind her.

"Gwenivier!" the blonde-haired woman said, beaming as she offered Gwenivier a flask of spirit.

Iseult was one of Gwenivier's oldest and closest friends. The girl was in many ways the older sister she'd never had. However, she couldn't help but resent the queen of Kernow's classical good looks. Her perfectly proportioned form. Her silky blonde hair. Her milky white skin. Her sing-song voice. ... oh and how every man who set eyes on her, always seemed to instantly fall head over heels for the Irish beauty.

As if to prove this point, Lancelot's predatory eyes shifted their gaze to the drunk Irish queen. "Your Highness, You are looking beautiful as ever. You have a glow about you. I know your husband hasn't yet arrived yet, so if you feel the need to work off any pre-battle anxiety, please consider myself at your disposal. Perhaps you would like to join us, Princess." Lancelot said with a smirk as he shot a sideways look at Gwenivier. "One last good galop before you get hitched."

However, no sooner had he taken his eye off Isuelt, she brought her knee up hard into his crotch.

Iseult smiled as Lancelot doubled over in pain. "Thank you for the kind offer, but I already worked off all my 'pre-battle anxiety' earlier today. Multiple times in fact. With a man who has a good deal more between his legs than you do."

Lancelot gave only a horse gasp in response.

" Size does matter Lancelot, any woman who tells you otherwise is probably one who you've had to pay." she said, grabbing Gwenivier by the hand, and dragging her away.

"What a total *gobshite*! Gwen, come on. The Rangers are going to play. Dance with me!" She said steering her towards where several of the Rangers had pulled out lutes, drums, and pipes.

Gwenivier was taken aback for a moment. Iseult had become rather haughty and reserved ever since her father had married her off to King Mark. However now, she looked like the fun-loving, free-spirited girl who Gwen remembered, back when she and King Anguish would visit her father's court.

It took only a glance over to where Tristan was standing, openly beaming at the Irish blond, to guess what had brought about that change.

"I guess the rumors are true," Gwenivier mumbled to herself, smiling as she joined Iseult by the fire. It felt like an age since she had danced to the songs of the partisans by firelight. Their music louder and wilder than that of the court bards and minstrels.

She once thought it strange for men, who survived by stealth, to sing and revel so loudly in enemy-occupied territory. However, after fighting beside them, Gwenivier had come to realize the purpose it served. The fast beat and distinctive almost unearthly tones they played would echo through the hills and forests for miles, calling in nearby allies. In this way a force of two or three Rangers could easily become ten or even twenty almost overnight.

It was a calculated risk. One the Rangers were always careful to mitigate. Enemies who tried to sneak up on their camps during these twilight revels often found themselves ghosted by night blades hiding in the brush outside, or sniped by archers stationed in the trees. For drawn in by the light and sound, it was easy to miss the ambushers hiding in the shadows beyond the camp. This only served to reinforce the commonly held belief that the Lloegyr Rangers worked with fairy familiars and goblin allies.

However, the primary reason for the song and dance was simply that it was fun!

To revel with the Rangers was to party like you might die in the morning. For, to them, each day could bring death. Many nights, Gwenivier had danced before the fire of the war camp while Rangers played their songs and warriors clapped and cheered. But these were not the men whom she had served with in the Orkneys. Those men were dead, and these strangers didn't cheer for her. Why would they, their chieftain's lady, she was no more. Now, they cheered for Iseult. For it was she who fought beside them, and shared the bed of their new allied captain.

It did not help that Isuelt was her friend. It still hurt Gwenivier to realize that she had been replaced.

She was about to leave, fearing that someone might see the tears that were welling in her eyes as she spun and skipped. But then came new claps and cheers, as men called out her name.

Spinning around, she saw that Lancelot and several of his knights had joined the Rangers around the fire. The Frankish mercenary smiled at her, and she smiled back, as he and his men sang and cheered for their future queen. Just as the Rangers and Outriders did for Iseult. And in that moment of drink, dance, and song, men who had moments before regarded each other, if not as enemies, then at least as rivals, became comrades and friends. While the ladies of Cameliard and Kernow spun and laughed. Free in a way neither had been for some time.

Chapter Eleven

Pudentius, Tribune of Leptis Magna

Leptis Magna
July 9th 543 AD

The wife of Belisarius... was the daughter and granddaughter of chariot drivers who had practiced their art in the circus at Byzantium and at Thessalonica. Her mother was one of the prostitutes of the theatre. She herself at first lived a lewd, life giving herself up to unbridled debauchery; and devoting herself to the study of the drugs which had long been used in her family, and learned the charms of those which were essential for carrying out her plans... The greater part of Belisarius's followers,

influenced by the natural weakness of his
character, were often more at pains to please
his wife than to show their devotion to him.

Procopius of Caesarea 555 AD
The Secret History of the Court of Justinian

Pudentius lay there in that hallway for what felt like an eternity. He could hear the clash of mettle; the screams of the dying. He could smell the shit, piss, and blood. However, in the fog of the Vandal witch's magic, he did not know whether this was his present or some memory of the past.

Dazed, he crawled towards the sounds of combat coming from before him. From there, came the cries of men he knew, men he had marched with, eaten with, sang with, and bled with. But, as he crawled forward, he saw not the palace walls nor the courtyard. Rather, it was the blood-soaked plain of Trichamoria.

He had seen that battle in his dreams many times over the years, as he had every blood-soaked engagement he had served in. But this was not the same memory. It was as if the furies themselves had conjured some new horrific parody of that battle.

He saw King Alba cut down by one of the Vandal brutes. While this happened, others grappled with the enemy. White forms struggled against black ones, until all were soaked in red.

Unable to rise, Pudentius could only lay there and watch as men he knew too well, fall to the enemy. Their throats cut and their bellies hacked open.

This was not the battle he remembered.

No! They had fought hard, holding out against desperate odds, but they had been victorious in the end.

Now, the dead and the dying looked at him with accusing eyes.

THIS WAS NOT HOW IT WAS SUPPOSED TO HAPPEN! Where was the general?

Where were Belisarius and the Caraphats? Why did they not come? Always they came, but not now.

Instead, he saw *her*. Not the Vandal witch, no, the specter before him was one he feared far more than any tattooed harlot.

The specters eyes were a shade too blue. It's lips a shade too red. The demoness's silky black hair cascaded down her back, highlighting her clear, ivory skin.

"I warned you what would happen if you failed us," she said, running her tongue almost seductively across sharp canines.

All Pudentius could see after that was the blackness of The Pit, the dark dungeons of the imperial palace where all of this had begun. As the darkness closed in on him, he tried to remember a time when things had been better.

A time when life had been good.

A time of hope and plenty.

Pudentius had known such a time, so long ago now that it felt like a dream.

Once he had lived in a gilded hall, honored and respected. A guard in the imperial palace of Constantinople.

Emperor Justinian and his wife, Theodora, had just taken power. Neither had been born to the purple. Justinian had been no more than a common soldier born to a family of peasants. The empress had been a dancer in the hippodrome. However, if any thought their humble origins would in any way temper their lust for extravagance or their hunger for wealth, they were sorely mistaken. For, as if to make up for their baseborn pasts, they draped themselves in purple silk, and their private pleasures were beyond every description of excess.

However, this simply made it easier to get caught up in the glory of the spectacle. For back then the imperial court had seemed a place of beauty and light. A world that made all he might hope for seem possible.

Pudentius had risen quickly through the ranks of the palace guard. The empress always favored men like him; those who, like herself, had risen from the undercity.

However, even when she had lived in the slums by the hippodrome, Theodora had still been far above a starving street thief like him. For she was the daughter of Acacius the Bear Keeper, Shadow King of the Blues.

Since the time of Old Rome, two factions had ruled the city streets and back alleys of the Empire. Officially the Blues and Greens, as they were known, were nothing more than guilds of circus performers who catered to the spectators that frequented the hippodromes and the chariot races. However, this was little more than a front. Over the centuries, the two groups had come to control every aspect of the empire's sordid underbelly. The Blues' income coming primarily from feeding the vices of the imperial citizenry. They controlled the smokey theaters, the opium routes, the gambling dens, and the beast shows.

Balanced against them were the Greens. A syndicate of thugs, and thieves. Serving as goons and enforcers for the old noble families, they ran the protection rackets; Extorting money from the lower class merchants, as to protect the monopolies of the aristocratic elite.

Yet, all the money they extorted and stole paled in comparison to what they made running the slave markets and brothels. For slavery was the business that drove the empire. Yet, the elites, who profited from the cycle of oppression, preferred to have the sordid workings of the enterprise kept out of sight and out of mind. Slavery was not the sort of trade that honest businessmen wanted to be associated with, for slavery could not exist without piracy.

To be sure, some captives came from wars. However, those windfalls were brief. Wars inevitably ended, with the captives eventually being ransomed and released. However, the demand for slaves remained. Thus, slave brokers were forced to turn to pirates and renegades to acquire their stocks. True, the corsairs might boast of capturing treasure ships or retiring off the proceeds of a rich ransom. Such exploits made these men famous. For in these daring stories, the raiders seemed in their way heroic. As if they were no more than brave men risking their lives to steal from the pockets of the fat merchants.

However, while pirates might brag about their refusal to bend knee to any king or empire. No one who had ever seen these men at their bloody work would believe them anything other than the scum of the earth. For it was not the plunder of treasure but rather the trade in human lives that drove their day-to-day business.

Pudentius had been twelve when Vandal pirates attacked his home village. He, his father, his mother, his brothers, and many others, had been packed into a leaky hold destined for where … they did not know.

His father had been wounded in the raid and did not survive the journey. The day after he died, the imperial marines of Byzantium boarded the ship and killed the pirates. Stringing the bastards up from their own mast.

Pudentius and his family had been taken to Constantinople. There, those who had been free men and women, before being captured, were supposed to be released. However, his two brothers were strong and healthy. They were valuable. Too valuable to set free. As such, when they reached the capital, the Byzantine captain sold them to the Greens.

Pudentius had been young and sickly back then. He had been spared. Abandoned, with his mother, to starve on the docks.

They had never returned to the shores of western Egypt. They could never afford to. Instead, his mother had taken up running a food stall by the hippodrome.

He remembered how the Greens would come. They would threaten his mother, demanding a lion's portion of their earnings, or all of them if they felt the offering to thin.

Always, they claimed that it was for protection. Not from thieves of course. After all, the thieves worked for the Greens. No, they claimed to protect the people from the monsters of the undercity who stole children and drank the blood of the innocent. The Blues.

At the time, Pudentius had thought them liars, and the thugs who did the collections probably were just that. Pudentius didn't believe for a minute that those morons knew the truth.

Like everyone else, all he'd seen of the Blues, growing up, were the beast tamers and the chariot drivers; the beautiful acrobats and the dancers. The fortune tellers and street women who drew men in with alluring looks, and unmarked ivory skin, did not seem half as dangerous as the thugs in cheep cut green silk who ruled the slave markets and robbed you in dark alleys.

Then everything changed. The son of a peasant and the beautiful dancer overthrew the fat, greedy nobles and their corrupt and incompetent bureaucrats. Without the protection of their noble masters, the Greens had been left at the mercy of those they had preyed on. How he had cheered watching the thugs dance in the air, after being strung up by their own innards. Perhaps if they had managed to hang them all, things might have gone differently. Unfortunately, a lynch mob is an imprecise thing.

Still, it had been a time of hope. It was why Pudentius had joined the imperial army in the first place. He had wanted to be part of the great new world, that seemed to be at hand.

He knew now that, all young men thought that way, regardless of their generation. Looking back though, that world still seemed so full of possibilities.

Then, it all fell apart.

Quickly, the Blues set to evicting the ancient noble families from their palaces, installing their own people in their places. Few saw the danger in this. Rather, the common people mocked the fallen nobility, and cheered their beautiful monarchs in these actions.

Justinian's new councilors, eager to line their own pockets, had quickly taken over the extortion rackets of the Greens. But extortion was a tricky business. There was a limit to how far you could push people. And, as corruption became official policy, those with political connections used their positions to drive their competitors out of business.

Soon new monopolies formed as the rising oligarchs cornered the market on commodities ranging from silk, to copper pots and sausages. When the courts sought to uphold the rights of the landholders, new judges were appointed who instead of favoring justice, sold verdicts to the highest bidder.

For centuries the color gangs had always been balanced against each other. That balance maintained by the absolute power of the imperial throne. However, Theodora was the daughter of the Shadow King himself. With her rise to imperial power, any hope for balance between the factions was shattered.

What happened next was perhaps predictable. The nobles, though diminished, still had power at their disposal. After being displaced by courtesans, opium smugglers, and chariot drivers, it shouldn't have been surprising how quickly the nobility threw that power behind the remaining Greens.

It had been all too simple to set the population against the emperor. All it took was for the granaries to run dry.

Some claimed that the Greens had made some deal with the Vandal usurper Gelimer to get him to halt the grain shipments from Africa.

Others insisted that Justinian and the Blues were preventing the grain ships from docking so they could sell the grain to the Gothic kingdoms for gold to pay for new palaces and lavish parties.

Who could say now, with any certainty, who was correct? For centuries the color gangs had always been balanced against each other. That balance maintained by the absolute power of the imperial throne. However, Theodora was the daughter of the Shadow King himself. With her rise to imperial power, any hope for balance between the factions was shattered.

In the end the people didn't care. Their children were starving, and so, spurred on by the Greens, they marched on the palace.

Pudentius had been assigned to the Emperor's Bodyguard. No longer the sickly boy the slavers had rejected. He had grown into a man even more impressive than his brothers had been. Strong, handsome, and intelligent; the sort of soldier who rose quickly in the ranks.

Service in the palace had been a good posting. One he had made the most of.

Lavish feasts would be laid out for the beautiful women and richly dressed men of the court. However, few members of the imperial inner circle were ever seen to touch the buffets, and fewer serving in the palace dwelled on such things. No one who had grown up on the streets ever questioned where the meat they were given came from. "Meat was meat," as his mother had always said. Why would they question the reasons the imperial court did not eat the meals set for them? Especially, since once the food went cold and stale, it would be given to the servants and guards.

Feasting on fresh fruit, veal, cheese, and wine made it easy to forget that people were starving in the streets beyond the palace. Even if someone did mention the suffering masses, it was only to point out how grateful they were to no longer be counted among them.

That is until the fires broke out, and the barricades fell.

Pudentius had been assigned to man the palace walls as the screaming mob set siege to the royal complex. From there, he watched as the people set fire to their own city, while men in green silk robes led bands of thugs to loot the markets and warehouses,

The Nika Rioters, as they called themselves, attacked anyone known to be a supporter of the imperial regime. They burned the palaces of the councilors and the homes of bankers, looted shops, and barricaded off neighborhoods.

Some were bloodthirsty scoundrels, hungry for plunder. Most, however, were simply caught up in the crowd. Given a choice between looting or being looted, they had chosen to get their share.

The rioters eventually seized the hippodrome. Fortifying themselves in the giant stadium but a stone's throw from the palace.

It was at that point that Pudentius had been tasked with escorting a noble named Hypatios and his family out of the palace. It had been easy enough to navigate them around the mobs of looters. Guiding them through the side streets and back allies where he had spent his youth.

It would have been easier had Hypatios and his family not constantly lagged behind.

Finally, having had enough, Pudentius had turned and challenged the senator. "You need to keep up!" he snarled.

"Are you going to kill us?" the man had asked, swallowing.

"What?... No Senator. My orders are to see you safely back to your home." The question made no sense. If they had been marked for death, there would have been no reason to bring them out of the palace to do it.

"I am the last surviving son of Paulus. I'm the only man in Constantinople with a hereditary claim on the imperial throne ..."

"I have my orders."

"Please, if you're going to kill me, at least spare my wife and daughters. I can pay you," the man said, holding out a purse of coins.

"My orders are to see you safely to your home," Pudentius said. Of course, he had taken the offered purse. No one who had ever lived in the undercity turned away coin when offered.

When they reached the senator's home, the Greens were waiting for them.

"Senator, we are so happy to see you managed to escape the palace," their leader said. He was a fat bastard, with scars across his face. However, unlike the men with him, he didn't wear his hair in a long Hunnic style, and his green, silk tunic was of a more conservative cut.

"What are you doing in my home?" the senator asked. "What do you want?"

"We are here to see you crowned emperor," the sneering thug answered, gesturing to the men who rushed forward to seize Pudentius.

"Stop! This man is my bodyguard," the senator yelled. "I will go with you, but please allow him to take my wife and children back to the safety of the Palace."

With a nod from their leader, Pudentius had been released.

Hypatios' wife, however, grabbed her husband around the knees and held onto him. Babbling incoherently, until she was beaten off of him by the Greens.

While the thugs bore Senator Hypatios into the heart of the firestorm, Pudentius had taken the women back to the palace..

At the time, it had seemed the right thing to do. Pudentius could not have held off the mob alone, and what chance did a wounded noblewoman and three teenage girls have wandering the streets during a riot. Plus, Pudentius had taken the man's money.

He had intended to explain everything to his superiors when he got back. However, before he could give his report, General Flavius Belisarius had grabbed him along with every other able-bodied soldier in the palace and led them out to put down the mob.

Later, the chroniclers would call the unrest The Nika Riots. More like the Nika massacre.

Faced with armored soldiers, the protestors and looters had fled to the hippodrome. However, as soon as they got there, they wanted out. For they soon found themselves trapped with neither food, nor water.

For three days, the palace guard had besieged the stadium as the people desperately tried to force their way out. On the orders, Pudentius had cut them down... men, women ... It didn't matter. The rioters had no way out, no chance of victory. They were fish in a barrel ... Sheep panicking in a fold.

When the army finally broke into the hippodrome, the horror he saw within the stadium had been beyond anything Pudentius could have imagined.

He doubted that even in the days of Caligula had a Roman stadium seen so much blood. Nor had it been the soldiers who had done most of the killing. Rather, as hunger and despair set in, the rioters had beaten and raped each other to death for handfuls of bread and gold.

It had seemed absurd ... there were countless passages out of the hippodrome. Tunnels that led to every corner of the undercity.

Why had the Rioters not simply escaped that way?

However, even before they broke through, there had been rumors of something that prowled the undercity. Something the rioters feared more than the spears of the imperial soldiers.

At the time, he had thought it ridiculous superstition. Now ... now, he knew better. He knew the demons that the Empress and her Blues had at their command, and he knew to fear them.

The rioters were dispersed or executed, and the fires were extinguished. However, empires don't forgive, and they don't forget. Those with any connections to the unrest were put on trial. Some were spared. Others were executed. All however, were stripped of any wealth or estates they possessed no matter how large, or small.

Pudentius had no property to take. They simply came for him in the night. Without charge or trial, he had been thrown into The Pit.

Rumors of the Empress's private prison did not do that hole justice. It was a labyrinth of cells and torture chambers. A dark netherworld where there was neither night or day.

At times, his jailors would drench him in freezing water and beat him senseless, asking him questions he had no answers for. Then, they would throw him back into his cell and leave him there, alone with the dark, as the insane whispers of the other prisoners echoed through the halls.

It would have been bad enough had they left him alone, chained to the wall in his own filth. It would have been bad enough had they only starved and beaten him. If you stayed in one cell long enough, you eventually grew comfortable. You counted the stones and learned each one's shape. You found the spot where it was best to sleep. If you were lucky, you might even befriend the rats. But, no sooner had Pudentius grown content with one place, than they would move him, dumping him in an unfamiliar hole with strange sharp stones and rats that bit. And sometimes, he wasn't alone.

The first time they put him in an occupied cell, he had not realized it for some time. For what felt like an eternity, he'd stayed pinned to the door, listening to what sounded like a giant rat scratching in the black.

The jailors brought food three times, so it might have been three days. Then again, food came randomly, so it was impossible to gauge time by such things. Eventually, boredom and curiosity got the better of fear, and he'd moved to investigate.

That's when the creature leaped upon him, screaming and scratching. He tried to reason with his attacker, but in the end, he was forced to throw it to the ground and split its skull open with a stone.

Only afterward would he come to realize that it had been a woman. She had not been that old either, barely more than a girl. Nothing but skin and bones covered in filth and scabs.

She had died terrified, and for what might have been hours, days, or even weeks, he had sat there with her dead-eyed, rotting corpse.

Eventually, he was moved to a thankfully empty cell. But all too soon, the door had opened, and they threw a half-starved skeleton of a man in with him. Day and night, he would rant about the "others." Screaming about how he had been locked away with demons. Sometimes even accusing Pudentius of being such a creature.

He had been mad. His madness all the more terrifying as Pudentius realized that he, too, might soon find himself in similar mental circumstances.

All too soon, Pudentius had met the demons the prisoner had spoken of. The first one had been an old man. Clever and sane. For days, he talked of escape, offering Pudentius knowledge and hope.

"If we got out, do you know a place we could go?" he would ask.

"The next time the guards move us, do you think together we could overpower them?"

"The mortar here looks weak. Do you think we could tunnel out?"

And so, they had started to dig their way through the wall.

However, in time, Pudentius realized that the man would never sit still. Nor did he ever once touch the food the jailors left. Then, one night, or maybe it had been day, the jailor had passed by to bring food, and his torch had illuminated the cell. That's when he saw the man in his true form. A red-skinned demon, his eyes yellow in the dim light.

Pudentius had screamed for help. Eventually, the jailors had come and dragged him from the cell. The old man simply laughed, his lips never moving, his eyes never blinking; as the guards kicked and beat Pudentius until he was broken and unconscious.

When he woke, she was there.

She had been cleaning his wounds, the sting of rough cloth on his wounded flesh making him jump. The dim beams of candles in the hall casting just enough light to show every perfect curve of her figure.

"Don't try and hurt me," she whimpered, leaping back as he'd reached out to her.

"Why would I try to hurt you?" Pudentius asked.

"You would not be the first," she said coldly.

Pudentius had not pressed the statement. He did not know how long he lay there, looking at her sitting on the mattress. Maybe it had been hours, or maybe days.

Eventually, she had crossed the cell, slowly like one would approach an unfamiliar dog. Sitting down, she had pressed herself up against him. "I'm cold," she whispered.

Pudentius had not known what to say. He just lay there, her body soft and warm against his. Then, she smiled at him to reveal a pair of sharpened canine teeth.

He had jumped up, pressing himself to the door, while she had simply sat smiling at him. Though it was no longer the innocent smile it of a moment earlier. It had become cruel and ... inviting. Behind her was the silhouette of a pair of shadowy wings; with her eyes shining an unnatural hew of blue.

"Is everything alright?" she asked almost conspiratorially.

In that moment, Pudentius gave into instinct. He banged on the cell door, pleading for help. Even another beating would be better than to be left in there with that monster.

The world went white, as her canine teeth bit deep into the veins of his neck. In those moments, he was overcome by a blinding mix of pleasure and pain. It had been even more potent than the magic with which the Vandal witch had assaulted him. After what felt like an eternity, she had released him. The attack leaving him with no strength to do anything but to lie on the floor, and curse the God that had abandoned him.

In the days that followed, she had ravaged his mind, forcing him to admit to things he had never known. Or worse, sometimes she would tell him secrets that no sane mortal would wish to know.

Then as suddenly as she had appeared, she had vanished. Leaving him all alone. Mind broken and body drained, but blessedly alone. However, in time, he would beg the empty darkness to bring her back.

Then, one day, the darkness had answered, and he was taken from the Pit.

When they brought him to the door of the jail, he had pulled back. He even had attempted to flee back to his cell, inexplicably afraid of the sun. But the guards had dragged him forward.

They placed him in a carriage and brought him to the home of General Belisarius.

Pudentius had wept for joy and relief when he saw his old commander standing in front of him. The general had asked him if he wished to bathe and rest. Pudentius had refused. He had not wanted to leave the general's side for fear that it might just be yet another cruel trick.

That's when she came in. The woman from the cell.

"My wife, Antonina," the general had said, by introduction. She placed her chin on her husband's shoulder, as she stared at Pudentius with hard, yet playful eyes, that were a shade too blue.

For a moment, he thought it was just a trick of his mind. For she was not as she had been in the cell. Her long, silken hair was now styled in intricate braids, with a long, flowing ponytail that reached down to her waist. She'd been wearing a sleeveless, silk tunic that showcased her slim form and toned arms that bore what looked like faded Scythian tattoos.

Yet, there was no doubt in his mind that she was the same woman that had been in the cell with him.

"Do you know why you are here?" the general asked.

"Husband, give him a moment. He must be exhausted. Such a trying ordeal. Was it very horrible? But, of course, it was. However, sadly necessary, we must ensure the loyalty of our servants," she said, floating across the room.

"My loyalty?" he asked. Perhaps a bit too sharply.

Antonia smiled and poured him a glass of wine. "You must see how it looked. You were assigned to return Hypatios and his family to their palace. To keep them out of the way. Instead, you allowed the Greens to seize a man with a claim on imperial power. You do know they crowned him Emperor in the hippodrome, don't you? True, it seems to have been against the man's wishes, but still hard not to see that as treason. We had to be sure that you had not conspired with enemies of the Empire."

"What happened to them?" Pudentius asked.

"Happened to who?" the woman purred.

"Hypatios and his family. What became of them? I never found out."

"Do you care? The man was a traitor," Belisarius asked.

"Of course, he cares," Antonia said sweetly. "Forgive my husband. He was born a nobleman and therefore often sees the world in black and white."

"Thirty thousand died in those riots, and half the city burned in the chaos," Belisarius said, as a servant filled Antonia's wine glass. "Hard to see that as anything but black and white."

"Hypatios and his wife were executed, of course. Corpses tossed into the sea. But his children are unharmed," she said giving her husband an exasperated glare, before taking a sip of the thick red liquid that filled her cup.

"Some would call being stripped of everything they owned a sort of harm," Belisarius quipped.

The icy look Antonia threw her husband had chilled Pudentius to his soul. "Please, husband, you sound like Theodora. 'May I die rather than be deprived of this purple robe. May I never see the day when those who meet me do not call me Empress,'" she said with mock dramatic flair as she impersonated the Empress theodora.

Pudentius had laughed. He couldn't help it. He had never heard anyone so openly mock the Empress. Or, more precisely, he had never heard anyone do it and expect to survive. His laughter died in his throat as Belisarius pulled out a dagger and placed it on the table.

"Hypatios' daughters have retired to a convent in the country," Antonia said, floating behind her glaring husband. Sparks and shadow moved around her hands as she ran them across the general's neck. Dark, silhouetted wings moving like a shadow behind her, as her predatory eyes remained fixed on Pudentius.

"Are you ok?" Antonia asked as Pudentius stood rooted to the spot in fear, not sure if what he was seeing was real.

"Why did you bring me here?" Pudentius asked thickly, trying to control his terror.

"Would you rather go back?" Belisarius asked, recovering himself.

"Husband, be nice. He needs rest, give him his assignment so that he may retire," she said, setting herself on her husbands lap, as her smile once again revealed teeth that were too white and too sharp to be human.

"I understand you and your mother were from Western Egypt. You speak the native North African tongues?" the general asked.

"Yes," he'd said swallowing.

"Our intelligence indicates that the Moors of Libya are primed to revolt against the Vandal King Gelimer. The Emperor wishes to ascertain the possibility of fomenting rebellion against the Vandals in eastern Africa. Since you speak the language, it's the Emperor's wish that you go to Egypt. From there, you will lead a unit of *experandas* into Libya.'

"The Bishop of *Bernici* will provide you with gold, mounts, and supplies. Gelimer is a devout Arian, and he's stepped up attacks on the Nicene Christians, so be assured the church has a great interest in your success. Once in Libya, you will make contact with the local tribal and city leaders and ascertain their willingness to engage in open hostilities with the Vandals. If they are willing, you are authorized to make any reasonable offers and concessions you feel will secure their assistance.'

"If possible, you are to raise a revolt. Otherwise, you are to determine the Vandal positions and strength in the region and report back to the bishop. That is, of course, provided you accept this mission."

"It would be a good way to prove your loyalty," Antonia purred, moving past him.

The threat was obvious. He either would accept the offer or find himself back in the dark. It was no choice.

"I am the Emperor's servant," he said mechanically.

"And ours," Antonia cajoled. "Come, I will show you to your chambers."

As she led him down the hall of the general's palace, Pudentius stopped short, paralyzing fear rooting him into place as soon as he became aware that he was now alone with her.

"You need not fear me," she said.

"What are you?"

"I am what frightens and excites," she said, smiling. "You are in good condition for one so soon from the Empress's dungeons. Sadly, she took the Nika Riots quite badly. Peasants with torches and pitchforks calling for one's blood can make a woman quite paranoid. It's amazing that she hasn't run out of room in those tunnels of hers. But a full dungeon does offer opportunities. We did have some good times did we not."

Pudentius shivered at the thought of the pit and all those trapped there. "The Empress ... she's like you?" he asked.

"Not exactly. Just like everyone else, we are all special and unique in our own way," she said, moving towards him to whisper in his ear. "Would you not be more comfortable having this conversation someplace a bit more private?"

"I'm fine here," he said thickly, not wishing to go anywhere with her.

She threw her head back and laughed before pinning him to the wall with the speed of a spider. Her hand sparking with black magic as she placed it against the side of his head. "My husband thinks you might be useful. I agree, but I am not the Empress. If you fail. If you run. If you betray us in any way, the pit I just pulled you from will seem like heaven after I'm done with you. You might tell yourself that you are free. One day you might even believe it," she hissed, her violet-blue eyes gleaming with promised violence. "But no one ever escapes The Pit."

Truer words were never spoken. Pudentius had seen what happened to those who had tried. There were always those who managed to escape the dungeons. Or, more accurately, there were those who were allowed to escape.

Wild-eyed, they would flee, only to be found hiding away, self-flagellating themselves. in the dark cellars of remote monasteries.

Pudentius knew this because he had been among those sent to find them. They would be hunched and bloody from their futile attempt to banish the memories and the fear. With some remorse, but without hesitation, he would drag them from their sanctuaries. Pulling them screaming from the altars as the monks and priests looked on.

In the end, Pudentius would hand the prisoners back over to Antonia, and her people. He would watch as they disappeared back into the dark. For no one ever escaped The Pit.

As the witch's magic slowly faded, he woke from the dream, returning to the present reality. However, as he found himself back in the brightness of the world, he was confronted by a new nightmare. Clear in the rays of the setting sun were the faces of the Lauathai delegation. The lifeless eyes of men he had known and fought beside now stared at him with accusation.

Not for the first time, Pudentius found himself wishing he could just crawl back into the darkness.

For no one ever escapes The Pit.

Chapter Twelve

George Bertilack, Prince of Caer Celemion and Chieftain of the Lloegyr Rangers

Badon
July 8th 543 AD

Often this wall, lichen-grey and stained with red, experienced one reign after another, yet remained standing under storms; the high wide gate has collapsed. Still the masonry endures ... bright were the castle buildings, many the bathing halls, high the abundance of gables, great the noise of the multitude, many a mead hall full of festivity, until Fate the mighty changed that.
Far and wide the slain perished, days of

*pestilence came, death took all the brave
men away ... The ruin has fallen to the
ground broken into mounds, where at one
time many a warrior, joyous with gold-bright
splendor, proud and flushed with wine shone
in war-trappings; looked at treasure, at silver
... at wealth, at prosperity, at jewellry, at this
bright castle of a broad kingdom. The stone
buildings stood, a stream threw up heat in wide
surge; the wall enclosed all in its bright bosom,
where the baths were, hot in the heart.*

*The Ruin
Unknown, aproximately 800 AD
Recorded in the Exeter Book 930 AD*

I WILL SEND FOR them when I once again require their skills.
Arthur's words were like sand in George's boot.

He had thought about pressing the issue, but Tristan had
persuaded George to wait and let Arthur get settled.

Anyways, attempting to speak with Arthur would require
getting past the archbishop, and the other priests, who
seemed to feel that this was the time to press their case for
spiritual dominance over Merlin and his druids.

George had resisted the urge to point out that such
arguments were pointless, as a Saxon victory would end with
both the Christian clergy and the druids, strung up with their
lungs torn out. A practice that the Saxons and Geats called
blood eagling. While George had done terrible things in his
life, he shuddered to think about what dark god, or deranged
psyche, had thought up that ritual.

In the end, he decided to let Arthur settle in. It wasn't like current events hadn't left him with enough to occupy his mind. There was the battle and the unfavorable tactical situation. Then, of course, there was the damn dagger that was chafing in his boot.

On top of all that, there was the issue of Tristan and Iseult. However, after some consideration, George had decided that the sex lives of his comrades' were not his concern.

On the other hand, the matter of the dagger was not so easily dismissed. He was now convinced the blade had not belonged to the Geat from whose corpse he had taken it from. The more he thought on it, the more likely it seemed that the slim blade had been slipped to the Northman by the woman George was .... he wasn't exactly sure how to define his relationship with Morgana, especially now.

If all that wasn't enough to twist his heart and mind into knots, there was the matter of Princess Gwenivier of Cameliard.

King Leodegrance and his redhaired daughter were not exactly the last people George had expected to arrive, but they were certainly not the first.

At one point, Leodegrance would have been counted as one of Caer Celemion's closest allies. Things were different now.

It was the way of the world. Inevitably, politics shifted, alliances changed, and betrothals were broken. Now, Gwenivier was marrying Arthur.

He had to admit, Arthur had played the game well. With the Saxon invasion bearing down on their heads, the Pendragon prince had used the situation to get the Archbishop to declare him High King. That gained him the support of the Christian lords. Meanwhile, by marrying Gwenivier, the daughter of the pagan King Leodegrance, he secured the loyalty of the followers of the old ways. Not to mention, combining the military might of Cameliard and Camelot in the bargain.

There would be a wedding, then a battle, and provided everyone was alive at the end, there might be a honeymoon for the happy couple. The whole thing struck George as all very Pictish.

However, political skill was a double-edged sword. For it was painfully obvious that the new King of Camelot didn't want to simply win the coming battle. He wanted to win it in a way that was politically advantageous to him.

George, however, would settle for just winning. That would be hard enough. Even after the arrival of reinforcements, the army of the Britons was still outnumbered. Not to mention half of the lords and knights on the Briton side would be just as happy to fight each other as they would be fighting Saxons.

Actually, they would much rather fight each other. A sheep-stealing raid against your neighboring Briton kingdom was a weekend's sport. A campaign against the Saxons, on the other hand, was the hard slog of war.

However, there was no arguing that Arthur's arrival had transformed the mood of the camp. No longer were people flinching at shadows while lighting extra fires in hopes of disguising their numbers. Now, they lit blazes in celebration, singing and cheering as Gwenivier and Iseult danced with the other battle-maids.

George had hardly been the only one enchanted by the vision of Gwenivier and Isuelt spinning and twirling around the fire. White-blonde hair and red curls moving in time with the music.

However, when the song finally stopped, Iseult had fallen into Tristan's arms while Gwenivier moved over to flirt and giggle with Lancelot. An unbidden surge of jealousy had heated George's blood as the Frankish mercenary's fingers grazed Gweniever's tattooed arm.

Now, George paced through the town, trying to sort out his feelings, as he looked out at the ruins of the old Roman temple complex.

Vortigern, Ambrosius, his grandfather, and Gorlois had all attempted to build fortresses on the ancient foundations of the Roman bath house. Yet, the great hall of Terrabil had never been completed.

There were rumors that the site was haunted. Some said that an ancient dragon slumbered beneath Britain. The beast's breath heating the ancient springs that dotted the island. Others claimed the waters were magical, watched over by the fairy queen Sulis, who cursed anyone who dared attempt to build on the sacred site. The ruin's strategic position alone made it valuable. A castle here would give a ruler command over the junction between the West Country and southern peninsula of the Dumnonii. Yet, for the past twenty-two years, the site had remained abandoned.

Twenty-two years ... that's how long it had been since Uther and the armies of Camelot had ripped through the area, plundering and burning. Uther had never tried to build on the site. A pity since a hardened base would not be without its uses at the moment.

However, there were rumors that the site was haunted. Some said that an ancient dragon slumbered beneath Britain. The beast's breath heating the ancient springs that dotted the island. Others claimed the waters were magical, watched over by the fairy queen Sulis, who cursed anyone who dared attempt to build on the sacred site.

Every ruin on the island boasted a similar tale. Sometimes it was fairy queens and dragons. However, other such places also had stories of shapeshifters, trolls, pixies, and puccas attached to them. It was in no small part because of these stories the Saxons dared not enter the ruined Roman settlements that dotted the island.

In this way, the tales of barmaids and bards served the Briton cause better than a hundred posted garrisons. For most of the Roman cities and forts had been built on strategic sites with access to the roads and riverways. Moreover, the Roman cities had been built with underground sewer systems and hidden passages, thus making them perfect bases and safe houses for the Rangers, and other such fugitives.

However, George didn't like trusting in his enemy's superstitions. Cedric of Wessex was clever. It was possible that he might attempt a night raid with a group of chosen men. If he did, the ruins would provide good cover for an approach. The enemy would then be on top of the Britons before their forces would have a chance to react.

"Time in reconnaissance is seldom wasted," George muttered to himself. Remembering his sainted ancestor's final words, he grabbed a bow and quiver from the rack before heading out.

"Where are you going?" Gwaine asked.

"To scratch an itch. If I'm not back in an hour, send out a rescue party," he said, heading towards the ruins.

"Give me a moment. I'll go with you," Gwaine said, standing up.

"I want to be alone," George snapped.

"I thought you said you were ok with my cousin marrying Arthur?" Gwaine asked tactlessly.

"Why wouldn't I be! Now, fuck off! I'm going for a walk. If Arthur comes looking for me, tell him I'm making sure the Saxons aren't planning on slitting our throats while he polishes his crown."

As he walked away, George tried not to think about Gwenivier; without success.

Any lingering feelings he might have for the Pictish princess were best kept in the past, or so he kept trying to convince himself. He could go weeks without thinking about her, but then he would hear a song or a joke, and her large, round eyes and tangled red mane would appear in his mind as if he had seen her only hours ago.

However, the last time he had seen the Pictish princess was when she'd dissolved their engagement, by throwing an ax at his head. Right up to that point, George had expected to marry her.

It was the sort of expectation that inevitably comes when allies have children of similar ages. They had grown up together. When they were young, they had played lord and lady. Then, when they got older, they became hunting and sparring partners, drinking, training and reveling together in their fathers' halls. While George probably should have been a bit more faithfull to the troth, for his part, he had not minded the concept of spending his life with Gwenivier.

Whatever else she was, Gwenivier was fun to be around.

Morgana was many things. However, no one would ever accuse Morgana of being fun. Rather, she was clever and intellectual. She frightened him and excited him. As for the dark-skinned woman from his dreams ... she was but that; a dream.

In his heart, George knew he and Gwenivier could never have made each other happy.

George had been taught that you used power and wealth to improve your people's lives and protect their freedom. Gwenivier, on the other hand, felt that wealth should be hoarded, and the people's only purpose was to provide their leaders with more wealth and means to defend it.

Despite this difference in opinions, they had been friends. That is, save for a few drunken exceptions where they might have been more. The memory of those nights still brought a reluctant smile to his face.

Moving silently through the ruin, he ducked down at the sounds of muffled voices. For a moment, he thought he might have imagined the sound. A laugh and a far too familiar moan ahead of him. Notching an arrow in his bow, George turned the corner and came face to face with the last thing he expected to see.

There, in front of him, was Gwenivier.

She was sitting on the edge of the steaming Roman bath, her lean, tattooed body taut in ecstasy. She had taken out her battle braids, so that her red hair now tumbled down to her waist, and right between her legs was a head, with sandy brown hair, that did not belong to Arthur.

George's immediate thought was to retreat and pretend he'd seen nothing. However, the shock of the unexpected sight caused him to hesitate a moment too long. Gweniever's eyes shot open to find George standing there looking like an idiot.

"By the love of Brigid and the gods!" she screeched, leaping forward and closing her legs. These simultaneous actions resulted in her dunking her lover's head under the brown, steaming water.

"George, what the five hells are you doing here?" she yelled. Most women would have attempted to cover themselves. However, Gwenivier was a Pict, and Picts tended not to place much import on such modesty.

The man, who had moments ago been between her legs, broke the surface of the pool with a choking gasp.

It was with some alarm and anger that George recognized Lancelot's squared jawed face. "*Merde*! He's seen us!" the Frankish captain gasp as he swam to the edge of the pool.

"Yes, Lancelot, he has seen us. Thank you for stating the obvious," Gwenivier said with an exasperated sigh.

"I haven't seen anything!" George babbled. "All I see are forty armored Frankish knights and roughly a hundred woad painted warriors. There are over two thousand Saxons marching on us. So I really couldn't give a fuck whose face is down in whose snatch. And unlike some people, I don't have any loyalty, perceived or otherwise, to Arthur that would compel me to tell him anything. In fact, he doesn't even want to talk to me, so fuck him."

"You do know you're being a jackass, George," Gwenivier said flatly, standing up. Indifferent to the fact that she was wearing nothing but her tattoos.

Lancelot looked a little surprised by the princess's lack of modesty. However, George knew to take this sort of thing in stride when it came to Gwenivier. Picts typically went without clothes when indoors and during the summer often walked naked in their villages. George knew all too well that Gwenivier enjoyed it when her exhibitionism made others uncomfortable. George had no intentions of encouraging her further. Rather, he had other worries, mainly the Frankish mercenary inching towards his throwing axes.

"Move even a hair closer to those *Franciscas*, and I'll pin you to the wall," George snarled, drawing his bow back.

"Leave it be, Lancelot," Gwenivier said, walking forward and laying her hand on George's arrow. "George won't say anything. It wouldn't be to his advantage. And, he doesn't do anything unless it's to his advantage."

"What should I say, Gwenivier? That this was a bad idea? You knew that before you decided to sneak off for this haunted-ruins hot tub session," George snapped before turning on Lancelot. "And you! Really ... did you have to fuck this particular princess tonight? You couldn't have found anyone or anything else to stick your dick in? I'm pretty sure I saw some sheep on the way in. You do realize our light infantry vanishes into the mist if she doesn't get married in the morning."

"Fuck you, George. You seem to be missing the fact that I'm getting married tomorrow. That is to say, I am not married tonight. No, tonight, I'm free to frolic around and fuck whoever I want," she hissed, before shooting him an almost playfull smile. "You know, you could have just asked to join in."

For a moment, looking at Gwenivier standing there with her white skin that seemed to glow in the moonlight, parts of George's anatomy considered this offer. That is until his brain reminded those parts what they were considering!

"Not my thing," George said hoarsely. "I mean, who the hell knows where he's been? Plus, last time I saw you, you threw an ax at my head. I make it a point not to get in beds, or baths for that matter, with people who might murder me halfway through."

"And yet, you're sleeping with the witch-bitch," Gwenivier scoffed, "Anyways, what are you even doing here?"

"I felt someone should check the ruins. If you had told me you were already planning to do the scouting, I wouldn't have bothered. Though, couldn't you have picked anyone other than Camelot's knight commander to escort you?"

"Who better? He is the greatest warrior in Britain," she said, smiling.

"He is the payer of his own minstrels!" George scoffed.

"I could kill you easy enough," Lancelot snarled.

"Put some pants on first," George shot back.

"What? Should I have chosen some nobody?" Gwenivier asked. "Would that have made you happy?"

"Yes, actually," George said nodding. "If you had to rub yourself off on someone, why not someone easily disposed of afterward? Isn't that what you typically do? That way, no one notices when you bite the heads off your bedmates afterward."

"How dare you talk to her like that!" Lancelot objected.

"Shut up, you. Manwhores don't get to preach to me about chivalry," George shot back.

"No, he's right. You don't get to talk to me like that!"

"My lady, perhaps you should put some clothes on?" Lancelot whispered.

"I think you're scandalizing your Frenchman." George smirked.

"Why, it's not like it's anything you haven't already seen before, and maybe I'm not finished with him yet," Gwenivier snapped, nodding to Lancelot. "After all, it wasn't like you were offering."

"I didn't break if off, Gwenivier, you did! I'll leave you to … whatever this is you're doing," George said, turning to walk away.

"Oh no, don't you dare walk away from me like that. You don't get to judge me! Not after the way you ran off to play Legendary Captain-Save-A-Ho to my soon-to-be, bitch sister-in-law. You made me a fucking laughing stock!" Gwenivier said furiously.

"You are aware that Uther was about to burn the last of the bloodline of Boudica at the stake? What was I supposed to do?"

"Don't lie to me, George, I know you too well. You could care less about bloodlines and titles. You would have happily played the part of George, Defender-of-Well-Stacked-Sluts, even if she had been a pig keeper's daughter. Anything to show off your skills with horse and lance for a wet and willing damsel. Scoop them up onto your saddle, carry them to safety, and they'll let you ride them any time you want, am I right?" she hissed.

"You flew off the handle, like a jilted peasant girl, all because you felt threatened by Morgana? You could have given me a chance to explain, rather than having your father play the messenger. That was a bit awkward, Gwen. Though, I grant that it was honorable for him to still pay the pensions for the men I lost in the Orkneys."

"What?" Gwenivier asked flatly.

"Fifteen walrus tusks, thirty pearls, and sixty pieces of silver," George said with a victorious smirk.

"My fucking dowry! He gave you my dowry? And you took it?" Gwenivier shrieked.

"I figured the families and villages of the men who died needed it more than Arthur did," George said coldly.

"It wasn't for Arthur! It was for me. It was my future. It was mine!"

"I'm sure Arthur has plenty of gold and silver to spare. Provided he doesn't spend it all on wine and whoring mercenaries," George said, glaring at Lancelot.

"You bastard!" she shrieked, picking up her clothes. "You should talk. Don't you have some damsel in distress to see to? Bet that pretty, young widow you rescued earlier today is back at your tent just waiting to suck the cock of her knight in shining armor!"

"Says the blushing bride I just found with her future husband's champion between her legs," George said, nodding over to Lancelot who was in the process of putting his clothes back on.

"It was a political alliance between us, George. That's all it ever was. I only slept with you so that you and the Rangers would fight for us in the Orkneys," Gwenivier snarled.

"And the other nights?" George snarled.

"I was bored and drunk. Don't insult both of us by trying to say it was love. A moot point now anyways. I have a new engagement. To a richer and more powerful husband. Or would you like me to refuse to marry Arthur? Watch my father's warriors, how did you put it, 'disappear into the mist?'"

"No," George said, letting his anger fade. "I've seen the army that's coming against us and what its purpose is. They're not coming to secure land or to raid. Cedric plans to kill us all. Picts, Britons... all of us. What you're doing, marrying Arthur, it's ... honorable. I know it can't be easy for you. I'm aware of how much you value your freedom. Best wishes on your wedding."

"What are you going to do?" Lancelot asked, picking up his sword.

"I'm going to finish scouting the ruins. You're going to go see her back to camp. Then, we are all going to get some sleep and pretend none of this ever happened!" George said, slumping his shoulders, before doing what he should have done in the first place.

He left.

Chapter Thirteen

Kaboan, King of The Amazigh

Leptis Magna
July 9th 543 AD

Beyond this is the city of Leptis Magna, which in ancient times was great and populous, but since has become almost entirely deserted, having through neglect been mostly buried with sand. Our Emperor rebuilt its walls from the foundation, not, however, enclosing so great an extent as formerly, but much less, in order that the city might not again be exposed to danger, either from human enemies or from the sand, by its great size. He left the buried part of the city as it was, covered with heaps of sand...
I cannot pass over in silence the thing which happened in Leptis Magna in our time. When

the Emperor Justinian had already taken over the imperial authority, but had not yet undertaken the Vandalic War, the barbarian Moors, those called Lauathai, overpowered the Vandals, who were then masters of Libya, and made Leptis Magna entirely empty of inhabitants. Being encamped with their generals upon some hilly ground not far away, they beheld a strange light in the midst of the city. Supposing that the enemy had entered the city, they rushed hurriedly to attack them; Finding no one there, they took the matter to the soothsayers, who, by an inkling of what had since happened, claimed that Leptis Magna remained inhabited...

Procopius of Caesarea, 555 AD
The Buildings of Justinian

BY THE TIME KABOAN reached the city walls, he could already hear the enemy moving through the town as they searched for him.

Once, he might have tried to fight his way out. But age and experience had taught him discretion.

There was always another day to die, but you only got to live once.

Now he just had to make it out of the city. If he could get back to his people, and tell them what happened then he could make a fight of it.

Run to fight. Live to die.

Silently, he rushed to the far side of the defensive walls, glad that he had taken the time to scout out the town beforehand. He breathed a sigh of relief as he reached the far western corner. There the sand had piled up High enough that it was possible to scramble up to the battlements. However, reaching the top of the wall, he heard the sound of a Vandal screaming. *"ER IST HIER!"*

Dropping the princess, Kaboan turned around and rushed the man. Closing on the guard quickly, he pulled out the dull dinner knife he had taken from the banquet table and plunged it into the man's throat. The screaming guard fell to the ground, his eyes wide with fear as he clutched his bleeding neck. Behind him, he heard Sabra moan as she started to regain consciousness.

"Where are we?" she asked as she tried to stand.

Without answering, Kaboan grabbed her hand and slid down the outer wall; leading her into the ruins that surrounded the city.

Sergius should have had the half-buried buildings torn down to give his soldiers a clear line of sight around the fortress. However, Kaboan was glad for the cover the man's negligence now provided him.

He felt Sabra slowing behind him as he led her through the labyrinth of charred timbers and scorched stone. He tried to pull her forward, only to have her collapse in his arms, still clutching the red, silk scarf her father had given her. As Kaboan moved to help her up, his hand slipped on the slick blood pouring down her leg. Sabra pushed his hand away as she tried to stand.

"Stop. Let me see it!" Kaboan said.

"I'll be ok, leave me here. You need to get back to the camp and tell them what happened."

"There is no way I'm leaving you," he said. Running his hand down her leg, until he found the deep wet gash. Without a word, he grabbed the silk scarf.

"No," Sabra cried, snatching for it.

"Without a tourniquet, you'll bleed out. Your life is more important," Kaboan hissed, wrapping the scarf around her leg.

"My father is dead." Sabra sobbed.

"If you wish to honor his death, then live!" Kaboan said, sliding the knife he had taken from the buffet table through the knotted silk and twisting hard to tighten the tourniquet.

Sabra bit down hard, crying out briefly before passing out from the pain.

Kaboan looked around and realized that he had been there before, back when the now half-buried buildings, had been part of a thriving Vandal city.

It was after he had defeated the Spetzcarls of King Thrasamund. Some of the Vandal cavalry had escape and retreated here. The nomads had pursued them and sacked the city. In the end, they had been forced to fight man to man in the streets.

It was in that same burned-out house where they now sheltered, that Kaboan had held his childhood friend Warmaksan as the man bled out in his arms.

The man whose name meant undefeatable had seemed just that. A giant of a man, unmatched in battle. Yet, for all his prowess, he had been slain by no more than a stable boy with a pitchfork. The boy's broken bones still lay bleached in the corner where Kaboan had, in his grief and anger, hacked the child to pieces before putting the city to the torch.

"It has to be for something. We owe it to the dead to live," Kaboan said lifting the unconscious princess up into his arms.

What do you know of the dead?

It was not one voice that spoke but many. Their words echoing through the ruins of the burned and buried houses. Buildings where men and women had lived, raised their families and made their homes.

Homes Kaboan had ordered burned.

Before him stood a phalanx of wraiths, their pale flesh transparent in the dark. Each was different. Some wore Vandal mail, with golden inlaid belts, and silver arm rings. Others wore the lighter armor favored by the desert tribes. He looked at the ghostly faces, and he knew them all. He had watched the life leave their eyes. Those he had slain, and those he had led to their deaths.

You killed us, they whispered without words.

"It was war. That is the nature of combat. Death is the harvest of war. You knew it as well as I did," Kaboan said, holding the unconscious Sabra tight to his chest as he backed away from the advancing wraiths.

I did not die in battle. I was unarmed and wounded. Yet, you cut my throat on the sands. The face was that of a Vandal Spetzcarls, the dark tattoos the man had worn in life now glowed bright on the specter's pale ghostly flesh.

Kaboan remembered him.

"That was justice," Kaboan shouted at the Vandal ghost.

I did not but follow the orders of my king.

"You and yours burned churches; tortured innocents. You deserved your fate!"

Did I deserve mine?

Kaboan knew what he would see before he even turned around. Standing before him was a little girl no older than his own daughter. Her blonde hair matted with blood, and a hole in her side where his spear had pierced her all those years ago.

"I didn't mean to kill you. It was dark—"

And there was fire. So much smoke and fire, another figure said coming out of the dark, its face burned beyond recognition. *I was terrified. I hid in my house even as it burned around me.*

Other specters came up behind the charred figure. These wore no armor, for they had never carried arms. They were women and children. Their clothes torn, their ghostly flesh burned and bloodied.

Who lit the torches? Who ordered the attack? Our soldiers were dead. What chance did we stand? A young boy, younger than the girl even, walked forward carrying a bloody pitchfork. The specter of the page who had killed Warmaksan.

Next to the boy stood the figure of his brother-in-arms. *We killed and died. You promised us freedom! You promised us an empire!*

We killed for you, we died for you, and you have let it be for nothing, others said coming forward.

You have forgotten us, came the accusation from another warrior.

"No, never. I never forgot you. Any of you," Kaboan yelled, looking around at the specters that closed in around him.

We died for nothing, the ghosts screamed.

"I made peace," Kaboan said.

Your peace is a lie.

Your wife died, and you lost all taste for battle. You gave up.

"My daughter ..."

I had daughters too. They killed them. You promised me vengeance. Warmaksan said, but before Kaboan could respond, the blonde-haired girl walked forward.

My mother tried to protect me. You cut her down, the girl said.

"What do you want from me?" Kaboan yelled. "Do you want me to swear I will shed no more blood, that I will go off and live a life of peace? I cannot do that, not now. They have killed my brothers-in-arms. They will kill more unless I stop them."

We do not want your peace.
Your peace is a lie.
"Then, what do you want?"
We want it to have been for something!
Sabra stirred in his arms. Kaboan looked back towards the walls of Leptis Magna. It would not take them long to find the dead guard. Once they did, they would track the blood trail right to them. He needed to get Sabra to safety. He needed to get out of there.

Holding the princess tight to his chest, he pushed through the blood-soaked wraiths that blocked his path.

Just as he thought he might get free, before him stood Warmaksan. *You promised us an empire. You promised us power and glory. That we might be forever free.*

"Brother, my life is yours to take. I hear you. I promise your death will not be for nothing. But she will die unless I get her to safety."

Many will die, the little blonde-haired ghost said.

Run to fight. Live to die. The wraiths said.

Kaboan pushed forward out of the ruins and onto the open sand. Before him, he could see the lights of the encampment on the hills above him. But looking back, he saw Warmaksan and the little girl whose name he would never know.

"I am sorry for your death. I will fight on. Our people will be free, brother," he said, nodding to the ghost of his old friend. He then looked to the girl. "More will die and for that, I am sorry."

You will betray her, the ghost of the girl said sadly.

As Kaboan carried the wounded princess back towards safety, forcing his aging limbs across the sands, the ghost's final words echoed in his mind.

So consumed was he by his grief, he did not hear what Sabra murmured in his arms. "He will betray you."

They were Alba's final words to his daughter. The prophecy the dragon had whispered to the king's ear that night in the temple. *Kaboan will betray her. He will join me. It has been foretold, it will come to pass.*

Chapter Fourteen

George Bertilack, Prince of Caer Celemion and Chieftain of the Lloegyr Rangers

Aquae Sulis, Territory of Camelot
July 9th 543 AD

"Unhappy that I am, I cannot heave my heart into my mouth. I love your Majesty according to my bond, no more nor less. ... You have begot me, bred me, loved me. I return those duties back as are right fit: Obey you, love you, and most honor you. Why have my sisters husbands if they say they love you all? Happily, when I shall wed, That lord whose hand must take my

plight shall carry half my love with him, half
my care and duty. Be sure I shall never marry
like my sisters, to love my father all."

Princess Cordellia's Answer to King Lear
520AD
As Recounted by William Shakespeare 1603 AD

George walked back through the ruins, attempting and failing to clear his mind. He had a battle to win, and it would likely be the most difficult battle he would ever fight.

He remembered vaguely being told by his grandfather that abstinence before battle was essential. George had been twelve at the time and hadn't really understood what he meant. Now, he did. However, part of him wondered if a good lay might just clear his mind. Though, when he thought it through, he realized that it would probably only make matters worse.

It annoyed George to discover that the red-haired princess of Cameliard still had a hold on him. Gwenivier was pretty, but not in the classical way that Iseult was. Rather, with her tattooed skin and mane of red hair, Gwenivier had a haunting kind of beauty. The type that stayed in one's mind long after the memory of other maids had faded.

That said, with her white-blonde curls and delicate features, the Queen of Kernow looked like she belonged among the ancient marble statues that adorned the Roman ruin. The fact that he could not seem to banish his friend's lover from his fantasies, was a new and shameful annoyance.

Of course, neither of them could match the nameless, dark skinned woman who had danced with him in his dreams. However, you could not make a life with a dream.

He wondered if it was that simple. Was it simply that Gwenivier was the first woman, the only woman really, who had ever felt real to him? He had once expected to build a life with Gwen. He could not say the same for anyone else.

Iseult was Tristan's and always would be. Morgana ... He reached down and pulled the dagger from his boot. Morgana belonged to a world of hate and vengeance. Even when he held her in his arms, she was never fully his. She was a dream, as much as the woman in red silk. Only fools fell in love with dreams.

Yet, he was certain that if he so much as closed his eyes, he would find the images of Gwenivier, Morgana, Iseult and the dark-skinned woman dancing in his mind. Chestnut brown, blonde, red, and midnight black hair moved in a seductive whirl of color, as the visions looked at him with clever, inviting eyes. The fact that all four were now spinning in his brain did not help matters. In the end, it just left George feeling very lonely.

Tired he sat down and set his back against the wall. However, as he did, the ruined masonry and rotting timber gave way, and George found himself falling back into the room beyond.

Looking up he saw before him two giants. Instantly, he drew his dagger against the two unexpected foes. However, as he did so, a dim moonbeam illuminated the room, revealing the giants to be nothing more than two unfinished statues.

These were not the ancient, broken statues of pagan gods and goddesses that decorated the ruined temples and baths. These were more recent. New images carved from broken Roman columns, to form two great kings of stone. Their eyes were fierce, and their brows furrowed as if each figure bore the weight of the world on their shoulders.

Even half complete, they were wonders. The image of his grandfather was unmistakable. King Lear of the Hundred Knights, the king who chose peace rather than endless civil war. The man who had given up his kingdom to live out his days as a monk, while watching his grandson grow up. He had in no small part, made George the man he was.

"So, this was the hall of Terrabil," he whispered, looking over to the steaming hot spring that sat in the center of the unfinished hall.

Growing up, he had heard the stories of Terrabil, but it had always felt like a fairy tale. Like the Court of Elphame on the island of Avalon. Even standing there, George could not bring himself to believe that the great hall had actually existed.

A great fortress that was never finished, to defend a kingdom that never was.

George remembered his grandfather describing it once. "It was a mighty hall, built wide and open like the ancient palaces of the Romans. So that all the kings and lords of Britain could meet together and be heard."

"But shouldn't a fortress be built like a labyrinth with chokepoints so that it can be defended by as few men as possible?" George had asked, always eager to show his grandfather that he remembered the old man's lessons on the art of war.

His grandfather had smiled and nodded. "A king is not a knight. A knight must build his fortress to protect himself from his enemies. But a king's enemies are those closest to him. They are often his friends and his family. The assassins of kings are seldom a foe with a knife or garrote. More often, the death-dealing blow comes from his bodyguards, his children... the woman with whom he shares his bed."

George looked down at the dagger in his hand. Running his thumb over the smith mark.

"I wish you were here, granddad," he said, staring up at the statue. "I could use your advice. Da is a good man. On the field, there is no better warrior. But he is no politician, and I am outmatched in this game of shadows."

With a sigh, George put the dagger away, and turned to the other statue. It was also only half complete, yet even though the man had died a half a century before George had even been born, he knew without a doubt that this man was Ambrosius Aurelianus. His iconic Roman-styled helm was the same that George still wore. An heirloom that had long ago been gifted to his grandfather by the dying warleader, and then passed down to him.

"You know, there are those who say you're not dead," George said, looking at the statue. "That you live still among the Faye on the island of Avalon. If that's the case, now would definitely be the time to come back. And if you feel like bringing an army of the fairy knights with you, that would be great."

After a moment, George turned to leave. As he did so, his eyes landed on another statue half-covered in ivy. He rushed forward, tearing the vines away from the bronzed image.

George's breath caught as he read the inscription below the figure.

Princess Cordellia, The Fair.

"My father always assumed it had been destroyed. My God, she was beautiful," George said, looking at the statue of his mother. As he reached out and touched the smooth mettle, he noticed the words scratched across the figure. Deep cuts made in malice and madness.

Better you had not been born, than pleased me better.

"So, this is where it happened," George said, looking around the room. "This is where the age of Lear ended and the tyranny of Pendragon began."

George looked back to the beautiful statue. "I wish I had known you," he whispered.

"She would have given anything to have been with you through your life. Instead, she gave her life that you might live. Not even I could save her."

George spun around. His eyes went wide with surprise as out of the fountain that dominated the center of the room came a beautiful woman. Her hair was the same white-blonde color as Iseult's, and her face had the same perfect symmetry, but this figure's skin shone like liquid quicksilver covered in green, glowing symbols.

"Who are you?"

"I mean you no harm. I am the Lady of the Fountain. Queen of the Sídhe and Vanir of Elphame."

"You are Sulis?" he said, remembering that the original temple complex had been dedicated to the Celtic water goddess of wisdom and war.

"I am one who has as many names as there are winds ... but yes, Sulis is one of my names. You are not afraid of me?"

"Why are you here?" George asked, ignoring the question.

"This is my place, my fountain. You are the intruder here, not me. However, the son of Cordellia is always welcome in my temple," she said, moving almost seductively around the prince.

"You knew my mother?" George asked.

"She was my friend. And I have so few these days, especially among mortals. It was because of your grandfather's cruelty to her that I refused to let him finish his castle here."

"He never mentioned that," George said.

"I don't think he knew," she said smiling. "You still do not fear me?"

"Should I fear you, my lady?" George asked.

"Many who bear witness to my kind do."

"You said that you wished me no harm. It is said your kind do not lie," George answered. "And we've met before. You used to visit my dreams when I was a boy. You built me a castle. I have it still."

"I'm surprised you remember. You were very young," the goddess said sweetly.

"You are not a sight to be forgotten, and I've seen other Faye since. Though none were as lovely as you."

"Charming as you always were," she beamed. "We seldom show ourselves to mortals without need. We are privileged to watch mankind through the ages, but seldom do we dare interfere," she said, walking over to the statue of his mother. "Your mother was a Christian, but she honored this place. She was my friend. I am yours. I offer you a glimpse into the Fountain."

She walked past him, touching the surface of the water. The moonlit surface transforming into a shining silver mirror.

"This is the Fountain, a window to the world between worlds. Few mortals look to this place and see anything but their own reflection. Fewer still enter it outside of their dreams. I can command the Fountain to reveal its truth to you. However, you must choose whether or not you will see what it wishes you to know," she said, moving over to a silver pool.

"What does your Fountain wish me to know?"

"The past perhaps or maybe the future. The water here shows what it wishes. I will not make this offer twice. Come if you will and see what you may," she said, gesturing George towards her.

Cautiously, George moved forward. Looking into the silver pool, he saw a dark cave.

"Where is that?" George said, reaching his hand forward.

"DO NOT TOUCH THE WATER!" she screamed, her voice like a thunderclap, but her warning came too late. As his fingers broke the surface of the water, pain shot through George's arm, causing him to stumble and fall forward into the silver pool.

Chapter Fifteen

Morgana an Spyrys

**Haustdesert Castle
July 9th 543 AD**

"... this is my desire: the first night that you shall lie by Igraine you shall get a child on her, and when it is born, it shall be delivered to me"... and King Uther lay with Igraine more than three hours after Gorlois' death and begat Arthur, and come the day, came Merlin to the king ... "When the child is born, let it be delivered to me at yonder postern gate unchristened." So as Merlin devised it was done.

*Sir Thomas Mallory, 1485 AD
Le Morte D'Arthur*

MORGANA IGNORED THE KNOCK on the door. They had been knocking, off and on, for the past few hours. Fortunately, the room she was in was one of the few in the castle with a lock. It was part of why she had picked the room to hide in. This time, however, when the knocking stopped, Morgana heard the hatch click.

"Pardon my intrusion, mistress, but I felt you should eat something," the old maid, whose name Morgana could never remember, said, walking in with a tray of bread and cheese.

"I'm not hungry," Morgana answered petulantly. "How did you get in here? I locked the door."

"My husband, Bernard. He keeps a copy of the key for every lock he ever forged," she answered. "I'll never understand why the young master chooses to stay in this closet. I guess it's familiar."

"Familiar?" Morgana asked puzzled.

"This has been the prince's room since he was a babe. The master stayed here with him, so he could get to the goat shed easily at night when George needed feeding."

"A goat," Morgana asked, surprised. "He didn't have a wet nurse?"

"Oh no, at the start of course, but ..." the woman fidgeted like she'd just realized that she'd said too much. "Well, I shouldn't say more. Let's say, in the end, his lordship preferred to do the feedings. It did the babe no harm. He was already eating mash by that point."

"Why didn't Lord Urien trust a nurse?" Morgana asked. She had a hard time seeing the gruff, old woodsman patiently feeding a fussy infant goat's milk and mash.

"Well, like I said, he did have one once," the older woman said in a conspiratorial whisper. "A comely pagan lass, who arrived claiming that her man and babe had been killed in the war. The master, well, he loved the babe, but you know how it can be with the father when the wife dies. Then one night, she stole away from the castle with the prince."

"What?" Morgana asked, astonished. "What happened?"

"No one knows, neither his lordship, nor the old high king ever said. One morning, the lass and babe were gone, and the master and Lear went after her," the cook whispered. "A few days later, they came back with the baby. Then he told my Bernard to fashion the biggest lock he could and put it on that door. After that night, the master wouldn't let anyone near the boy alone. Not until George was almost old enough to wield a blade himself."

"Why did she do it?" Morgana asked, taking another bite of cheese.

"Who's to say. Perhaps she wanted to replace the babe she'd lost and didn't think the master would mind so much. Though, some claim that she was one of the *bandraoi*, a druid woman of the old ways, and that she took the boy on the orders of the High Druid Merlin."

The cheese in Morgana's mouth felt like it had turned to ash. "When did this all happen?" Morgana asked.

"Oh, I don't know," the maid said, pondering. "Let's see, the prince was just about a year old. It must have been nine months or so after the sacking of Terrabil. So about the time Prince Arthur was born to your mother."

Morgana's mouth fell open.

It couldn't be a coincidence. She remembered everything about the night her brother, Arthur, had been born. How could she forget how Uther had held her mother down, as the woman screamed for Merlin to give her back her baby?

For three days after that, her mother had refused to eat or drink anything. Then, as suddenly as he had vanished, Merlin had returned with the child. What could be the odds of two princes being taken by the druids simultaneously, only to have both mysteriously return?

The aging cook, oblivious to Morgana's thoughts, suddenly spied the bound lock of soft, dark hair on her pillow and exclaimed, "Oh, is that yours? I see now. You didn't get a chance to give it to the young prince. He did leave so quickly."

Morgana looked down at the lock of hair and snatched it up. The lock of hair was not hers, nor had it been meant for George. However, the cooks words still brought to mind the last time she had seen the prince of Cear Celemion.

She had been angry, and he'd had that confused, hurt look on his face. Thinking about it, she realized it was the same look he'd had that day at the joust when he had come to her in the stands—the day they had met in Camelot.

She felt her guts clench as she suddenly understood what that look meant. He was about to risk his life, and all he had wanted was a small indication that he had something worth fighting for. A simple sign of gratitude. It would have cost her nothing to offer him a ribbon or a lock of hair, but she had refused him.

Tears welled unbidden to her eyes. "I've never given him a favor. Never." She sobbed.

"Oh, dear. Don't fret. He will be back. You'll see. He's a great warrior, our prince. Greater than his father and grandfather both if what they say be true. He could wield a mace and lance when he was but eight years old. He will come back to ye', you'll see," the older woman said, giving her a hug. "I have to get home to Bernard. You should eat, mistress. I'll come back in the morning for the tray."

As Morgana listened to the heavyset maid move up the stairs, she looked down at the lock of hair in her hand. Clenching her fists, she walked up the stairs to her old rooms, moving quickly before she had a chance to change her mind. Eldol was still there sleeping as she grabbed a pen and parchment and wrote a quick note. Then taking it, she walked over to the cage where a captive raven glared at her.

The ornery bird squawked at her from its perch. She smacked its beak as it tried to bite her and fastened the message to its leg.

"Listen, you evil bird. Take this to your master, and don't bother coming back," she said as she threw the raven out the window. It was not much, but it was something.

It was all she could do without jeopardizing her plans. Despite everything, those plans were all the more important now. She didn't know what purpose Merlin had in taking Arthur and George all those years ago.

But whatever the druid's plan was, it involved her somehow.

Her and her child.

Morgana looked down at the lock of hair that was there. The color so close to her own that it was no wonder the cook had believed it hers. Instead, it represented the one thing that mattered to her.

It didn't matter how many had to die ... Uther, Arthur, Merlin, Lancelot, Elod ... perhaps even Urien. All that mattered was that the Pendragons would fall, and she would see her child again.

Mordred, the child she could never speak of. The child she had been forced to leave in Camelot.

Chapter Sixteen

George Bertilack, Prince of Caer Celemion and Chieftain of the Lloegyr Rangers

The Otherworld

Who was the first that forged the deadly blade?
Of rugged steel his savage soul was made.

Albius Tibullus 41 BC

GEORGE FOUND HIMSELF SURROUNDED by strange voices that seemed to echo across space and time. Before him was a room; darker and more ancient than his grandfather's unfinished hall.

George was aware of himself, but he did not feel like himself. He was a child, an infant, yet he wasn't. It felt like a memory, yet it was not. For he was there, in a time and place he could not possibly have remembered.

"Anoint the sacrifices," a hooded man said, holding up his hands.

George's infant self was set down on a freezing altar as fresh blood was poured over his head.

Around him were inscribed pagan symbols of the old gods. However, these were not the gods his father prayed to. The symbols spoke to spirits of death and hate. In almost obscene contrast to this, stood a wooden Christian cross set before the altar.

Across from him was another platform, that bore a second child. This one a squealing newborn. The two altars connected by a set of lines inscribed on the floor that formed a five-pointed star, and in the center was a rock with a square iron anvil set upon it.

"By the blood and water of Britain, your sacrifice will be honored," the hooded figures surrounding the circle chanted.

"Did you bring the claimants?" an alien voice hissed in the darkness.

The tallest of the hooded figures stepped forward. "Oh, great son of *Balor*, we have done as you ask. Before you are two unbaptized scions of Britain, descendants of the line Aeneas by Brutus."

"Then, why do you bar me from my meal with these symbols of suffering and punishment?" the voice snarled as two eyes like red hot embers burned in the shadows. "These Christian totems offend my eyes."

The man then removed his hood to reveal the face of Merlin. However, this was not the aging, grey-bearded man who slunk around the courts of Britain. No, this man was young and strong, and there was a fierce ambition in his eyes.

"We seek not to offend you my lord, but times have changed," Merlin said, bowing as he hid his face from the creature's withering glare. "We have been too long without your favor. Too long without your guidance and protection. An age has passed since the Romans murdered the Keepers of Knowledge. Our sanctuaries and sacred places are no more. We have lost almost all knowledge of your teachings and magic. Thus, we have been forced to resort to the sorcery of our enemies," Merlin said, gesturing to the crosses. "We know not how to call on you without causing offense. Only by the magic of the Roman Christ God are we able to treat with you."

"And yet you fools know nothing of that God or the tyrannical magic of the light that holds this world in bondage! Though in your stumblings, you have hit upon some truth." The dragon said, glaring at the crosses. "But that's always the way with hedge wizards. Your magic is of no concern to me. You wish for a king. You will have one. I even allow you to choose which one of these offerings will be spared to rule. For this, I demand the other." The eyes vanished for a moment, and black scales reflected out of the darkness as the creature moved in its lair.

"My lord, you are old and wise. Tell us, will a king be enough to drive off the invaders and restore these islands to the old ways?"

"You demand a greater boon? Fine! I will forge a sword of power for your king so he may wield it in this island's darkest hour. But only the rightful King of Britain may wield it, for any other to hold it will bring only sadness and woe."

"For the ruler of our people to wield such a weapon would be a great honor," Merlin said.

"Yes, it would. You have a blade, sorcerer?" the dragon hissed.

"Yes, my lord," Merlin said. "Shameful for a sorcerer to lower himself by wielding steel, but such are—"

"Why should it be shameful for a sorcerer to carry a blade?" the dragon growled. "It was on an anvil such as the one before you that Azazel himself taught the first savage men to shape metal into sword and ax. What greater act of sorcery could there be, than to use fire, earth, air and water to forge the tools by which men do labor that is against their nature?'

"Of course, no smith among man, however, can smelt true steel. Your forges are weak attempts to create the heat I can produce with a single breath. For it was dragon fire that forged the swords of the ancient kings of the Sunken Empire. For my meal and your fealty, I will forge a sword for the Last and Future King of your choice," the hateful voice snarled. "Take out your blade, and hold it above the anvil."

George watched as the smirking Merlin walked forward and held the sword above the square iron anvil at the center of the chamber.

"I forge for you, Excalibur!" the dragon hissed, and a gout of flame shot from the shadows. In that brief flash of light, George saw the creature clearly. The same horrible, bat-winged monster that invaded George's dreams.

Merlin screamed as fire engulfed his hand, fusing it to the steel of the hilt. Meanwhile, the sword itself began to wilt into gory icicles. It was not like the way a blade was forged. It was a more wonderous thing. Like ice melting in the sun, only to freeze in the winter wind.

Eventually, the charred remains of Merlin's hand broke from his arm, and the red hot blade plunged down into the anvil, burying itself in the smooth iron block.

"My hand!" Merlin cried, as two of the other druids rushed forward to help their wounded master.

"There is always a price to be paid. I assumed even a hedge wizard would know this," the dragon chuckled.

"The sword," Merlin said, clutching his teeth against the pain as he gripped the charred remains of his wrist. "Get the sword."

One of the hooded figures moved cautiously to the anvil. "It won't budge," he said, exerting all his might to free the blade.

"Did you think I would give you such a weapon, wizard?" The creature laughed. "A blade like that is quite a dangerous thing for one such as me to give to one such as you. It may be wielded by the Rightwise King of these lands and no other."

"Then ... begin the incantation," Merlin said, grimacing in pain as he moved behind the altars. "We bring before our great dragon lord, two trueborn princes. One born to the kingdom of Camelot in lust, and one born to the kingdom of Caer Celemion in—"

An arrow flew out and took the druid standing beside him in the chest. George saw his father and grandfather as they charged into the cavern, Their blades flashing in the dim light as they cut down the attending druid novices.

"Remove the crosses. The bargain must be fulfilled," Merlin cried out to the other druids, as he retreated down a side passage with the infant Arthur in his arms.

George watched one of the hooded figures knock away the cross by the altar. The druid's reward for this was to be immediately engulfed by a gout of dragon fire as the beast moved forward to collect its due.

"No!" He heard his father's deep voice boom as he rushed forward and snatched George up in his arms.

George felt his infant self relax as the comforting scent of his father overpowered the sickening smell of smoke and blood.

The monster's hateful laugh echoed through the cave. "I had forgotten how good it was to witness true bloodshed." The dragon chuckled. "Now, give me the boy!"

"Never!" Urien yelled, clutching him protectively.

"Warrior of the old ways, you know what is demanded! That child is mine by right. For this amusement, I will allow you to leave here alive. I care about nothing but my claim!" the dragon snarled.

"You have no claim, demon!" He heard his grandfather yell. The king walking forward clad in the black armor and mail George now wore. Dropping his sword and shedding his armor to the floor as he went.

Reaching the center of the room he dropped his sword and shed his armor. The man who moments ago had seemed invincible, as he cut down his enemies with a mad fury, suddenly appeared quite old. Yet, in his age, there seemed to be a new strength.

"That child," he said, " Is my grandson. Born of the love between my noble daughter and this righteous lord. He is a descendant from the blood of the warrior saint, Sir George of Lydda, he who was martyred under the Emperor Diocletian for choosing the path of God and righteousness. I, Lear Abbot of Green Chapel and Once King of the Britons, renounce your claim! I renounce you, your master Satan and all the works of your demon kind, and in the name of the Father, and the Son, and the Holy Spirit, I baptize this boy, George, a child of God!" he said, pulling out a water skin and pouring it on George's face to wash away the blood the druids had smeared on him.

"Fool, do you think that a splash of water will stop me from claiming what is mine?" the dragon roared.

"I do. I do believe it, as I know you believe it," Lear said, stepping forward. "Otherwise, I imagine we would be charred cinders by now," Lear said, chuckling.

"Do you think I will be denied by a mad old king and Christian superstition? I am Ripper ... Tearer ... Slasher ... Scorcher. I am the teeth in the darkness, the talons in the night. Mine is all things unseen. I AM PAIN, HATE, AND WRATH; VENGEANCE, LUST, AND WAR! I AM GURZIL! Give me the child!" the beast roared as it paced in the shadows.

George saw his grandfather laugh, the look of madness, for which he had been famous, clear in his eyes. "Mad I must be to stand and laugh at a live dragon. Mad I am, but king I am no longer, I have no land, no knights, no power... nothing but my faith, and these hands. But if you name me king, then perhaps I have power still. I, Lear of the Hundred Knights, heir to Ambrosius Aurelianus, and Rightwise High King, as my last and final act as ruler, banish you, dragon, from these lands."

"You dare banish me!" The beast roared.

"Hear me, recreant!" Lear yelled as if he was chastising a rebellious peasant. "Put thy hated backside to our kingdom. By the power of God and my crown, you are banished, Gurzil, servant of Satan. You will leave my island before the sun next sets upon it."

"This is not finished." The dragon hissed, retreating back to the shadows. "The doom of this land has been foretold. It will come to pass."

Chapter Seventeen

Gwenivier of Cameliard

Aquae Sulis
July 9th 543 AD

Warriors who are to be exposed to the perils of battle, offer human sacrifices. For the performance of which they employ the Druids. For they believe that the only way of saving a man's life is to propitiate their god's wrath by rendering another life in its place ... The sacrifices are set to fire, and the victims burnt to death.

Julius Caesar 49 BC
Commentarii de Bello Gallico

Gwenivier was furious as she stamped through the ruins. It was dangerous to move alone in enemy territory, and she knew it. However, she didn't care.

She was angry and frustrated; anyone stupid enough to get in her way would die. Quite painfully if she had it her way.

She couldn't believe Lancelot had left her. True, George's arrival had completely killed the mood. But still, she had totally intended to finish what she had started. If only to spite him. However, she didn't get the chance.

Rather, Lancelot had gotten up, dressed, and left her!

Worse, he'd said that George was right, and that he should never have betrayed his king.

She couldn't believe it.

"How dare he say that George was right! How could he say that?" she mumbled to the moss-covered stones.

Even if George was right, and Gwenivier did not accept that, didn't Lancelot realize that once you had sex with a woman, you were obligated to disagree with their exes in all things unless otherwise specified? If George said that the sky was blue, then Lancelot should have insisted it was a different color ... any other color but blue!

Nor did she believe for an instant that George had "stumbled across them" while scouting the ruins. He was a fucking Ranger. She had watched him sneak into enemy camps without anyone realizing he was there until their throats were cut. Yet, he expected her to believe that he had just "stumbled upon" her and Lancelot in the middle of a haunted ruin.

Moreover, where did he get off judging her? After all, he was being all buddy-buddy with Tristan and Iseult. He didn't seem to care that Iseult was married to a rich and powerful king, all while she was fucking the man's nephew. He didn't seem to have any problem with that.

Yet, in her heart, Gwenivier knew she couldn't put her and Lancelot in the same category as Tristan and Iseult. After all, they truly loved each other. It was the sort of love that could never be concealed. They needed to only look at each other, to light up a room.

Gwenivier going off with Lancelot had been more an act of rebellion and self-sabotage. He had been kind to her. He was tall, charming, and ... well he'd been there.

He had seen her. The real her. Not the queen Merlin demanded she be. Nor the princess Arthur and her father wanted her to be. No Lancelot had seen Gwenivier as she was, with all her strengths and all her faults, and he liked what he saw. It had been the same with George for a time.

In the Orkney's when she had danced at the war camps, George's Rangers had cheered for her. She had fought beside them and been respected by them as an equal. Those days were over, and the Rangers she had fought alongside in the North were all now dead. All except for George. Now the Rangers had a new lady to cheer for. And when the dance was done, Gwenivier had watched as the beautiful queen Isuelt collapsed into Tristan's arms. However, there was no one to hold Gwenivier close, as George once. That is before war had turned him cold.

The Orkney's had been a bad war. A war of wolves. A war with no glory, and no honor. The savagery of the conflict eventually forcing the Northmen to send to the Danes of Heorot for reinforcements.

Gwenivier could remember standing on the rocky beach as the sails of their longships broke the horizon.

Even outnumbered, the Picts and Rangers might have held out. However, somehow the invaders had learned the locations of their hidden bases and secret paths across the island. It was only by the efforts of George and the Rangers that they had not all been slaughtered. George and his heavy cavalry had cut a path through the Viking lines, before heading for the coves where they kept the large barges needed to transport their giant warhorses. At that point, George alone had held the rearguard so that Gwenivier and her father could get their people to the longships. Unable to reach his own men, he'd been forced to evacuate with her and her father's forces.

Gwenivier remembered how George had stood on the stern barely breathing until he caught sight of the Rangers rowing out. However, that relief soon turned to horror as the swift longboats of the Northmen appeared over the horizon.

Like a pod of killer whales, the Danish longships hemmed in their prey. Weighed down as they were by horses and men, the Rangers never stood a chance. With oar, hook, and spear, the Viking raiders pushed the gunnels of the Ranger's barges under the waves, causing them to swamp and capsize.

Even had they been close enough to render aid, the fleet of Camliard would have stood little chance against the Danish pirates. As such, all they could do was watch as men and horses floundered in the freezing water. If she closed her eyes, she could still see the hard-faced Northmen bearing down on the capsized boats. Pitiless and efficient as spring sealers at their bloody work.

George blamed her. Why wouldn't he? After all, she blamed herself. However, he always seemed to forget that those men had been her friends too!

Not that it mattered anymore, she was marrying Arthur. The past, it seemed, would stay in the past.

It wasn't that she didn't like Arthur. He was a completely acceptable match, and marrying him would make her the most powerful queen in all of Britain. She would have fame, wealth, and respect.

She would be a queen of renown. Regardless of what Merlin, her parents, George or any of them might imagine.

"The Dark Lord Balor can take the fucking lot of them!" she yelled. However, no sooner had Gwenivier voiced her frustrations to the ruin, than the shockwave of a thunderclap nearly knocked her off her feet.

Come quick! Help him! a voice demanded.

"Who's there?" Gwenivier cried out, looking around before realizing that she had not so much heard the voice as thought it.

No time! He is trapped. The pool is safe to enter—the magic is now within him—but you must pull him from the water before he is lost forever. If I interfere, others will know. You must save him, Gwenivier!

Looking over, she saw a strange glow coming from the fountain at the center of the ruined hall in front of her. Moving forward to investigate, she saw George sinking to the bottom. His body was seized tight like in a fit, and his veins glowed a strange incandescent golden-yellow.

"George!" she screamed.

Dropping her weapons, she dove into the pool without a second thought. Grabbing George around the middle, she pushed off against the muddy bottom and made for the surface.

As she dragged him out of the shallow water. Laying him on his back, she stripped away his breastplate and armor. The yellow light that had been pulsing through his veins dimmed and disappeared.

"Don't die on me. Come on, breathe!" she yelled, slapping George's face, as the yellow light that had been pulsing through his veins dimmed and disappeared.

"This is not how you go out! No, everyone knows if you're going to die, it's going to be saving some pathetic damsel in distress. *Like, oh no, look an evil monster, if only there was a brave knight around to save me.* Wake up, Captain-Save-A-Ho! I said save me!" she yelled, pressing down on his chest to no effect.

"Damn it! The best horseman in Britain does not get to drown in a puddle the day before battle! That's just ridiculous!" she shouted at him, before locking her lips over his to fill his lungs with air.

George's response was immediate. He vomited into her mouth.

As the putrid bile struck the back of her throat, she fought back the urge to vomit herself. However, she soon had other problems, as George, now awake, drew the *seax* from his belt and lunged forward at her.

Startled, Gwenivier lost her footing and fell backwards into the water.

"Put that away this instant, or I swear I will put you back the way I found you," she said pulling herself back up out of the water, before walking over and kneeing George hard in the crotch.

He gave a pained grunt as he fell to the ground, hacking up more water as he did so.

"I wish I was dead," he groaned, clutching his sides.

"Yes, well, you're not," Gwenivier snarled. "What exactly were you doing?"

"No idea," George said.

"You're lying," she said, kicking him hard in the stomach.

"Please stop hitting me," he moaned, clutching his sides.

"Then, tell me what you were doing drowning yourself at the bottom of the world's creepiest fountain," she said, pointing to the sacred spring at the center of the ruined hall.

"I wasn't trying to drown myself. I tripped," George answered. "Thank you for saving me."

"I'll be sure to think twice before doing it again," the princess said as she picked up her weapons.

"I'm sorry about attacking you... I... I wasn't in my head. Are you ok?

"I'll be fine. What about you?" Gwenivier asked, once again swallowing back the urge to vomit, as her tongue found something soft and partially digested lodged in her cheek.

"I don't know. My lungs feel like they're on fire, and it feels like my brain is going to burst. I'm freezing to my bones, yet I'm hot and itchy all over," George moaned, finally sitting up.

"You were covered in some kind of magic or something. I swear it looked like your veins were on fire," she said, casting a suspicious glance at the pool.

"Feels like it too," George moaned.

"You got lucky. Few who touch the waters of Avalon survive," a voice said. Startled, she looked back to see Merlin leaning on his staff.

"Oh great, it's you," Gwenivier said, glaring at the leering wizard.

However, she was distracted from her seething thoughts by the sight of George standing up on uncertain legs. "What did you do to me?" he asked the druid.

"I did nothing. The vision was the fairy queen's doing not mine," Merlin said.

"I'm not talking about the vision. I'm talking about before when I was an infant."

"George, what are you on about?" Gwenivier asked.

"When I was a baby, he tried to sacrifice me to a dragon."

"Oh, the Lord Gurzil is so much more than just a dragon. So, your father and the old king never told you? That's interesting. Well, now you've seen the past with your own eyes, so I guess there's nothing more to tell," the one-handed sorcerer said and started walking away.

"Where do you think you're going? I have questions for you, old man!" George yelled.

"George, what's going on? What did he do?" Gwenivier felt like she was missing some important part of the story.

"I'm not entirely sure. He and the other druids took me and another child, who Im going to guess was Arthur, to a cave. They did something ... Not exactly sure what, but it was supposed to secure the dragon's favor. Then, my father and grandfather arrived. My grandfather baptized me and banished the dragon. Only Merlin here got away," George said. "A mistake I think I'll correct."

However, as George picked up his blade, Gwenivier jumped up between him and the glaring druid. "No, George! He's too important. Right now, he's the basis of Arthur's entire claim on Camelot. Think about it! If you kill him now, any unity our army has is gone. Whatever you saw in that pool, it's over, it's done."

"It's hardly over." Merlin chuckled. "Don't you see. Lear banished the dragon from this island. Now Lear is dead, and a new king is crowned. You broke Arthur's sword that day at the joust. Now he has a better one. Excalibur has been pulled from the anvil. Arthur has proven himself the Rightwise King of all Britain. The banishment your grandfather imposed on the Lord Gurzil holds no more, and when the Son of Balor returns, he will claim his due. The Faye will return to their places of power, and the druids will rule these islands as we did in the days of old. We will drive the Saxons and their dark gods from this island, and the Christian pestilence will fade and die. "

"Dear God, you really are crazy. You truly believe everything that demon told you?" George asked.

Merlin tapped his finger on his staff before commenting. "Your Christian sorcery can't defeat the Saxons. Only the old ways can bring lasting victory. Soon, the people will see that."

George laughed, holding his sides as he grimaced in pain. "Your old ways are dead and gone. They will not come back."

"They will when the people witness the power of the old gods. When they see the dragon for themselves." Merlin said spreading out his arms.

"You know nothing of the other world. Nothing of the Faye."

"And you do?" Merlin sneered.

"I have walked the mists. I have met the spirits you worship. Most are as devoted to the Holy Trinity as any Christian."

"Only because it has been forced upon them. The Faye were kings and queens here once. Your Christ-God has stripped them of their thrones and reduced them to nothing but imps, fools, and jesters. The being who keeps this fountain was once a mighty goddess. What is she now?"

"She is what she chooses to be," George answered.

"When the dragon returns, I will be the one who gives them back their thrones."

"The spirits you deify laugh at you. You're nothing but a joke to them. I'll tell you a secret about your druids of old. Do you know why they demanded human sacrifices? It wasn't to appease some dragon's hunger. No one who laid eyes on it would ever believe it possible to sate that creature's bloodlust. No, the priests of old gave it blood and gold because once people had given up what was most precious to them, they could never go back. A parent who gives their child to be consumed by dragon's fire must believe that it was done for some higher purpose. You tell them it was a noble sacrifice to sate a dragon's hunger and gain the god's favor. They believe it because otherwise, they would be facing the reality that it was all in service of nothing more than the insane vanity of evil men like you."

"You are not completely wrong," Merlin said, leaning against his staff. "However, it is not a lie. It is a rite of faith. A commitment to something greater than oneself. Through sacrifice, men and women bind themselves to their gods, and by doing so, they free themselves of the shackles of fear. That they may rise to levels of greatness, they would otherwise be incapable of. That is the power that Gurzil offers. He stands before all in his power, consumes all in his path, and by his fire, we are made strong," Merlin said, holding up his mutilated stump of a hand.

"You have sacrificed. So has she," he said, turning his owl-like eyes on Gwenivier. "You have been bled and burned. You have endured loss and pain. To ensure that sacrifice was not in vain, you will fight to the death? You regret the sacrifice, but enjoy what the pain has made you. Would you deny others that same sense of purpose?"

"I had a choice. We had a choice. What choice does an infant stolen from his family have?" George yelled.

"Choice is irrelevant. Whether a child is given by its parents willingly or ripped from a screaming mother's arms, it matters not. Their mind and soul will still demand that the loss be in service of some greater purpose. They may hate their gods for it, but they will honor them all the same."

Gwenivier needed Merlin to stop talking. Otherwise, George would kill the crazy old baby-killing magician, consequences be damned. And if he didn't, she would.

"Merlin, don't you need to get back to Arthur? I mean, what if he tries to have an original thought while you're away, or, God forbid, tries to take a piss without you holding his cock for him?" Gwenivier said, sneering at the druid.

"Oh, the refinement of the noble ladies of these isles." Merlin sneered. "They seem so lovely, right up until they open their mouths to speak. Then, the lot of you could put an Irish dock whore to shame. I do agree with those

Christian fools, the ones that call themselves bishops, about one thing. The queens of the Britons are all harlots."

"There are advantages to being a harlot," Gwenivier snarled. "After all, sluts don't get sacrificed to dragons."

"This is true, it is best if the offerings are pure." Merlin nodded. "Few cry when the village whore gets eaten alive. Though the Christians do love to cheer when they find a bitch to burn. But, by all means, Gwenivier, be proud of your bedroom conquests. I hear they also put the dock whores to shame."

"Merlin, do you think I'm going to stop her from killing you?" George chuckled, as Gweniever's hand tightened on her short sword.

"She won't harm me. She's too ruthless, and I am the key to the life she desires. She won't kill me, for the same reason she will marry Arthur."

"And what is it you think I desire?" Gwenivier snarled.

"Fame, and fortune, my lady. To be loved and renowned. To have men despair in their desire for you. You want a life of safety and comfort in a court of silk, pearls, and gold. Thanks to me you will have all of that."

"You think I'm for sale?"

"My lady ruthless, you are not for sale. You are bought and paid for. With me by his side, Arthur will be the greatest king this island has ever known. You will be the queen of the Britons and the Picts. The Hen kings and lords of the North will pay you homage, the Irish will be brought to heel, and the Saxons and their Northmen allies will be driven back to the sea. Peace will reign, and you will rule in fame and glory."

"That is not peace, it's subjugation and genocide!" George yelled.

"You would rather have freedom and anarchy; war and chaos?" Merlin asked sharply.

"I would live with men in peace rather than wade through the blood of women and children. The Saxons have been here for generations. There is no justice in forcing men and women from lands they were born to."

"Yet you come to fight them all the same," Merlin observed.

"I would make peace with the Northmen and the Saxons, on fair terms, if they would have it. If that means I must see Cedric and his bloodthirsty following in the dirt first, then I will fight and bleed for that cause. Not for yours."

"Says the Black Knight who scalps and burns his enemies alive, a prince whose inheritance is marked out with human skulls." Merlin sneered.

"To know one's enemy, you must become them. I know my enemy very well, and I know my people and how they fight best. If you let them, the Saxons will advance in an ordered shield wall, and as patient as winter, they will drive through an army like a wedge through wood. The only way to fight them is to force them to react, piss them off, and pull them out of their formations. To do so requires dark methods. I fight like a wolf, and it blackens my soul. But if saving my people means I scream in my sleep some nights, then that's the price I have chosen to pay."

"Say what you will, darkness is darkness. You and I are no different," Merlin said sagely.

"Evil is not in the thing. It is in the way in which it is used. Brutality is a tool. Use it as a crutch and the whole enterprise becomes counterproductive. And answering genocide with genocide leaves no one left alive!" George yelled.

"The winners in war are those who survive to the end," Merlin said. "I doubt I will live to see the end of this war. However, I do not think you will either. For I know the doom that stalks you. It will not be long before you walk the paths of the dead."

"Why did you choose Arthur?" George asked, ignoring the druid's dark prophesies. "You gave me to the dragon but Arthur was to be spared. Why?"

"Uther was the strongest of the lords. By his father, the blood of the ancient Roman emperors runs through his veins. From his mother he claims the inheritance of the great warrior queen Boudicia of old. He was the right choice to be king," Merlin said. "And had you died in that cave, your father would have had nothing to hold him back. Urien Bertilack would have been the champion of our people."

"My father loves me. That much I have always known. That love has never made us weak. It is our strength," George bellowed; his knuckles white as they gripped the hilt of his blade.

"Do not your own Christian scriptures tell of how your God demanded that Abraham sacrifice his son, Isaac, to the fire to prove his faith? It is true your father loves you. As he loved your mother, body, and soul. As Uther never loved Arthur.'

'That was the reason you were chosen. Had you been given to the dragon, we druids could have offered Urien a way to vent his grief. Urien would have freed us from the Saxon scourge, and Arthur would have inherited a free land. For we would have seen to it that your father had no living heir."

"But I didn't die. I was saved. Just as God made sure Isaac was spared at the last minute. Seems to me I was not meant to die."

Merlin shook his head, "you should have been the martyr who freed our people. Instead, you lived, and the greatest warrior on this island spent his strongest years hiding away in a forest raising a spoiled child."

"Don't you see, you fucking fool?" George laughed. "Your dragon couldn't kill me. When my grandfather baptized me, that protected me from your demon. I suspect that protection still holds. So, if your dragon does come back, what's keeping him from taking Arthur rather than me? You did not keep your end of the bargain, and your gods aren't known to be forgiving."

"You think the ways of your God are so different from mine? Look at the symbol you wear. A cross, an instrument of torture and oppression. Do you have any idea how many druids the Romans crucified on this island?"

"I wear it to remind myself that Christ died for my sins, that he suffered at the hands of fanatics and tyrants for the sake of their vanity and power. As you say, sacrifices have power. His sacrifice was the greatest of all. It reminds me that faith and belief do not come from giving men like you what is most precious in this world," George countered.

"So clever. A student of the old ways and the Christ-God both. You're nothing but an amateur. Arthur is protected as well. I had him baptized and fostered by Sir Ector. He has been raised in the new faith to guard against just such an eventuality as the one you speak of. It won't matter in the end. When the old ways return, the thin water of the Christ-God will be rinsed away with sacrificial blood," Merlin said, turning to leave.

"The old ways are no more," George said, weighing his dagger in his hand. "I could kill you now, Merlin, but I don't need to. The days of blood are over. If your dragon dares return, we will kill it and be done with both it and you."

"You mock what you could never understand. I serve the deep magics that bind the worlds together. You cannot even comprehend the questions to ask," Merlin proclaimed.

"I do have one question. Who is the woman?" George asked.

Merlin looked puzzled. "Who? The wet nurse who brought you to us? She was no one, a follower of the old ways. She is long dead."

"No, not her. The woman from my dreams," George answered. "The one the dragon is after."

A dark look came across the old druid's face. "Describe her!"

"Raven hair and coal black eyes. Dressed in red silk," George said. "Skin dark as midnight."

"The Southrons! Damn the daughters of Dido! Interlopers! The faithless beast has returned to his old masters!" Merlin screamed. "Do you know what this means?"

"That you're both raving lunatics," Gwenivier ventured.

"A lifetime of work wasted because of one pious, old madman!" Merlin ranted.

"So, I take it the dragon's not on its way to eat me?" George said.

"The Horned Lord will have his due, believe me. The magics of this island are potent. Crosses and holy water will not banish them. The old ways will return. The dragon is your doom. It was foretold, and it will come to pass!"

Chapter Eighteen

Pudentius, Tribune of Leptis Magna

Leptis Magna
July 9th 543 AD

The Moors who are called Lauathai came to Sergius with a great army at the city of Leptis Magna, spreading the report that they had come so that Sergius might give them the customary gifts and insignia to make the peace secure. Sergius was persuaded by Pudentius ... to receive eighty of the most notable men among them into the city, promising to fulfill all their demands, but commanded the rest to remain in the suburb.
After giving to these men pledges concerning the peace, he invited them to a banquet ... When they began a discussion with him, they

brought many charges against the Romans, and in particular said that their crops had been plundered wrongfully. Sergius, paying no attention to these things, rose from his seat and wanted to leave. One of the barbarians present, laying hold of his shoulder attempted to prevent him from going .... and one of the spearmen of Sergius drawing his sword killed that Moor. As a result, a great commotion arose in the room, as was natural, and the spearmen of Sergius killed all the barbarians. But one of them, seeing the others slain, jumped out of the house where these things were taking place, and unnoticed by anyone returned to his people and revealed what had happened to their fellows.

Procopius of Caesarea, 544 AD
The Wars of Justinian

FINALLY WILLING HIMSELF TO stand Pudentius, had staggered towards the courtyard. There he had looked out blankly at the scene in front of him for hours.

He had been an imperial soldier his entire life. He had walked battlefields of blood and bile. Yet, looking at the slaughterhouse that had once been a palace courtyard, he felt the contents of his stomach heave up into his throat.

The Vandals had done their work thoroughly. As he looked among the dead, he saw faces of men he had known and lived amongst. Men he had fought side by side with at Bulla Regia and Tricamarum. Among these was King Alba of Saline.

Pudentius felt sick remembering how he had convinced Alba to ally himself with the Empire during the Vandal wars.

God only knew how many days he had spent crossing the barren sands in search of the legendary desert kingdom. So many times, he'd imagined he saw the great lake of Saline only to find that it was simply a mirage. Only after he had washed the grit from his mouth with the water of the city's lake had he allowed himself to believe his eyes.

Saline had been a marvel. A city of commerce and life in the middle of nowhere.

Looking down at the dead king, Pudentius remembered how Alba had welcomed him into his home, introducing him to his mighty queen and their beautiful daughter. How proud the man had been as he showed Pudentius his palace and homeland.

Little more than a decade had passed since that time, but it felt like a lifetime ago.

What plans he'd had back then. They would drive out the Vandals and bring unity to the land once again. A caravan road would be established across the deserts. Diamonds, ivory, slaves, exotic beasts, and gold would flow north from the southern jungles. Finally, under the guidance of the imperial engineers, they would build great canals. Artificial rivers would turn the desert into fertile farmland, and supply the whole of the Empire with grain.

None of these great dreams had come to be. All of the promises he had made the man had come to nothing. In the end, all that imperial occupation had brought was slavery, anarchy, war, and death.

The king's lifeless eyes stared up at Pudentius full of just accusation. All of the promises he had made the man had come to nothing. In the end, all that imperial occupation had brought was slavery, chaos, war, and death. Yet, somehow shame escaped him, but fear did not.

It was not fear of the Vandal cutthroats who were now stripping and looting the dead. Nor was it fear of the army of Moors that would certainly seek retribution for this crime. All he could think about was that, for this stupidity, he would be doomed to The Pit forever.

All fears paled when compared to The Pit.

Once after the Battle of Tricamarum, he had found himself alone with General Belisarius. Battle-weary, Pudentius had asked the man if he knew what manner of creature his wife was. "Of course! I share the woman's bed. Do you think I am blind? I know what Antonia is. I know what *They* all are."

He knew, of course, who *They* were. *They*, were those who would prowl the imperial palace day and night, or lounge in their beds for days on end yet never sleep. *They* were those who demanded elaborate feasts, and yet ate nothing.

"But if you know ..."

"Why do I share my wife's bed? Why do I serve my Emperor? Why did I put sword to the rioting mob that wished to depose them?" Belisarius said, asking the questions Pudentius had not yet voiced. "I am an imperial soldier. I serve the Empire."

"But why not oppose them. You could overthrow them?" It had seemed so achievable at that moment. There, they were with an army, allies, a strategic port, and a base of supply. They had everything needed to launch a revolution. However, Belisarius only laughed.

"Do you truly think I would make a good emperor? I promise you I would not. Those who lead us are no worse than any other for what they are. Many men have been born in every age who, in one way or another, have shown themselves to be true born monsters. They have been the ruin of cities, and destroyers of countries. Can you name any form of evil that a demon could perpetrate that could not also be done by mortal hands? I doubt that even the devil himself is all that different from your average mortal despot."

Staring at the bleeding and bloated corpses before him in the courtyard, Pudentius realized the truth of the general's statement. These men had been slain by no demon. Rather, it had been mortal steel wielded by the hands of ordinary men that had ended them. Whatever threats, promises, or lies they had been told to drive them to this crime, it did not change what they were. These assassins were men, and that made their actions all the more monstrous.

Then again, had he not done such deeds himself?

The truth was that, in the end, it didn't matter. He had a job to do. This was a mess, and it was his task to see it cleaned up. Pulling himself from his thoughts he walked up to the man closest to him.

"Where is the witch?" he asked.

"Don't know. Stupid bitch botched the job. Gunthuris got pissed and sent her away."

"Then where is Gunthuris? Where is the *Dux*?"

The man gave a huff and continued rifling through the pockets and purses of the dead. But Pudentius was in no mood, he grabbed the man and hurled him onto the blood-soaked table. Drawing his dagger as he did so.

"Tell me what I want to know, or I will personally start slitting throats until I get answers. Starting with yours."

"Calm down. I'm here," Gunthuris said, walking up with Sergius close at his heels.

"What have you done?" Pudentius yelled.

It was the question he kept repeating. Unable to move past it in his mind.

"I did your job. I protected your *Dux* when the Moorish King attacked him."

"That is bullshit. He was an old man."

"Old men can be dangerous. I just saw one with a blade to the throat of one of my best," Gunthuris said.

"None of this would have happened if you hadn't provoked him. You did it deliberately so you would have an excuse for this massacre."

"Prove it," Gunthuris scoffed,

"It's all for the greater good, Pudentius. Gunthuris has simplified the problem," Sergius said, smiling at the pile of corpses. "You were right. They were never going to agree to give us the grain for nothing."

"We don't have the grain. Right now, it's in the middle of an army of Moors!" Pudentius shouted.

"Which, thanks to their leader's assault on my person, we now have *cassa belle* to attack. We can legally seize the grain by force," Sergius said brightly, picking a piece of fruit off the blood-soaked buffet table.

"Did any of them get away?" Pudentius asked soberly.

"We lost Princess Sabra. She and one of the other Berber lords escaped through a window into the city. It won't take us long to find them. The man looked to be a few seasons past his prime, and the girl was ... injured," Gunthuris said, gritting his teeth, as he cast a nervous glance towards the sky.

"I want them found. We need to give Ierna's people as much time as possible to take control of the Berber tribes," Sergius said. Yet the decisive tone felt unnatural, almost ridiculous, coming from the pampered man-child. "See Pudentius as I told you everything is in hand. By removing all the secular heads of state, the people will now have no choice but to fall in line behind the priests of the temple of their great horned ... whatever. No more dealing with factions. No more tribal bullshit. It's enough to give a man a headache. From now on, there will be one group running all of it."

"Ierna and his followers are a pack of wild dogs!" Pudentius yelled.

"Gunthuris assures me the man can be reasoned with, or at the very least, that he can be bought. I'm confident that with the kings and chieftains of the Lauathai dead, Ierna will be able to secure power over the native tribes."

Pudentius shook his head. The idiot was going to give the whole fucking lot to Ierna and Gunthuris. Did he truly think that he could control either man? Worse Sergius wasn't even doing this to gain power or wealth. No, he had butchered innocent men and handed power over to a fanatical cult simply because he couldn't be bothered to do his job. All this blood, all the suffering that would come after it, all so Sergius could sit content in his bath water and fuck his slave girls all day.

That was, of course, saying it all went down like Sergius expected. Pudentius seriously doubted it would. Too many ways for this plan to go terribly wrong. He could already see it falling apart. Sooner or later, the Vandals and/or Ierna and his cult of crazies would turn on them. When that happened, they would probably just start killing everyone.

However, these were concerns for another day. For now, he was an Imperial Tribune, and he had a job to do.

"Who was it that escaped with the princess?" Pudentius asked.

"An old man, blue robes, long scar down the center of his face," Gunthuris answered.

"Kaboan," Pudentius sighed, looking across the desert towards the Amazigh encampment. "Well, you'd better catch him, or we are all going to die. If the Eagle of The Desert makes it back to his people carrying their bloodied princess, it won't matter what deals you have made with man, God, or the devil. They will rise for him, and he will kill us all."

"Did you say the Eagle?" Gunthuris asked, a haunted look crossing the Vandal warlord's face.

"Yes, Kaboan, the Eagle of the Desert. King of the Lauathai Amazigh. Defeater of Thrasamund, Sacker of Leptis Magna. A man who fought in the vanguard side by side with General Belisarius at Tricamarum, and you thought to slaughter him like a spring lamb."

As he spoke, a roar of outrage sang out over the sands from the Amazigh encampment.

"Beware the eagle, the lion, and the bear. For the righteous will resist you," Gunthuris whispered to himself, as he stared off across the sands.

Sergius turned white. "What do we do?" he asked.

Pudentius resisted the urge to laugh.

What should he do? Now, the boy asked the question.

Pudentius could have told him what not to do. He could have told him not to send away the gold he needed to pay the Moors for the grain. Not to hire a bunch of two-faced Vandal mercenaries. Not to slaughter the local kings and all their men, and most of all after he'd done all that, not to let the most fearsome and respected North African cavalry commander since Hannibal escape!

"I need five of the best horses you have. Rig them with packs, water, and supplies for a journey, but don't weigh them down," Pudentius said to one of his officers.

"Escape. Yes. Good idea." Sergius nodded.

"The horses aren't for us," Pudentius snarled.

"What?"

"You can't even stay on your horse during a hunt. How the hell do you expect to evade the Moors in their desert? And when they catch you, and they will catch you, they will kill you and I guarantee they will get extremely creative about it. No, you and I are going nowhere but to the vault, or wherever it is you've hidden your treasure," Pudentius said, grabbing the panicking nobleman's arm and dragging him towards the palace. As he went past, he called out to one of his officers. "Gorcus, come with me and bring a bag."

Arriving at the vault, Pudentius forced Sergius to open the treasury, sickened by the sight of the hoarded wealth before him. He grabbed the bag from his second and filled it with treasure.

"You greedy fucking idiot! You do realize all of this would have been enough to buy you the grain and secure the peace." Pudentius snarled at the meek-looking Dux.

Turning to his second in command, Pudentius asked, "Gorcus, do you have any friendly contacts among the tribes? Or should I say, any friendly contacts who don't have a brother or uncle among the dead in our courtyard?"

"Maybe," the officer answered.

"Good enough. Take three of our best riders. Go east. There is a port town on the Egyptian border called Bernici. You'll find an imperial intelligence outpost there. Now, I don't care what it takes. I don't care who you have to bribe or kill. You get there, and you find a man name Artabanes or his brother, John."

"Who the hell are they?" Sergius asked.

"They are Armenian imperial intelligence officers in the service of the Prefect of Alexandria," he said to Gorcus, ignoring the *Dux*.

"What are agents of the Prefect of Alexandria doing in Libya? Why wasn't I informed?" Sergius complained.

"Corruption, embezzlement, imperial renegades, the creepy black-robed priests in the desert, your Vandal friends. Take your pick as to what they are investigating. All of it's kind of a moot point now since your stupid schemes are about to cost the Empire the whole of Africa! Over ten years of my life for nothing. What matters now is that

Artabanes has the ear of the Prefect of Alexandria and Senator Areobindus, and both men have soldiers and ships."

"Why aren't we trying to get to my uncle in Carthage? Or General Belisarius in Italy?" Sergius asked.

"Maybe because Egypt might actually send help. Even if he wanted to, Belisarius can't help us because your uncle and Procopius managed to convince the Emperor to pass an edict making it an act of rebellion for him to so much as step foot on African soil. And even if your uncle decided to send aid, it's unlikely the imperial garrison in Carthage would march out to fight an army of righteously pissed-off Moors to save your skinny dick."

"They serve the Empire."

"They're owed over six months back pay! Don't think; you're no good at it. Do me a favor, make yourself useful and take the remaining gold, go down to the port, and arrange for ships for an evacuation, and I suggest you don't haggle," Pudentius screamed as he walked back down the hall.

"You really think this is over, sir?" Gorcus asked.

"It's not over until it's over. Find Artabanes, bring help, and pray we live long enough for it to get to us. You leave now," Pudentius ordered as his quartermaster rushed up to him.

"Tribune, the Vandals are demanding access to the armory!"

"Give it to them," Pudentius said, without stopping.

"After what they did, sir?" the man asked.

Pudentius sighed. The quartermaster had been stationed in Libya since the Vandal wars. He had inevitably known some of the men who had been slaughtered.

"They did what Sergius and Solomon paid them to do. Regardless of our feelings on their actions, we are imperial soldiers, and they are our commanders," Pudentius said with a sigh.

"With all due respect sir, fuck that."

Pudentius wheeled on the man. He did not have time for a mutiny. "Right now, the only way we live is to wade through blood until we are out of this mess. Arms and armor do us no good in the armory! Anyone who wants to fight, issue them a fucking kit! Do you hear me, soldier?"

"Yes, Tribune," the quartermaster said, snapping to attention.

"Then, assemble the men, full infantry armor, shields, and spears. Have all of them and the Vandal auxiliaries meet me at the gate."

Chapter Nineteen

George Bertilack, Prince of Caer Celemion and Chieftain of the Lloegyr Rangers

Aquae Sulis
July 9th 543 AD

I don't care how tactically or operationally brilliant you are, if you cannot create harmony—even vicious harmony—on the battlefield based on trust across service lines, across coalition and national lines, and across civilian/military lines, you need to go home,

because your leadership is obsolete.

General James "Mad Dog" Mattis, USMC
Address to the US Joint Forces Command
Conference 2010 AD

After leaving the ruins, George had walked back to the war camp alone.

"Where have you been?" Urien demanded, walking towards him from the direction of the command tent.

George just stood there, remembering the vision he had seen in the fountain. He remembered how his father had protected him, shielding him from the monster.

He had never had a mother. It had been his father and grandfather who had raised, protected, and trained him. The training had been hard, and the discipline rough, but they had loved him. He had never doubted that.

Without a second thought, George did something he had not done since the day he had returned from the campaign in the Orkneys. He hugged his father.

"What's wrong?" the grizzled warrior asked, as he held George close.

"I'm sorry I took the Rangers to the Orkneys. I should not have disobeyed you."

"I did not forbid you nor the Rangers from going, only the riders of Haustdesert. You did what you thought was right. I was proud of you for that. You are a son any father would be proud of. Where have you been? And why are you wet?" Urien asked.

"I didn't want to wait around like a dog to be summoned by Arthur. I went to check the ruin. I fell in one of the pools."

"You shouldn't have gone alone at night."

"Shadow walkers don't sneak up on camps of drunk soldiers during the day," George countered.

Urien looked over his drenched son's shoulder to see Gwenivier walking back into camp, wringing the water from her curls.

Urien's hand swung out fast, cuffing his son in the head. "Are you daft, boy, or just suicidal?"

"What?" George asked in surprise.

Urien nodded over to the future queen of Camelot.

"I wasn't with her. She was there, but it's not like that," George whined in protest.

"You're going to lie to me? On the eve of battle," his father snarled.

"I'm not lying. I went to check the ruins. She was there, the end. If there was anything lingering between us, it's gone now, trust me," George answered.

"You're not telling me everything."

"You don't want to know everything," he snapped. "I'd prefer not to know everything right now, and I'm doing my best to forget much of what I know."

"We will discuss this later. We are needed at the war council," Urien said, letting the matter drop.

"I saw mother's statue," George added.

Urien stopped. "I thought your grandfather destroyed it."

"I know, but I saw the inscription," George said.

"After this is over, I think I'd like to see her again," his father murmured.

"I saw Merlin as well," George added.

"And what did that old cat owl tell you?" Urien asked without turning around.

"Things you should have told me, a long time ago," George answered, and in that instant, he saw his father age before his eyes.

"You're right. Come. We should talk," he said, slumping his shoulders and gesturing over to a bench. However, before they could sit down, Galahad came rushing up.

"There you are," he panted. "There is a problem."

"We have so many problems. Be specific," George said.

"We have a new, rather immediate problem-"

"What! What more could possibly have happened?" George said, throwing up his hands, surprising himself with the venom of his response.

Galahad stepped back. "There is a debate going on about who should be in command of the army."

"That's Arthur's problem," George snapped.

"And yours," Galahad added cautiously. "You have some friends and more than a few strong voices are calling for you to remain as warleader."

"What the hell!" George yelled. "I swear to God! If all we ever had to do was fight each other, the Britons would be counted as the greatest masters of war in the circle of the world."

As he walked into the pavilion that had been set up as a war room, he saw Iseult standing in front of the table of knights and lords. "Tradition dictates that the lord who arrives on the field of battle first and sheds blood is the warchief," she said.

"Since when do Irish slags dictate the laws of the Britons?" Sir Kay shouted.

"How dare you? She is the Queen of Kernow," Tristan shot back.

"I agree with her ladyship. George has the experience in battle, and he has already scouted both the field and opposing force. Perhaps it is best that he remains in command," Leodegrance added.

"We have an agreement, Leodegrance!" Arthur shouted.

"Lear was the last rightful High King of Britain," another lord yelled.

"Lear abdicated his throne. He died a mad monk," Sir Bedivere retorted. "His claim is null and void."

At this Sir Ciaus grabbed the knight herald by the collar. The aging knight lifted the younger Bedivere over his head, before hurling him to the ground. "Listen well you base, proud, shallow, beggarly, three-suited, hundred-pound, filthy, worsted-stocking knave! Lear was a great man, and a greater king. The greatest I have ever had the privilege to know. Only for the sake of my family, my lands, and my people did I serve Uther in silence for all these years. My forced fealty kept as a prize by a tyrant; in the foolish belief that it transferred with it some of the noble authority of my former master. But I tell you truly not one day in all that time did I not consider how I might kill the usurper."

"I'll see you dead old man." Bedivere snarled, leaping to his feet.

"Sixty winters I have seen. In that time I have fought more battles than any man here. This shall be my last, the Morrigan herself even now whispers to me. It makes little difference to me if I die tonight or tomorrow." Ciaus shouted, as he swiftly drew a dagger from his belt.

"It makes a difference to me," George said calmly, as he walked up behind the old knight. "If this is to be the final battle of Sir Caius, the Sacker of Cent, then I would like to say that I was there beside you."

Caius turned, tears wetting the old man's eyes, as he touched his forehead to George's. "My deepest regret, my lord, is that I did not come to serve your authority sooner. You are your grandfather's very image."

"You were my grandfather's most loyal captain. He often spoke of you. He bid you serve your lands and people, and he respected you for doing so. Peace, for we all now face a common enemy."

Walking to the center of the tent George looked around at the angry faces that filled the room. "In this tent are those I have known as friends, and those I have known as enemies. But know that I am happy to see every single one of you here. I would be happier still if all those who were slain on Sarum plain were here with us, along with those who have died in all our pointless civil strifes. We shall miss their spears and swords tomorrow. For right well over two thousand Saxons march on us. It is an army with one purpose. Its single goal, is to wipe this world of ours from existence. We will not fight amongst ourselves here. Nor will we be such fools as to divide our forces under two commanders. There is no question who is in command. One hundred and fifty men came to this place at the call of Haustdesert, almost three times that many came on the behest of Camelot. Tomorrow, we all ride under the Pendragon banner, or not at all."

Arthur quickly leaped on the opportunity offered. " Yes! and I say we make our stand here and avenge ourselves on the Saxon horde. For the blood of every Briton they have slain, we will spill the blood of twenty!" he said to cheering applause.

"Good. Now, that's settled. Arthur, may we talk in private?" George asked soberly.

"Whatever you have to say, you can say before all," Lancelot said, walking in with Gwenivier suspiciously in tow.

"I was speaking to Arthur," George snarled.

"And Lancelot speaks for me. You can say your piece before all assembled," Arthur said defiantly.

"Fine. I suspect the Saxons will be here by dawn," George said. "Now, unless we plan to fight amongst ourselves until they get here, might the warchief wish to confer privately with a humble scout?" George asked, gesturing off to the side.

Arthur seemed unsure but eventually nodded and followed George out of the tent. His bodyguard Bors following him closely.

"I said a private word," George said, turning to the fair-haired executioner.

"I go where my king goes," Bors answered.

"Leave us, Bors. I trust the prince isn't planning on killing me here," he said, waiting for the man to leave before turning to George. "Alright, let's talk about the Saxons."

"Like I said, Cedric's army is at least two thousand strong with maybe three hundred or so housecarls and chosen men. I saw no women, camp staff, or livestock. This isn't an expeditionary force. It's an army of destruction, one that plans to supply itself on the raid."

"All on foot," Arthur asked.

"Some thanes and mounted raiders. No heavy cavalry, and they have lost many of their light horse and scouts over the past few days."

"Good. One mounted knight is equal to eighty men on foot. We press the advantage of our heavy horse," Arthur said, heading back towards the council.

"With all due respect, the Saxons have withstood our cavalry before," George said.

Arthur strode back. "What would you have us do?" he spat. "Would you have us run?"

"No, this is Badon. These are the hills the Britons must fight or die on. I believe we can win this if you listen to me," George added.

"Listen to you?" Arthur snarled. "Didn't you hear them? Half of them think it's you who should be leading us. What do you think they will do if they learn I'm following your battle strategy?"

"As I said, Arthur, I brought a hundred men here. That's what I could muster. You brought four hundred, and, given time, Camelot could muster twice that. I'm not laying siege to your golden hall anytime soon. True, my grandfather was High King, but that's only because he had an entourage of a hundred armored knights and squires. Once he didn't have that, he was just a tired, half-mad old man," George said sternly.

"If renouncing my claim on the kingship over the Britons is what it takes to get you to listen, then I renounce it, Arthur."

"You'll swear allegiance to me as king?" Arthur asked.

"Don't push it, I won't do that," George hissed.

"Yet, you still expect me to trust you," he snorted. "What about the claim my sister holds on my western territories?"

"Me and Morgana aren't married. Even if we were, I would still have no right to renounce her inheritance," George said, grinding his teeth. "I prefer to ride into battle as friends, but that is not a requirement. Like I said that day at the stones; Urien and Uther were enemies, George and Arthur don't need to be. You don't need my oath. You just have to trust that I have no interest in civil war."

Arthur looked up at the stars. "You know when we jousted, I wasn't knocked out. I had my eyes closed so I didn't have to yield. You could have killed me that day, couldn't you have?"

"It was an honest contest. I had no reason to see Arthur dead, and I still don't. Together, you and I have a chance to give our people freedom and peace. Something they have not had in recorded memory. That is why I didn't kill you on the field, or at the henge. One day, we will have to decide where we stand in respect to each other, but first, we need to drive the Saxons back over the border!" George answered.

Arthur gave a sigh and sat down on the bench. George sat down next to him, but no sooner had he done so than Gawaine came rushing out of the tent with Tristan and Lancelot following closely behind.

"What's wrong now?" George asked.

"Uncle Leodegrance and Gildas got into an argument," Gawaine said.

"Please tell me he didn't kill one of the priests." Arthur said, looking back at the sky.

"No, but Leodegrance says the Picts won't fight tomorrow," Tristan answered.

"What!" Arthur and George both exclaimed.

"Is Gwenivier backing out of the marriage?" George asked, glaring at Lancelot.

"No ... I mean, yes ..., I assume the wedding is off," Gawaine babbled. "I guess Merlin had told my uncle that the old gods had chosen Arthur, to be king, when he brokered the marriage with Gwenivier. Leodegrance started asking questions and discovered that Arthur is in fact a Christian. Now he says he doesn't believe the old gods would choose a Christian to be High King. Worse some of the lords are now questioning whether Arthur is in fact Uther's son. Some apparently hold that he's in fact the son of Gorlois,"

"That's ridiculous," Arthur shouted.

"It's also irrelevant. Gorlois had as much claim on the title of High King as Uther did," Tristan added. "But Leodegrance now says he wants proof of the gods favor before he will commit his troops to battle."

"Find Merlin!" George and Arthur replied in unison.

Chapter Twenty

Qaseem

**Leptis Magna
July 9th 543 AD**

Many witches possess one or more hyenas which are branded with their mark, and ... The elders tell a number of supposedly true stories about the sorrow and rage of witches whose hyenas were killed.

*Some Structural Aspects of Mbugwe Witchcraft
Robert F Gray 1963 AD
Witchcraft and Sorcery in East Africa*

FINDING THE AMAZIGH HAD not been hard. Sneaking into the encampment, however, proved more difficult.

The camels surrounding the camp had been quick to react to the appearance of a hyena in their midst. Qaseem had been able to dodge their kicks and teeth; however, the commotion drew the attention of the human guards. Qaseem barely managed to dodge the two javelins, they hurled at him, as he rushed into the camp. Quickly, he went to ground under a pile of crates and camel saddles. Stifling the reflexive laughing growl that formed in his throat.

He was angry at himself for being spotted. Sneaking past the human's unseen should have been easy. After all, Qaseem had been sneaking into human camps since he was a pup.

After a moment, Qaseem carefully, sniffed the air to see if the coast was clear. That's when he smelled it. The perfumed scent of smoke and death barely covered by frankincense cologne. Qaseem would know that smell anywhere. His upper lip rose in a reflexive snarl.

It was Ierna. The man who had left him for dead on the sands.

The high priest was walking with another masked figure. He knew this man's smell as well, the stench of hashish and body odor was unmistakable. It was Wahb ibn Hudhafah, an Arab who'd come to the Maghreb with a cult of mystics from the east. Wahb claimed to be a follower of Baal, who had come to answer the call of his son Gurzil. However, Qaseem had known Wahb before he had pledged himself to the cause of the Horned God.

He had first met him years ago in the village of Jeddah on the Red Sea. Back then the man had been a charlatan, hawking useless spells and idols, to the desert tribes. However, it had been obvious to Qaseem, back then, that the man had never believed in the gods he claimed to serve.

He suspected Wahb had come west hoping to profit off the superstitions of the cult, only to come face to face with the might of the dragon. Now the man believed every one of his earlier lies, with a blind fanatical devotion that appealed to Ierna and his dragon master.

The two men were no more than five feet from where he was hiding. Qaseem could have rushed forward and torn the throat out of both men in an instant. However, that would expose his position.

Had he been human, he might have taken the chance. But there was no stronger drive in a hyena than that of self-preservation. Qaseem would not give up his life. Not for revenge.

"We should have had men present at the meeting. It was an insult to be barred from attending," Wahb said haughtily.

"There is no reason for us to attend. It would only lead to awkward questions later on." Ierna said, placing his hand on the other man's shoulder. "It is better this way. King Alba and Kaboan will both be killed by Gunthuris and his Vandals, along with their loyalists. The Imperials will take the blame for the massacre, and no one will suspect our involvement."

"What of our Lord Gurzil's bride?"

"The Vandals will capture the Princess Sabra and deliver her to us," Ierna said with a wave of his hand.

"Can we trust them?" the masked Arab hissed.

"They have now borne witness to the might of Gurzil. What trust is required." Ierna answered.

"But what if they decide to deliver the princess to our lord themselves?" Wahb whispered.

"Let them. All that matters is that the blood of Dido comes to our Lord Gurzil. Let the Vandals have their war. Let them conquer. In the end, we will hold the true power ..."

Qaseem heard fast footsteps approaching. "Have you seen a hyena pass this way?" the perimeter guard asked.

"Why would there be a hyena in the camp?" Ierna asked.

"One of the guards said they saw one sneak past."

"It was probably just a dog," Wahb scoffed.

Qaseem let out a sigh of relief. He was now glad that he had always been careful to keep his true nature from the high priest, and it seemed the dragon had not told the man Qaseem's secret either. If he had, Ierna might not have dismissed the news of a hyena's presence so quickly.

It was then, that screams of grief and outrage rose from the other side of camp, to echo across the sands.

The guard who had been pursuing Qaseem immediately gave up his hunt and hurried to investigate. Wahb moved to follow him, but Ierna restrained him.

"Let's wait and see what is known before rushing in blindly," Ierna said leading the man away.

Taking advantage of the distraction, Qaseem rose and made his way towards a tent on the far side of the encampment. Following the familiar smell of herbs, marble dust, and magic.

He was almost there when she emerged. Beautiful as ever, Kahina stood there bathed in the dim torch light, as a crowd clamored towards her. At the mob's head was a blood-soaked warrior bearing an unconscious, wounded woman.

. He recognized the man. He was Kaboan king of the Amazigh. Which meant that the woman in his arms was most likely Princess Sabra. Qaseem's mouth watered at the smell of blood and death that hung over them. She was wounded and badly.

That would not please the Horned Lord.

"Someone's going to be in trouble." Qaseem chuckled softly to himself, ducking back into the shadows. Slowly, he forced his belly to the sand as he snuck under the edge of Kahina's tent. The coarse grit rubbed against the raw flesh of his open wounds, pulling on the poorly formed scabs, and causing the blood and pus to run.

"Bring her in here and set her down," Kahina said. Qaseem ducked under a table, as she led Kaboan inside.

"Did anyone else survive?" she asked.

"It was only luck that we were able to escape," the warrior, Kaboan, say hoarsely.

"I need to cauterize the wound," Kahina said. Grabbing some herbs from her bags she dropped an iron knife into the brazier burning in the center of the tent. Then placing a piece of leather in the girl's mouth she brought the heated knife to the girl's wounded side.

The princess bucked with pain as hot mettle met flesh. Kahina then moved to check the injury on her leg. She removed the silk tourniquet and was about to cast it away, but the princess snatched it from her hands.

"No," the princess said, desperately clutching the blood-soaked scarf to her chest. She let out another scream of agony as Kahina brought the hot blade down to sear the wound on her leg.

"Will she live," Kaboan asked, after the girl had passed out from the pain.

"We will have to keep an eye on the leg to be sure infection doesn't set in, and she has lost allot of blood. It will be a close thing. But I think she will live?" Kahina said. She checked the girl's pulse, before turning back to the warrior king. "Are you wounded?" she asked.

"No, I'm fine. Take care of her. I need to see to things," he said, standing up.

Only after he was certain the desert chieftain had left, did Qaseem dare emerge from his hiding place.

"Kahina," Qaseem said, limping forward to where she was tending to the girl's wounds.

"By all the gods!" she screamed, jumping back in surprise.

"I'm not going to hurt you," he said, collapsing as exhaustion and pain finally overcame his stubborn will to survive.

"Qaseem?" she hissed, turning to the tent flap where two guards were rushing in.

"We heard a scream."

"Yes, I'm fine, I just dropped something. You should go find Kaboan. He will need all his soldiers at the perimeter. I'll watch over the princess."

The two men nodded and left without a word.

"Thank you," Qaseem whimpered.

"Shut up! I should have just told them you were here and let them kill you."

"Please, mistress. I'm hurt," Qaseem pleaded.

"Oh, mistress, is it?" she snarled. "Not witch woman, slave, prisoner, or my personal favorite, 'Hey bitch.' Oh no, it's mistress now."

"Please, Kahina. Don't let me die," he whined.

"Why shouldn't I? For that matter, why shouldn't I just finish you myself?"

"You wouldn't do that," the hyena man protested.

"Why not? I need a new rug. I can kill you, skin you, chop you up and sell your most valuable organs."

"But I'm your mate," Qaseem said, letting out a soft, pathetic whine as the gril lying on the mattress in the corner started to stir.

"Who are you talking to?" the princess asked, as Kahina tossed a blanket over Qaseem to hide him.

"No one."

"What happened?" Sabra asked.

"You don't remember?" Kahina asked.

"I remember yelling, blood... PAIN!" Sabra screamed, disoriented from the blood loss.

"Drink this," Kahina said, giving her a dose of what smelled like some kind of poppy extract.

"Where is my father?" she asked.

"You need to rest," Kahina said, dodging the question as she moved back over to Qaseem, grabbing up a needle and catgut thread.

"You're not going to tell her?" Qaseem asked.

"No, I need her calm," Kahina snarled as she inspected Qaseem's injuries.

"You should tell her. Family is important," Qaseem said, resisting the reflex to bite as Kahina washed the grit from his wounds.

"You should talk. I met your sister," Kahina snapped.

"You spoke with her?" Qaseem asked, with no small amount of alarm. The last time he had seen any of his clan they had been tearing his mother apart for the crime of teaching him the magical arts.

"Yes, and She Who Must Be Obeyed was most interested to know where you might be."

"They found you. How are you alive?" Qaseem asked.

Kahina did not answer as she silently dressed his wounds, but Qaseem could smell her fear. She was always so still and composed. For as long as Qaseem had known her she had always smelled of fear, but never had she had shown it. Not when he had captured and tortured the scholars she had been living with in Persia.

She had been so scared of him in those early days. The smell of it had excited him, but never did her voice so much as waver as she would recount to him tales of the magical world of man and nature.

For years they had travelled together, seeking out shamans and mystics from the wild remote corners of the world. A hundred times they had nearly died on their travels.

Yet, never once had she ever shown any outward sign of fear. Her willpower always exceeding her terror. It was a marvel.

Now, however, even a blindman could have seen she was afraid.

"Kahina?" Qaseem asked softly.

"They didn't find me. I summoned them," she said, her voice cracking.

"Why would you—"

"I needed their help," she spat, jabbing a needle into his tender flesh as she stitched his wound. "I had no time. It was all I could think to do."

"Who did you give them?" Qaseem asked.

"Some shepherd. Don't know who he was. Don't know if he had a family, wife, kid, a little dog ... and I'm not going to find out," she said sharply, before adding, "I made a mistake. I sent the princess into the dream world. I thought I would be able to pull her back. I was wrong."

She paused for a moment, turning her head for a moment as if listening to someone only she could hear speaking. That's when he smelled it. The unnatural stench of sulphur and sickness.

"You're listening to the shadows again!" Qaseem said, his upper lip lifting in a snarl.

"You don't get to judge. You left me! You sold me to Alba ... all so you could buy your way into a demon's favor." Kahina snarled jabbing her needle back into his skin.

"The dragon is no demon. He was born of flesh and blood, as was I. Like my kind, he dwells in the darkness, but he was not born of it," Qaseem growled.

"I've met your sister. Don't try to convince me that you are some innocent freak of nature."

"I never claimed to be. But my goals are those of a living thing. I know hunger, pain, desire, and love. The *Mbwiri* are born of the dark. They do not know hunger, seek no gain, nor have any will to power. They are darkness, and they desire nothing but darkness. All that listening to their whispers will bring is death and madness."

"It is no concern of yours!" Kahina snarled.

"You are my mate, all—"

"Who are you talking to?" the princess moaned, as she attempted to stand.

Kahina rushed to grab her before she collapsed. As the young woman stumbled forward, the hyena man found himself looking right into the coal black eyes of the princess Sabra.

She did exactly what most human's do when they find themselves face-to-face with a hyena. She screamed.

With lightning speed, Kahina clasped her hand over the girl's mouth. "Sabra, stay calm. It's ok," she said.

"That's a hyena!" Sabra said with alarm.

"Yes."

"It was talking!" Sabra exclaimed, her eyes wide. "I heard it!"

"I won't hurt you," Qaseem said.

"That hyena is talking!" the princess shrieked.

Kahina glared at Qaseem before turning back to the panicking girl. "Some of them can do that. Sabra, stay calm. He's in worse shape than you are. And if he tries anything stupid, he is getting turned into a throw rug."

"I would never harm one in the care of my mate," Qaseem whined.

"It's a talking hyena!"

"Yes, it's a talking hyena. Qaseem, Sabra. Sabra, Qaseem. Now, everyone needs to calm down while I keep both of you from bleeding to death," she said with an exasperated sigh.

"Why did it call you its mate? What does that mean?" the young woman asked.

"She is mine, and I am hers. Hyenas and humans are not as different as both might wish to believe."

"It's not as bad as it sounds," Kahina added quickly.

Sabra's eyes went wide with alarm. "You! ... with a hyena?" she babbled.

"No ... well, yes ... but not like that!"

"What do you mean? You either fucked a hyena or you didn't!"

"He can take on a human form as well. Though one might argue that he is even more detestable as a man," Kahina hissed.

"I was a good mate," Qaseem whined.

"Maybe by hyena standards. By human standards, you were awful," Kahina snorted.

In truth, by hyena standards, Qaseem had been a terrible mate. If his mother was still alive, he wagered she would probably tear him to shreds for the way he had treated Kahina.

The sorceress was a beautiful, strong, cunning, domineering woman, and a master of magic. She was everything a well-brought-up hyena male looked for in a mate. However, she had been stubborn and refused all his early attempts to court her.

In hindsight, murdering her former lover and torturing her traveling companions might not have been the best way to earn her affection. In his defense, it would have worked had she been a hyena. But she wasn't, and it hadn't. So in the end, he had been forced to resort mind games, and threats to hold onto her.

In the beginning it had been pure practicality. He had needed her. It was in their scrolls and stories that the humans hid their knowledge of creation. However, Qaseem had never been able to master the basics of the human practice of reading or writing. That made it hard to understand the nuances of the human magics.

Kahina had known many stories, and every night before they went to sleep, she would tell him part of a tale. She would never finish a story the same night she started it, and she was always careful to start another one before the night was over.

Even now, he didn't entirely understand how the stories held their power. But power they held all the same.

Only when she finally ran out of tales to tell, had he considered giving her up. However, since leaving her in Saline, not one night had passed that Qaseem did not long to hear her tales again.

"I never forced you to mate with me," Qaseem put forward in his defense.

It was the truth. She had always come to him willingly. In fact, even when he had traveled with the slavers and bandits, he had never forced himself on any woman. Among hyenas, women chose their mates. Males did not force them. That was the sort of thing lions and humans did, not hyenas. However, this didn't seem to impress Kahina.

She turned on him, her face thunderous. "Oh, really? How sweet of you. How romantic. You're right. Thank you for not raping me! Would you like a prize? A meaty treat? You realize that I lost count of the number of times you threatened to kill me. For what, nearly four years, you had me deciphering whatever spells, moldy scrolls, or star charts you could manage to swindle, rob, or torture out of every two-bit hack stargazer, priest, and shaman you could track down. Then, you left me." For the first time he could remember, he saw tears in his mate's eyes. "You traded me away like a lame camel. Sold me off to King Alba and marooned me in Saline without a word. After the queen died, do you realize how close I came to losing my head?"

"If that was the case, why would you sleep with him?" Sabra asked.

"Oh, he had his moments. We traveled from the western sea to the great wall of the Han kingdoms. Together we found the Hindu priests in temples of India, and the Vodun witch doctors of the southern jungles. He even found the kingdom of Shangri-La hidden in the mountains above the clouds. I know of no other outsiders who have ever stepped foot in their great library or walked the hidden gardens of the monasteries. He's a rotten, sadistic coward. But he showed me the world, and he still kept me safe. Sometimes, when we traveled alone, he could even be sweet," she said.

Qaseem gave an affectionate whine as he moved his nose under her wrist so her hand would come to rest on his head. However, as soon as he touched her, she stood up, causing his head to fall painfully to the table. "Then, one day, poof you disappeared. No explanation, no apology. You just packed up your stuff and left me at the edge of the fucking world, with nothing! No money, no mounts, not even a change of clothes. You took everything," she snarled, as a young girl no older than twelve, barged into the tent.

"Sabra!" the girl yelled, rushing in.

Kahina moved quickly to intercept the girl before she could see Qaseem.

"Lunja, wait outside!" Kahina said.

"I heard Sabra was hurt."

"Yes, she is, but she's going to be ok."

"I want to see her," the girl pouted.

"You can see her later. Right now, I need you to do something for me. I need you to be very brave and watch the door. Can you do that for me?"

"Yes," the girl choked.

"Good girl," Kahina said, walking back to the princess.

"Aren't you going to finish stitching my wounds?" Qaseem whined.

"Stay there and bleed to death quietly. I'll tend to you later, provided you're still breathing," she said, turning to the mattress where the young, dark-skinned woman had once again drifted out of consciousness.

"Is that truly King Alba's daughter?" Qaseem asked.

"Who else would it be?" the witch asked, checking the girl's pulse and letting out a sigh of relief.

"Gurzil will not be happy."

"Why? What is she to him?" Kahina asked, but before he could explain, there was a commotion at the front of the tent.

"Out of my way, little girl," came the snarling voice of the High Priest Ierna as forced his way into the tent.

"Kahina said no one could see her ... Sabra needs rest," the girl protested loudly.

Kahina flipped the blanket over Qaseem, hiding him before the priest entered.

"What is that stench? It smells like a hyena died in here," Ierna protested as he walked in.

"Very astute of you. I was mixing potions for divination. The main ingredients are several hyena organs. I'd offer you some but I'm bit busy, so you can fuck off."

"Save your poisons, witch. I am not here for your wares," Ierna snarled. "Where is the princess."

"The princess is wounded."

"Don't try to play me witch! I see through your deceptions. I suspect the princess is fine. You are simply attempting to hide her from her destiny. Again!" the priest bellowed.

Qaseem lay still under the blanket as his lips pulled back over his fangs. But wounded as he was, an attack would be a gamble, and a lone hyena did not gamble with his life.

"I don't care what you believe. Look for yourself." Kahina said.

Walking into the interior of the tent, Ierna's eyes went wide with terror as he looked down at the princess lying on the blood-soaked sheets.

"How did this happen?" he yelled.

"Uh, she was stabbed. Given that she and Kaboan were the only two to survive out of a delegation of eighty, she got lucky."

"Will she live?" Ierna asked, choking back obvious panic.

"She's lost allot of blood."

"Is she fit for travel," Ierna snapped.

"She's hardly fit to stand."

"Where is Sabra going?" the little girl asked.

"That is none of your concern. The Byzantines may attack at any moment. We need to get her out of harm's way," Ierna said, shoving the girl away as he made for the tent's entrance.

"Out of harm's way? She is injured. If the wound festers, she could die," Kahina shouted in protested.

"You will do as you are told, witch," the desert mystic snarled. However, Qaseem could smell the fear oozing out of Ierna's every pore.

As Ierna left, Kahina walked back and tore the blanket off Qaseem.

"Talk. What do you know?" she said, looking over at the unconscious princess.

"You will help me?" Qaseem whined.

"Talk now, or I WILL be brewing potions from your organs!"

"Gurzil wants the princess as his mate."

"Why?" Kahina asked before throwing up her hands. "Oh, wait. I forgot you never ask why. You always had me do that. Hyenas never ask the why of a thing ... gets in the way of killing, pillage, and plunder."

"Why doesn't help you on the savannah. What does it help to ask why a zebra turns a certain way, or why a lion will kill you on sight? It is simply in their nature to do so. The dragon wants her because it's in the beast's nature. It has something to do with her bloodline. For some reason, Gurzil believes she can give him a child. That's all I know. I suspect even Ierna doesn't know the why of it."

"How do I know you're not lying?"

"Why would I lie?" Qaseem asked.

"Because it's in your nature!"

"Check your witch bones, or tea leaves, if you don't believe me. The King of Saline is dead. I suspect Ierna would have certainly preferred Kaboan die with him. However, I suspect the dragon will be happy he is still alive. Gurzil will offer your desert king a victory he could only dream of. Provided that the Eagle of the Desert, gives up the girl. That is his plan. That is Gurzil's nature."

"Kaboan is a good man. An honorable man. He's not like you," Kahina snapped, glancing over at her various mirrors, runed bones, and star charts.

"You all want to believe that you're different from us, but humans and hyenas are one and the same. Just as greedy. Just as cowardly. Just as deceitful. Just as cruel, and just as honorable. Why do you think I can imitate your kind so well? Twelve years, I have lived as a man. Only you, ever even considered me outside the normal for a man." He sighed before continuing. "Your chief will hand her over to the Horned God. Why? Because the beast knows his nature, and so Gurzil will offer the man a deal that is in his nature to accept. See if your bones tell you otherwise?"

Kahina walked over to the tables and chests where she kept her bones and star charts, but she did not touch them. Rather, she just stood there, stone-still in thought, before glancing over at the block of chiseled marble in the corner.

After a few minutes that felt like hours, Kahina came to a decision. Tossing a number of various items into a straw-woven travel sack she walked over to where Sabra was sleeping.

"We need to go. We are not among friends," she said, waking the princess.

"You were right, she has lost a lot of blood," Qaseem observed.

"As long as I can keep her sitting on a camel, she should be ok," Kahina said.

"You might run, but you won't be able to hide. She is marked. The dragon will be able to sense the magic in her wherever she goes," Qaseem said.

Kahina grabbed a rough talisman of bones and herbs and said, "Sabra, put this on."

"What is it?" the princess asked, yawning.

"Something to help keep you hidden. It's not much but ..." Kahina went silent as she pulled back the princess's soiled dress to reveal a brilliant chain of gold filigree and bright gemstone.

"Where did you get this?" the soothsayer asked, gently lifting the strange necklace.

"In a dream. The prince gave it to me," Sabra whispered, weak and dizzy from the loss of blood.

"Well, your dream prince has good taste, and apparently, the services of a *djinn* smith. The good news is the magic in these gems will hide you from your scaly suitor better than any charm I can craft for you," she said, tossing the carved-bone charm away before helping the princess up onto the back of her camel.

"Mistress, what about me," Qaseem asked.

"You're not coming."

"But I'll die if I stay here," Qaseem whined. "They will kill me."

"You forget that I know you, Qaseem. You would sell your own mother for a magic spell. For all I know, your plan is to flush us into the desert so you can give us to the dragon yourself."

"I swear I won't betray you," he spoke.

"Really? You won't betray me," she said, glaring.

"I swear I won't betray you again," Qaseem said meekly.

"Oaths have no power over you. You would break your word as easily as breathing!" she snarled.

"When the Vandals cut me down, Ierna and Gurzil left me for dead. I owe them nothing. They are my clan no longer. You are my mate."

"So, I should believe you're on my side? A hyena only ever looks out for his own interest, did you not tell me that once?"

"As do humans. If you don't take me, I'll ... I'll ... I'll kill the little girl."

"Threats like that are not the way to earn my trust. Don't forget, I can still just finish you now," Kahina said, burying a knife in the table next to his head.

"Please, mistress. Don't leave me for dead. Everyone leaves me for dead," he begged, inching towards the front of the tent after her as she packed, but he realized it would be no use.

"Will you at least tell me a story, before you go?" Qaseem asked. If he was going to die he would at least like one last story.

"Seriously, you want a story now? I told you before, you've heard them all. I have no more tales to tell," Kahina said curtly.

"You could tell me one I've heard before. I don't mind," he said sadly.

Kahina stiffened, her knuckles turning white, as she struggled with some internal debate. "Fine! I'll take you with me," she said, covering him with a blanket. Grunting she picked him up, and carrying him outside, dropped him onto one of the camels, like a sack of meat.

"What's that? It stinks," the little girl asked.

"Lunja, I want you to stay here, stay hidden, and after the battle, find your father," Kahina said, kneeling down next to the girl.

"No! I want to go with Sabra," the girl said, stamping her feet in protest.

"That is not your destiny, little one. You must stay here. Your father will need you," Kahina said before turning and mounting her own camel, holding the wounded princess on the saddle in front of her.

"Before that though ... I need you to do something very important for me," the soothsayer added, looking at the unfinished marble sculpture sitting inside her tent.

Chapter Twenty-One

Galahad of Corbenic

Aquae Sulis
July 9th 543 AD

*And there I saw the mage Merlin ... and near
him stood the Lady of the Lake, who knows
a subtler magic than his own... She gave the
King his huge cross-hilted sword, whereby to
drive the heathen out ... There likewise I beheld
Excalibur before him at his crowning borne,
the sword that rose from out of the bosom of the
lake, and Arthur rowed across and took it ...the
blade so bright that men are blinded by it;—on
one side, graven in the oldest tongue of all this
world, 'Take me,' but turn the blade and ye shall
see, written in the speech ye speak yourself,
"Cast me away!" And sad was Arthur's face
taking it, but old Merlin counselled him, "Take*

*thou and strike! The time to cast away is yet far
off." So this great brand the king took, and by
his will, beat his foemen down.*

*Alfred, Lord Tennyson, 1st Baron Tennyson,
1859 AD
Idylls of The King*

"DOES ANYONE ELSE THINK this is a terrible idea?" Galahad asked.

He was standing on a hill with George, Tristan, Lancelot, and Bors. All five of the knights were trying to keep a neutral expression on their faces as they watched Merlin and Arthur row out to the center of the town's fishpond.

"No one said the Picts were coming in full battle regalia," Bors hissed through a forced smile. Looking out at the blue-painted woad warriors who stared expectantly at the mist-covered lake.

"I think It's a good sign," Tristian countered. "It means they expect to fight. We do the whole sign from the old gods, then it's the wedding, followed by the battle. If they didn't expect Arthur to pull off the whole blessings of the gods bit, they wouldn't bother getting all decked out for battle."

"Sure they would," George said, looking at the army of blue-painted soldiers. "Because when this goes to shit, they're going to try and kill us all."

"It's not going to go to shit. It's a simple plan. Merlin and Arthur row out, Merlin does his monologue, Arthur drops the sword in the pond, and Iseult throws it back to him," Tristan said, his eyes on the water.

"Why is Iseult the one in the pond again?" Galahad asked.

"She insisted, and it was her idea," Tristan answered. "She's the daughter of a fairy queen. That might buy us some forgiveness if Leodegrance figures out what we are doing."

Lancelot snorted. "More likely she's the result of some fisherman's daughter turning King Anguish's head when he was out hunting,"

Tristan turned towards the Frank with his fists clenched, but George stopped him.

"Tristan, keep smiling. Lancelot, shut up!" George hissed through gritted teeth as Merlin started his 'incantation.'

"Lady of the Waters, you who is clad in purist shimmering samite, we hand to you this sword forged in dragon fire, and if you deem this king be worthy ..." Merlin shouted.

"Do you think she's ok in there?" Tristan asked, looking pensive. "I mean actually when you think about it, lying on the bottom of the lake with a reed in one's mouth is hardly foolproof. That water's pretty cold."

"Well, I did tell you that it was a mistake to put Iseult in the pond," George said, looking around. "If you haven't realized, her absence here is noticeable."

"He's right. If this goes sideways, I don't think they're going to buy the whole 'she's the daughter of a fairy' argument," Galahad asked nervously. "I was praying last night. So out of curiosity, do we have a plan B?"

"You say that like this princess in the pond bull shit was plan A," George growled.

"I don't see how it ended up being the plan at all. Is this really how the Britons choose their kings?" Galahad asked.

"How should we do it?" Tristan snapped.

"I don't know. Elections, judges, a council of nobles ... something resembling legitimacy," the young warrior monk said.

"You want to do a *witan*? Here? Now?" Bors asked.

"We don't have time for a civil war," George agreed.

"Maybe we should just line up and do an old-school Roman decimation. Count off by tens and then beat each other to death. That wouldn't take too long. Would that be legitimate enough for you?" Tristan offered.

"I didn't say civil war," Galahad said defensively.

Lancelot laughed. "Yes you did. Around here, all that election shit always ends in war. Then, when there are enough dead bodies piled up, they cut off the heads and mark out the borders in human skulls. Whoever collects the most skulls gets the most land. Very democratic when you think about it. However, we are on something of a truncated timetable. No time for mass human sacrifice, so the savages have decided to go the with blonde-hanging-out-in-a-pond method of royal succession."

"And ... what happens if Leodegrance isn't convinced?" Galahad asked.

"You see those warriors all painted blue?" George said, indicating the Pictish woods. "You four are going to have to restrain them while Merlin and my father try to appeal to their sense of reason and better judgment."

"Reason? From men who go into battle painted blue?" Lancelot snorted.

"I didn't say we had a good backup plan," George answered.

"Wait! That's why we are here?" Galahad snarled. "You left that part out. How are the five of us going to restrain an entire army of angry Picts?"

"With great difficulty, I imagine," George answered. "And it will only be four of you. If it comes to that, I'll be busy."

"Doing what?" Bors hissed.

"Keeping my father and Merlin from killing each other?" George answered. "Happy to switch if you want, Saxon."

"Damn it, George. He's taking too long," Tristan said, a worried look crossing his face as he listened to Merlin's lengthy monologue. "You were right. We should have got a stand-in."

"Told you," Lancelot said. "There's a perfectly good brothel five miles up the road. All we had to do was go there, and find out which bitch could hold her breath the longest."

"The building your talking about isn't a brothel. It's a Christian convent," Galahad countered.

"Maybe there's a whorehouse next to the convent?" Tristan asked.

"No, there is just a convent," Galahad hissed.

"Well, I guess it wouldn't have worked, then. From what Im told Christian nuns don't give head," Bors asked.

"They do in Frankia," Lancelot countered.

"No, they don't, they swear a vow of chastity" Galahad snarled.

"Believe me you were not a virgin birth?" Lancelot said, laying an almost fatherly hand on the shoulder of his estranged son. Only to have Galahad knock it away.

"Whether nuns give head or not is irrelevant, to the business at hand!" George snapped. "The girl we put in the pond didn't have to blow anyone. She just had to lay down in a freezing pool of water and toss the sword back to Prince Pompous at the appointed time. For that, we could have used a whore, a nun, the wife of the muffin man ... really, anyone other than the Queen of Kernow would have been a great fucking choice! But it's Iseult in the pond now, so there is nothing to do but wait, pray, and hopefully enjoy the wedding. It's set to be such a lovely occasion after all. Princess Gwenivier is all decked out in her something blue warpaint, that matches perfectly with that of her heavily armed wedding party. Arthur's wrapped up in all that silk and shiny armor that just brings out his megalomania. It's such a pity that the Saxons will be arriving any minute to crash the wedding feast. I was so looking forward to it!"

"Are you ok?" Tristan asked.

"Why wouldn't I be ok? We are a few hundred about to go up against a few thousand! A battle that goes from a risky gamble to mass fucking suicide if Leodegrance and the Picts don't fight."

"What's your point?" Tristan asked.

"My point is that it's too late in the game for what-ifs and substitutions!" George said through gritted teeth, giving Tristan a pointed look as Merlin finished his monologue.

Arthur looked down and dropped the sword into the water. A few moments later, to everyone's relief, a white feminine hand rose up bearing the sword above the misty pond.

Arthur took the sword and held it up to the cheering assembly before hopping off the boat to stride up to Gwenivier and her party. Leodegrance glared at Merlin before nodding his assent and walking over to Arthur with his daughter.

"Wife, Queen, and Lady, thy doom is mine. Let chance what will, I swear to faithfully love and defend thee to the death," Arthur said kneeling down before her.

Gwenivier dropped her eyes before answering, "King, Lord, and husband, I shall faithfully love and honor thee unto death!"

"Looks like we might actually pull this off," George said before turning to Tristan. "Make sure no one sees our girl get out of the water."

A cold look crossed George's face as he watched Arthur take Gwenivier into his arms and kiss the Pictish princess. To Galahad's surprise, his father, Lancelot, wore the same pained expression.

"Alright," George said at last with a sigh. "We have our light infantry. Let's get this bloodbath over with."

Chapter Twenty-Two

Cedric, King of Wessex

Mount Badon
July 10th 543 AD

*We shall defend our island, whatever the cost
may be ... We shall fight in the fields and in the
streets, we shall fight in the hills; we shall never
surrender!*

King Arthur Constantine Pendragon 543 AD
The Battle of Badon Hill
&
Winston Churchill 1940 AD
The Battle of Britain

As the Saxon army snaked its way through the hills of Badon, Cedric kept casting glances at the ravens circling overhead. In the hundred years since the Saxons landed on Britain, the carrion birds had learned well that death followed the Germanic raiders.

It was a good omen. The Ravens were sacred to the dark Aiser gods. They would take the news of his victory to Wodan, Thonar, Surt, and Hellia. Tonight, the gods would toast his victory.

For a hundred years, weaker Saxon kings had tried to share this land with the other tribes. Some even going as far as to breed with the native Celtic, and Roman mutts. Diluting the sacred Saxon bloodline. He could tolerate mixing with the Angles and the Jutes. They were at least of the blood. But to breed with the Romans and the savages was a sin he would not tolerate.

His predecessors had forgotten who they were, and what made them strong. Cedric would remind them. He would put them back on the right path. He would purge the land with blood and claim it for his people!

Watching the ravens, it wasn't long before he saw what he was looking for, a bird with white wings. Placing a wooden whistle to his mouth, he called to it. The white-winged raven circled low before landing on the king's gauntleted hand, allowing the Saxon king to remove the small piece of parchment attached to its leg.

"What news from the Briton witch?" his son, Cynric, asked.

"George of Haustdesert ... That is Urien Bertilacks son, am I right?" Cedric asked.

"Yes, the grandson of the old High King. He calls himself the Black Knight. Though he reportedly rides a great white Sarmatian-bred hell-steed." Cynric answered.

"The soldier from the bridge?" the old Saxon king growled.

"And our Angel of Death from the other night," his son answered, taking a swig from his wineskin. "Why do you ask?"

"The witch wants us to spare his life." Cedric laughed, passing the small strip of parchment to his son.

"Women," Cynric sneered. "Doesn't she know mercy is for fools?"

Cedric gripped the black bird on his hand by the neck, and gave it a rough twist. The unfortunate messenger died with a squawk.

"If you see him today, kill him and send his head to the witch-woman. She's outlived her usefulness," Cedric said, handing the parchment to his son before wiping his hands on his greaves.

"With pleasure," Cynric answered, tucking the note into his armor.

As they strode back to the head of the column, the call came down from the forward scout. "Briton riders. Heavy cavalry arrayed for battle. Coming fast."

"Form shield wall!" Cedric bellowed.

With practiced precision, the Saxon forces formed a solid wall of interlocked shields.

"Did you see any infantry or archers with them?" Cedric asked.

"No, just horsemen coming through the mist," the scout answered.

"They never learn, do they?" Cedric chuckled before shouting. "Spears and broad axes to the front! Hedge formation!"

The shield wall opened as Cedric's Housecarls moved to the front line with their giant bearded axes. They were the Saxon answer to the Briton heavy cavalry. A trained axman could cleave both armored horse and rider in half with a single blow. Alongside them were their attendant spear-wielding light infantry. Trained horse cutters adept at disemboweling cavalry horses with their polearms.

Confident they stood stone-faced, watching the British knights close on them.

"Britons, always so attached to their horses," Cedric observed. Had Cedric been a horseman himself he might have noticed how the mist swirled around the hooves of the approaching mounts as they advanced at a controlled slow canter rather than a fast charge.

But he did not notice, and right as the housecarls raised their axes to cut down the advancing knights, the lead riders raised their lances and turned. Breaking off their charge they moved around the Saxon forces like water around a stone, with only a handful of riders discharging arrows and javelins into the enemy ranks.

"The fools are trying to go around us to take out our camp." Cedric laughed.

Attacking around the enemy to threaten their war camp was a tactic Cedric himself often used. The intention of such was to sow chaos in the enemy ranks as men retreated to protect the wives, children, and camp followers that fools would bring to war with them. It was one of the few effective uses Cedric had ever found for horsemen.

However, it was a gambit Cedric had foreseen. As such there were no women or children behind his lines in need of defense. The Saxon's strength was their shield wall and Cedric would not risk his men breaking formation. The foolish Britons were separating their forces for nothing.

"This will be over sooner than I expected," he said to no one in particular.

However, no sooner had he voiced this thought, then out of the mist came the shrieking sound of bagpipes, and the whistling of arrows as they flew from the fog to cut down his front ranks. The horsemen had been nothing but a screen, hiding the enemy archers and light infantry.

As the enemy projectiles cut down the best of the Saxon fighters in front of the shield wall, the forward shield bearers rushed forward to defend their fellows.

The Saxon king saw the danger too late. The Celtic archers had been waiting for that moment. Cedric watched as the shield wall opened, leaving them exposed to the skilled Celtic bowmen.

"Close ranks and lock shields!" Cedric yelled, but his orders were lost in the bagpipes' screaming and the din of dying men.

While Cedric and his captains worked to bring the shield wall back into order, the savages' infantry charged forward past their missile troops. There were border men and Rangers in rough leather armor, and mail-clad spearmen from Camelot. With them, were men and women from the North, wearing no armor but their tattoos and warpaint. At the vanguard of this force was a troop of green-painted monsters; the hosts of Haustdesert and Gore. Leading them was the giant Urien Bertilack.

The Briton warriors battered against the Saxon line. The enemies more mobile brawlers pulling men from their positions, before hurling them back to be butchered by those behind them. Cedric heard his men scream in grief and terror, as the heads of the Saxon dead were cut from their bodies and thrown over the shield wall.

It was in this chaos that Cedric looked beside him to see his son. "They're coming back. They're going to flank us!" Cynric shouted.

With horror, Cedric looked behind him to see the Briton cavalry charging their rear at full gallop. Leading them were two knights. One on a mighty black horse, armored in polished mail and a golden helm that shone like a beacon in the early morning light. Riding a white charger, the other had sprigs of mistletoe woven through a rough cape that billowed out behind his black varnished armor. Behind the two princes followed a hellish wave of horse and steel.

"Rear rank, turn and lock!" Cedric yelled out over the roar of battle, his shouts echoed by his son and captains. As the rearguard turned and locked shields, they cast worried glances over their shoulders at the carnage behind them even as death charged toward them.

Cedric's world slowed as he found a cadence to the chaotic din of combat. The thunder of approaching hooves, the squeals of the bagpipes, the hammering of steel against shield, even the screams of the dying all became one harmony for him.

Removing his helmet, he sang the battle hymn of his forefathers. Summoning the valkyries that would bear him to the corpse hall of Woden.

Lo, there before me do I see my father
Lo, there do I see my mother, my sisters, and my brothers
Lo, there do I see the raven-winged maidens of battle
They come for me
They bid me go to them
For the Fates decree
NO MAN SHALL LIVE FOREVER!

As he finished his battle psalm, he turned to see the distant sky-blue eyes of what he assumed could only be a valkyrie. Her blonde hair shining in the morning sun as she drew back her bow.

Iseult's arrow took the Saxon warchief in the eye. The self-proclaimed King of Britain was dead before his body hit the mud. He was spared from seeing the Saxon shield wall shatter under the hooves of the Knights of the Britons.

Chapter
Twenty-Three

Pudentius, Tribune of Leptis Magna

Leptis Magna
July 10th 543 AD

When the army of the Lauathai came near
the city of Leptis Magna, Pudentius confronted
them with his whole army. The battle came
to hand-to-hand combat: at first the Romans
were winning and slew many of the enemy,
and prepared to plunder their camp ... Then
Pudentius driven forward by reckless daring
was killed ...
Procopius of Caesarea, 544 AD
The Wars of Justinian

PUDENTIUS STOOD BEFORE THE gates of Leptis Magna, and looked out at his men.

They were scared, confused, and angry. Some of them had served with Pudentius for years.

Among them where those who had come with him all those years ago when he had been sent to scout out the Libyan coast in preparation for the invasion. Back then the Emperor and his propagandists had tried to say the war had been about God. That it was their holy duty to liberate the Nicean Romans living under Vandal rule. In the end, it had all boiled down to gold and grain.

However, that was as good a reason as any to fight a war. After all, the empire needed grain. People needed to eat. As long as Carthage was in Vandal hands, the Arian kings could starve Constantinople and plunge the Empire into chaos at will.

Having witnessed the horror of the Nika riots, who wouldn't agree it was better to fight, kill, and die in the deserts of Africa rather than slaughter your own people at home? Now ten years into the occupation, he no longer knew what this war was about.

Maybe, Sergius had a point. Just kill everyone in charge and leave it all to the desert mystics and the warlords to sort out. Make a deal with whoever was still alive in the end.

However, all one had to do was look over the walls at the righteously angry army of Moors now arrayed against them to realize the folly of this.

Pudentius and his men might have no idea what they were fighting for, but the men, women, and children ready to assault their gates harbored no such doubts. This was their homeland, and if they did not fight for it, they would forever be slaves to the empire.

"I know you're all wondering why we are here," Pudentius said, looking out over his men. "You're asking why it has come to this fight. I'm asking myself this same question. The answer is that whatever it is that has brought us to this point doesn't matter. The affairs of kings, consuls, and emperors don't matter here. Right here, right now, we must fight for nothing but our lives. If we stay here, the enemy will grow in number and swarm over us in force. These walls will not protect us. There is no way out of this but to wade through blood."

The officers nodded as they checked their men's gear.

"The plan is simple. Our spearmen and shield bearers will charge in on foot. We will cut down the camels to make a hole that will allow the Vandal cavalry to charge on the encampment. Don't worry about the Moors or their soldiers. The shield bearers will keep the enemy javelins off us, and the cavalry will deal with the enemy soldiers once the camels are dead and we have a clear shot at their central camp. Keep your shields tight, trust in the Lord and in the man beside you, and we will live to see home again."

As the gates opened, he moved his men forward in formation. It was mid-day by the time they reached the enemy. Iron-cored javelins rained down on their shields as they set to the day's bloody business. It was mid-day by the time they reached the enemy. The sun beat down upon the soldiers covered in blood, sweat, and gore. Pudentius lost few men, but those who had died had died badly. They died wallowing in the intestines of disemboweled camels, while flies swarmed around the corpses.

At last, they broke through to the enemy camp. Their the waiting enemy set upon them from all sides, desperate to seal the breach in their defenses.

"Signal the Vandals! Soldiers of the empire back out!" Pudentius ordered, breathing a sigh of relief as his bugler signaled the cavalry to attack.

But no cavalry came. Looking back, Pudentius saw the Vandal horsemen galloping away down the coastline. The mercenaries taking advantage of the enemy's distraction to make good their escape.

"Where's Gunthuris and the cavalry?" one of his men asked.

"Gone!" Pudentius yelled. He could already tell that the enemy's overwhelming numbers were taking a toll. Their momentum was stalled as exhausted Imperial soldiers now floundered in the blood-soaked sand.

"Fall back in formation! Back to the fortress!" he shouted.

But it was too late. No sooner had he spoken than he saw the Amazigh cavalry emerge from the center of the camp. Arrows and javelins sailed before them, cutting down the Byzantine soldiers as the desert horse lords charged home with swords and lance.

As his men died around him, Pudentius did the only thing any soldier could do under the circumstances. He ran. However, he did not get very far. For as he turned, his foot caught up in the guts of one of the disemboweled camels. Pudentius fell hard into the blood and gore as he watched his men flee, tossing away shields and spears, as they made for the temporary safety of the city.

Unable to join them, Pudentius hid himself under the rotting guts as the enemy cavalry thundered past him.

Then, he saw him. Sitting grim-faced on his horse was Kaboan, the Eagle of the Desert.

Once, Pudentius had fought side by side with the man. He realized then that all he had to do was stand and surrender to his old comrade, and he might be spared.

There was a part of him that thought he should take the chance. Yet, fear and shame bid him keep still. For even if he did surrender, what could he offer in exchange for his life.

Nothing but promises that they both knew would never be kept?

No, if he revealed himself, his fate would be sealed. He would be dragged across the desert behind a camel or ripped to pieces by horses. Better to go out like the old Roman fools with his own dagger in his belly. However, he could not yet bring himself to do that either.

"Have a detachment of cavalry archers track the Vandals. I don't want them doubling back on us. And find me that priest Ierna!" Kaboan shouted.

"No need to send your flunkies to find me. I am here," the black-clad mystic said, riding up, flanked by a cadre of armed attendants.

"Where are the Vandals going?" Kaboan asked.

"How would I know that? You're the desert scout, not me," Ierna answered.

"Save it. I know you've been selling your own faithful to the slavers," Kaboan snarled.

"I have done no such thing. The horned god demands tribute, in gold and meat. Those with no gold to offer may give of themselves. The temple simply facilitates the transaction."

"You are forcing people to sacrifice their children, and sell themselves into bondage. You are pillaging your own country!" Kaboan shouted.

"Faith sometimes takes persuasion. And not everyone loves their children as much as you." he said and gestured to his men.

Two men came out of the crowd carrying a young girl, a knife to her throat.

"*Baab!*" the girl cried.

"Let her go," Kaboan screamed, his hand going for his sword.

"Draw steel, and she is dead. She is nothing to me!" the desert mystic snarled. "I want the Princess Sabra. Tell me where she is, and your daughter goes free."

Kaboan paused.

"You can't think your way out of this one, my friend. I'll find the princess on my own eventually. I'm only doing this to prove a point. By all means, make me prove it," he said, raising his hand. The girl squealing as the blade tightened.

"Don't hurt her. Why do you want Sabra?" Kaboan asked, letting his sword fall to the sand.

"My master wants her. It is not my place, nor yours, to ask why."

"She is injured. She will likely die. Your master can have her corpse when she's dead!" Kaboan snarled.

"She will live. Your own witch says so," Ierna said, his eyes darting around like a trapped animal.

"You believe Kahina. The woman cannot say three words without lying," the desert warrior scoffed. "I know wounds, I know blood, and I know how much of it she left on the sands. Look around. Killing is what I do."

"You're... You're lying." Ierna said, his eyes wide with fear.

"Why would I lie? The Vandals stuck a knife in her side and sliced her leg deep. If blood loss doesn't kill her, gangrene will. Maybe the witches skills can prevent it but I have my doubts," Kaboan said. However even from a distance, Pudentius could see Kaboan's fingers tap on his sword. A slight tell that you would not know unless you had played chess or dice with the desert chieftain. Kaboan was simply playing for time, but Ierna had bought the lie.

"No, No, NO! What have they done!" Ierna cried. "The master was very clear she was not to be harmed."

Without warning, a wind like a hurricane flared around the killing field. A choking mix of smoke and sand whirled around, blanketing the land. In the chaos, the girl broke free, rushing to her father who clung to her tightly as he tried to shield his daughter from the storm.

"You have failed me!" came a booming voice that dripped with anger and malice. As it spoke, the whirlwind opened, sand circling them in the eye of a storm.

"Master, it was not my fault ..." Ierna whimpered as the monster walked out of the vortex.

It was a thing out of a nightmare. A beast covered in hard, horned scales, with claws, and broken teeth.

"Please, oh mighty Gurzil, spare me ..." the priest babbled, dropping to his knees.

"Enough! I tire of the blubbering and blundering of scheming mortals, I will not be denied my bride!" the beast snarled, before turning to Kaboan. "I will have my bride! You will tell me where Princess Sabra is. She still breathes, this I know, but I cannot sense her! You will tell me by what craft she is hidden from me!"

"You will have nothing from me, demon!" Kaboan snarled, holding his daughter tight.

"You cannot deny him!" Ierna cried out. "He is of The Deathless Gods. He will smite you ..."

"Silence!" the dragon hissed, and with a swipe of his tail, he sent the desert priest flying backwards into the sand. "Fools such as you have cost me dominion, time, and tribute before. NEVER AGAIN! Do not pretend you know anything. I cannot harm this man. He loves this girl as he loves the princess, and they love him. By that love, I am denied, and he is safe. Not even a god dares challenge the deep magics. Empires have been sunk for less than this man's murder under these conditions. I will not call down the avenging angels today simply to satisfy your ego!"

"Brave mortal," the monster said. Speaking to Kaboan with what sounded almost like respect. "I come not for your blood or that of your daughter. I want only what is mine, what was promised to me in an age long past ... my bride! I want Princess Sabra. You shall give her to me."

"I would die first!" the desert warrior answered.

The beast let out a chilling, booming laugh. "Of course, you would. You don't value your life so highly. You would give it in an instant; but would you give up your cause ... your beliefs? Would you give up the future of your people? Would you give up your dream? You have risked the princess's life for your cause before. Would you not sacrifice her for the certainty of success?"

Kaboan stood before the dragon but gave no answer.

"I know you, Kaboan. I know what it is that you have fought and sacrificed for. I know what you want. I know what the dead cry out for," the beast hissed. "I can give it to you. Listen and believe. Desert power will sweep across these lands, raising an empire from the sands. An unstoppable army of conquest will sweep across the desert. The great city of Alexandria will fall, Carthage will be conquered, and the walls of Constantinople will crumble, as the nations of Europe tremble in fear. This is what you want, is it not? It can be yours. This can be your legacy if you wish it. You can be the one to give your people the empire they deserve. It has been foretold. It will come to pass."

"You can grant this?" Kaboan asked.

"That which is written on the runes of destiny will come to pass. How and in what manner it comes is still unknown. But the destiny of these sands is fixed. Give me what I ask, and you will have what you wish."

"What of me? Have I not served you faithfully?" Ierna babbled. The desert mystic clearly not wishing to be supplanted.

"For your blundering, I should give you nothing. But I am a generous and forgiving lord. You will have what you desire.

You will be King of Saline. I assume the desert warrior has no objections to this?"

"You will keep your word?" Kaboan asked hesitantly.

"There is no word to keep. This is done. It has been foretold. It shall come to pass. Now, TELL ME WHERE IS MY BRIDE!"

"She is in the tent of Kahina the soothsayer," Kaboan answered without hesitation, hugging his daughter tight.

"No, she's not," the girl whimpered. "She's not there. Kahina took Sabra and left before the battle started. They told me to wait, but I got scared, so I came to find you."

"Where did they go? Tell me, or I will tear you limb from limb!" the dragon roared.

"You will not harm my daughter. That was the agreement," Kaboan shouted, leaping to his feet and grabbing a discarded Byzantine shield as he did so.

"You dare oppose me," the dragon roared, but the beasts growing rage soon turned to hateful laughter. "You have the courage and the skill. It would be an interesting contest. There was a time when I traveled and warred across the world simply to test myself against men such as you. A pity how quickly you would die ... perhaps had we met when you were younger. Sadly, I have no time for such diversions now. Know this, I knew another like you once. A great war master and leader of these same lands you now inhabit. He too, refused me, to the ruin of his people; your people. His name was Hamilcar, father of Hannibal, and I can assume you well know how his drama ended. You will not fight me. Nor will you oppose me."

"Oh, Great Gurzil, you credit this man too highly," Ierna said, stepping forward. "He is nothing but a desert warlord. Your faithful will find the princess. How far can two women get? She is wounded after all."

"Oh yes, you will find her, and this man will help you. You will deliver the princess before me. But you will do it quickly and you will do it quietly. This chaos has already attracted too much attention. Soon this bloodshed will draw the intrest of the blood sucking leaches from across the sea. I had hoped to settle this matter without their interference. However, it seems that even now their spys and servents watch us."

With a roar, the dragon rushed forward to where Pudentius was hiding and tore the camel carcass away, crushing the Roman officer under his talons before tearing his head off.

So, ended the life of Pudentius.

Chapter Twenty-Four

George Bertilack, Prince of Caer Celemion and Chieftain of the Lloegyr Rangers

Mount Badon
July 9th 543 AD

When a commander has won a decisive victory ... that is the time to exploit success. It is during the pursuit, when the beaten enemy is still dispirited and disorganized, that the most prisoners are made and the most booty captured. Troops flying in a wild panic to the rear, may, unless they are continually harried, by the pursuer, very soon stand in battle again,

freshly organized as fully effective fighting men.

Edwin Rommel, General Field Marshal, Greater German Reich 1943 AD

THE BRITONS DID NOT hold the momentum of the battle for long.

Arthur had been too quick to celebrate his initial victory, and as such, failed to press his advantage. By the time George and others had advised him of the danger, Prince Cynric had already rallied the remaining Saxon forces.

As the evening rain started to fall on the blood-soaked field they found themselves fighting a running battle through the mud. While Arthur attempted to regain the initiative with an infantry assault against the Saxon center, George was busy using his mobile force to keep the scattered Saxons from rejoining the main formation.

However, turning back, George saw too late the danger in reckless Arthur's assault. Standing at the vanguard of his forces, Arthur was hammering away at the shield wall with his dragon-forged broadsword. The Saxons withstood the attack untill they saw the young king start to tire.

It was in that moment when Arthur paused to catch his breath that the Saxon line opened. Four chosen men with short blades and bucklers rushed forward to seize the young king. Arthur cut the first down easily. However, before he could pivot, the other attackers grabbed him; dragging him behind the Saxon shield wall.

They should have killed him on the spot; hacked him to pieces right then and there. Instead, the Saxon Prince Cynric stayed his men. Walking forward, he picked up

Arthur's fallen sword, before approaching the King of Camelot.

George was not the only one to witness this. Gwenivier was quickly attempting to lead her own woad warriors in a flying charge in a bid to rescue her captive bridegroom. But George could see that she would not make it in time.

"Gwenivier!" George yelled, galloping up towards her.

During the campaign in the Orkneys, the two had developed a tactic. It had been an evolution of the Pictish practice of moving champion warriors around the battlefield on chariots. The pair had taken this an almost suicidal step further, developing a maneuver that was made possible only by Gwenivier's acrobatic agility and George's strength and skill on horseback.

Riding forward, George flipped the chain of his flail over his shield, leaning low as he passed by the Pictish princess.

Gwenivier grabbed the heavy ball of the chain and heaved herself up, setting her feet flat against George's shield as they charged the Saxon line. At the last instant, George wheeled his horse hard to the side, bracing himself as Gwenivier springboarded off his shield; catapulting herself over the Saxon line.

She landed on her feet in the soft mud behind the enemy. Losing no time, she launched two throwing knives from her belt into the throats of the Saxon housecarls who were holding Arthur. Then, drawing her sword and battle ax, she whirled around in a spinning attack. Striking low and savagely under the enemy shields to hamstring her foes.

As she did so, George wheeled his horse and charged the wall of men and iron, Cordellia's massive ironshod hooves hammering against the Saxon shields.

Faced with such a savage attack on their front and the unexpected appearance of a Pictish battle-maid at their rear, the Saxon line began to split and shatter.

Freed from his captors, Arthur reacted quickly, leaping on Cynric as the Saxon prince turned to retreat. Wrenching the dragon-forged sword from Cynric's hand, he brought the blade up tight under the man's throat.

"I, King Arthur of Camelot, by the sword Excalibur, claim you, Cynric of Wessex my prisoner!" he shouted, as the remnants of Cynric's broken shield wall formed up with their rear guard.

"Surrender!" Arthur yelled. However, apparently indifferent to this threat, the Saxons began advancing in formation, grunting with each step.

"I will kill your lord!" Arthur yelled.

"They don't care!" George yelled as Gawaine rode up behind him. Tossing him a fresh lance as he did so.

Arthur, realizing his threats were useless, yet still not wishing to lose his hostage, forced Cynric to his feet. There he held the Saxon before him like a shield, as Gwenivier, and the nearby Briton forces formed up beside him.

"I hear fifes," Gwenivier said, as the wind shifted, whistling hard from the west.

As she spoke, George heard it too. The sound of high-pitched flutes, whistling out the battle anthem of Kernow. Looking up, George saw an army advancing over the hill from the southeast. They were all dressed in polished leather and mail that bore the sigil of Tintigle.

"It's Mark! Kernow has come!" Gawaine cried out next to George.

The Kernish forces sounded their charge, and the soldiers and light cavalry of the western kingdom surged forward to join the fight. The fresh troops made short work of the scattered Saxon stragglers, as they advanced to join the assault on the main Saxon force.

"This isn't over!" George said, looking to where the Saxons were attempting to form into a defensive triangle.

"Then, let's finish this!" Arthur yelled, knocking Cynric cold with the pommel of his sword. "Rangers, soldiers, kings, and princes. Christians and pagans. Nobles and commoners. Today, here and now, you stand as equals! Today you have proven yourselves, knights of this island all. For all those who have fallen. For oath and honor! Wrath and justice! For Britain!"

"For Britain!" George and the rest of the army bellowed in reply before rushing the Saxon line.

With their chieftains dead or captured, and facing enemies from all sides, the Saxon lines crumbled. And as the last of the enemy forces surrendered or died, George rode forward to greet the Kernish captain.

"I'm Sir Candor. Is this all that remains of the Saxon forces?" the man asked.

"There were more of them before. What took you so long? Your prince and queen got here days ago." George laughed, slumping down into his saddle.

"Prince Tristan and Queen Iseult are here?" the man next to Candor asked.

"And did Kernow credit? It was the queen's arrow that felled King Cedric. May the evil bastard rot in hell," George said, surveying the battlefield.

"King Mark will be most interested to hear this," the Kernish lord said darkly and rode away.

In that moment, George felt his mouth go dry as the thrill of victory turned to dust.

"What's wrong?" Gwenivier asked as George rode past her.

"Find Iseult. Tell her to run! I'm going to look for Tristan!" George yelled and took off across the field.

Chapter Twenty-Five

Unahild of House Gieseric, Priestess of Gurzil

Praetorian Prefecture of Africa
July 9th 543 AD

*The naked dragon of fell heart that flies
wrapped about in flame: him do earth's
dwellers greatly dread. Treasure in the ground
it is ever his wont to seize, and there, wise with
many years, he guards the heathen gold, and
not a whit doth it profit him.*

Beowulf
Unknown Approximately 640 AD
Recorded in the Nowell Codex 975 AD

No one had tried to stop Una as she stole out of Leptis Magna.

She doubted she would be missed. The last she'd seen of Gunthuris and Sergius, they had been busy securing anything shiny and valuable on ships so they could make their escape. The *Dux* eager to flee the danger back to his uncle's skirts.

Once she was safely away from the chaos, she pulled out the simple-looking golden ring. Yet, the ring was anything but simple.

There were many entrances that would lead to the dragon's temple. Most were hidden, even from her. However, Gurzil had trapped a djinn inside the ring for her. If she looked at it in the right light she could just make out the spirit frozen in the gold, like a bug in amber.

"Djinn of the ring. Return me to my lord and love," she whispered to the creature trapped in the metal.

As she spoke, the sands shifted under her feet. She fell through darkness and shadow, landing hard on a pile of gold. The temple however was darker than she had ever seen it before.

"I considered confronting you on the sand," Gurzil hissed in the shadows, the dragon's voice dripping with malice. "But then, I realized you would return here."

"Where else would I go?" Una asked, moving forward towards where the dragon crouched in the dark.

"You mean where else could you go! I say many things, but every word I say is carefully chosen. I move men with words, and fate with men. That is the art of *seidr*."

"My lord, what is wrong?" Una asked, squinting into the shadows. "It's dark. I can't see."

"There are many paths that fate may take. Many roads lead to the same place. For this reason, I let my minions do as they will, but one thing I was clear on ... DO NOT

HARM PRINCESS SABRA OF SALINE!" Gurzil roared, and Una dove for cover as a pillar of fire came flying toward her. "I have protected you! Honored you! Given you position and pleasure! This betrayal is how you repay my favor?"

"My lord, it was an accident. There was so much chaos!" Una whimpered, hiding behind a pile of treasure.

"DO NOT LIE TO ME! I have read the Tablets Of Fate, I know every language spoken, every war waged, every empire that has existed since the dawn of man!" the beast bellowed, charging like a bull out of the shadows and hurling her into a pile of gold. "What were you thinking? She is the one, the only one who can bear the seed that may give birth to my line!" the dragon roared. "I have waited for one such as her for over a thousand years!"

"Why obsess over her? Why her?" Una sobbed. "If it's only her body you need, then just take her, my lord."

"It must happen in the way fate demands. Otherwise, this could have been settled centuries ago. I thought the ancient bloodline lost. For centuries, I studied the prophecies and meditated on their meaning, searching for a solution. Only to stumble upon her by accident after being banished from my northern lair. I am the last of my kind. It falls to me alone to give rise to my race, restore the fallen empire, and build the city of New Babylon."

"But why her? Surely another could bear your child. I could—"

"Is that why you have done this? You have jeopardized centuries of planning because you thought you could take her place?" He bellowed, his talons cutting deep into the flesh of Una's arm. "You know nothing of magic! Nothing of fate! Do you even know the reason I have amassed all this gold, all this wealth?"

"It... it is power," Una answered with a sob.

"You think this is power? This is nothing! Men live and men die, but I endure through time. Time is all that matters. Time is the one thing I cannot afford right now. AND TIME IS WHAT YOU HAVE COST ME!'

"This shining metal serves no purpose. Endless suffering curses it. It echoes with the groans of the slaves who mined it. The madness of those poisoned by the mercury used to refine it, and the pain of the men seared when they smelted it. It sparkles with the blood of the countless innocents who died for it. It is the pure elemental foundation of heaven, cursed on this plane by the endless pain it has inflicted. I keep it because its infernal sparkle amuses me. Just as your sad sapphire eyes and golden hair amused me! But in the end, this gold is worthless! It's beauty means nothing! As you are nothing!"

"Please, master, forgive me. I will do anything." Una sobbed.

"No, I will do what I should have done with you in the beginning," the dragon hissed, its reptilian eyes fixed on her with a look that froze Una to her core.

The dragon roared, and fire engulfed her. Una's blonde hair vanished in a whirl of flame, but the rest of her did not burn so quickly. Her screams echoed off the piles of gold in the subterranean cavern.

The dragon smiled, for the sound amused him.

Chapter Twenty-Six

George Bertilack, Prince of Caer Celemion and Chieftain of the Lloegyr Rangers

Mount Badon
July 10th 543 AD

AD 543- This year died Cedric, the first king of the West-Saxons. Cynric his son succeeded to the government and reigned afterwards twenty-six winters.

Alfred the Great, King of Wessex, 886AD
The Anglo-Saxon Chronicle

WHEN POETS SING ABOUT battles, they always sing about the end of a battle. The dead are tallied, while the spoils and honors are divided amongst the victors. Such songs speak of the grief felt by the survivors, the feasts that toast the fallen, and the dishonorable enemies who are put to the sword.

They don't talk about how mighty heroes vomit and collapse from fatigue as the adrenaline of combat fades. They don't record the screams of dying men and horses, nor the din of crows and hogs as they fight over the carrion. Bards may sing of fair and foul days, yet the stories always end with clean and honored heroes.

There were plenty of heroes who stood, fought, and died on Badon Hill. But when the battle was done there was no song, no feast, no honors given on that day. Just the fatigue, nausea, and hard bloody labor that comes with hard won victory. Allies needed their wounds tended, while wounded foes were dispatched with dagger and ax. That labor was already underway by the time George found Tristan.

He was at the bottom of the hill where rain had flushed the blood, piss, and shit of the battlefield. Tristan was kneeling in the filth as two Kernish knights held him down. Before him stood King Mark of Kernow, Tristan's sword in his hand.

George charged his horse down the hill, and without a second thought, knocked down the two men who held his comrade.

"Run, Tristan!" he shouted.

Bloody and unarmed, Tristan fled for the woods, while Lancelot and his Franks closed in behind George.

"Drop the lance, or we drop you!" Lancelot shouted.

In that moment of indecision, George found himself wishing that he had another ten Saxon divisions before him, rather than this one troop of Franks behind. Yet, in the end, he complied, driving his lance into the soft turf.

"Off the horse," Lancelot demanded.

Reluctantly, George dismounted.

"Now, the mace. On the ground."

In compliance, George took the flail from his belt and tossed it down.

"What are you waiting for? Kill this traitor!" King Mark yelled, striding forward.

"That's not happening," George snarled. Pulling the slim dagger from his boot, he grabbed the king and brought the Kernish forged blade tight to the man's throat.

"Enough, George! Release him," Arthur boomed, walking up, his shining sword drawn before him.

"Like hell! I'll let him go when I have guarantees that Tristan and Iseult are safely away and will not be hunted," George yelled, tightening his grip on the King of Kernow.

It was at that moment that Iseult came forward. The afternoon sunlight reflected off her golden hair as she made her way past the standoff of armed men. Her milk-white skin was caked with blood, yet she was still as beautiful as the dawn. Yet her easy smile was gone, as was the bow she had wielded so brilliantly over the past few days.

"George, put down the dagger. I will go with my husband," she said, walking forward, slow and sad.

"Say the word, and I will make you a widow this instant," George said, holding his ground.

But Iseult shook her head, and walking up to George, she gently placed her hand on his to lower the blade.

"You will regret this," King Mark hissed as he pushed himself away from George, tripping as he did so to land face first in the mud. As he recovered himself, he grabbed Iseult roughly by the arm and led her to his horse.

Seeing her handled so roughly, George felt his blood rise again. But any response from him was prevented by Gwenivier and Galahad.

"George, you need to calm down!" Gwenivier whispered.

"You two are ok with this?" he snarled.

"She is going home with her husband," Galahad said, "For better or worse, that is what he is."

"*And that which God has joined together, let no man tear asunder.* I must say the Christian wedding ceremony is quite beautiful. Did she tell you that we converted? Well, I did at least. I think she is still having trouble with some of the commandments," King Mark said darkly.

"Leave, before I am tempted to kill you," Galahad snarled.

"See, I think that is a sin as well, isn't it? I don't know, I must confess, I'm still new to this, haven't finished the whole book," he said, placing his arm around Iseult who flinched at his touch.

George snarled, but his father's large hand held him back. George was suddenly aware that Haustdeserts own green-liveried soldiers had come up around them, lances and bows pointed at the Franks and Kernmen.

"There is nothing we can do about it now," Urien said, dispelling any hope of armed intervention.

"It was her arrow that slew Cedric. She has been fighting on this field before any of the rest of you even got here. I would be dead if not for her, and for this valor, her reward is to be abandoned?" George screamed. Turning on King Mark, he yelled, "I swear on all that is holy on this island, king or not, her husband or not, if you harm her, I will kill you! And damn be the consequences!"

"You know when I first saw him, I couldn't believe he was your son, Urien," King Mark said as he mounted his horse, placing Iseult on the horn of his saddle like a trophy. "But I see it now. A bit shorter, but definitely yours. I remember you said something similar to me and Uther. Do you remember? Right after he married my sister, Igraine. You said it the same way too. You need not worry on my wife's account, young prince. I would never jeopardize my peace with the Irish King Anguish by doing anything permanent," he said before turning to Arthur. "I must return to my own lands. My men will remain to assist with securing the area. Arthur, I honor the alliance between our kingdoms and offer my condolences on your father's death."

Arthur returned the gesture, as the sneering king rode west with Iseult.

"Get off me!" George snarled, lashing out at those holding him.

It was Galahad who spoke first. "George, listen to me—"

George, however, wasn't in a listening mood and fired a hard left hook to the side of Galahad's head, sending him hard into the mud.

"You were their friend, you self-righteous piece of shit!" he screamed.

"George, leave him alone," Gwenivier snapped. "It was her choice to go with him. She was offered protection. She refused it."

"Where is Tristan?" George asked.

"He took off west," Galahad said, getting up.

"Son, I know how you feel," Urien said quietly. "But part of being a leader is accepting things we may not like." Then turning to Gawaine said, "Take five men, scout east—"

"No," George said. "You may be King of Caer Celemion, but you named me warchief of this field. Gawaine, round up our men, get our wounded in wagons, and gather our fallen and captives. We are leaving! The Kernmen and Camelot can handle the mop up."

Gawaine looked at George in surprise, carefully glancing over at Urien who gave a nod of assent.

George quickly walked away, striding past the row of secured Saxon captives.

"So, you're the mighty George of Haustdesert. The Black Knight, cowed by a monk and Pictish whore."

George looked over to see Prince Cynric's hands bound, blood still flowing from where Arthur struck him in the head. George paused for a moment before continuing on without a word.

"Hey, hold on! I got something to show you. Trust me, you want to see it," the fair-haired prince called out.

"What do you want?" George asked, kneeling down a few feet in front of him.

"In my pocket. Right breast," Cynric said, nodding. "Come on, I won't bite."

Cautiously, George reached forward, his hand closing on a piece of parchment. As he did Cynric snapped his teeth, causing George to fall back into the mud as he jumped away, drawing the dagger from his boot.

"Can't blame me for trying." the Saxon laughed as George unfolded the parchment.

He looked down at the slim blade in his hand, with its Tintigle markings, as he read what was written.

The green riders have left Haustdesert, George Bertilack Prince of Caer Celmion rides ahead of them, he is not to be harmed.

M

"I wonder what your fellow Britons will say when they find out. What do you think they will do to the witch?" Cynric called out behind him.

George looked out over the blood-soaked hill and tried to calculate the number of dead.

He wondered about the kings and nobles slain at the stones on Sarum plain. *Were they still there, bloated food for crows and foxes, or had the dead been claimed and buried?*

Cynric's words echoed in George's mind. "What do you think they will do to the witch?" George knew what justice and honor demanded, what the dead demanded. Yet, the dead were dead, and they were victorious ... as for justice and honor ...

Justice and honor demanded that Tristan and Iseult pay for their infidelity. Despite the fact that they loved each other. Despite the fact that her husband was an unworthy piece of shit.

Justice was blind, and George found he had no stomach for it.

Had Morgana's treachery changed anything?

Regardless, Cedric would still have brought his army west sooner or later. The war would still have happened. This battle would still have been fought, and the dead would still be dead.

He looked back at the sneering Saxon prince. "I can't wait to see the look on the boy King Arthur's face when I tell him," the man mocked.

"Can I be there when you do? I can't wait to see him laugh in your face," George said with a smirk.

"What?" Cynric asked frowning.

"Look around. You lost," George whispered in his ear. "You and your father ... you fell right into our trap. Morgana told you what we wanted you to hear. Think about it. Uther and his loyalists are dead, Arthur now takes the throne uncontested, Camelot and Caer Celemion are at peace, your army is crushed ... all because you and your father were stupid enough to believe the word of Arthur's sister. I wonder what ransom your tattered hide will bring. Not that I'll see a penny of it, since it was Arthur who took you prisoner. So, by all means, tell Arthur, threaten to expose him. I wonder will he slit your throat himself to keep you quiet, or will he be like his old man and have his executioner do it? Oh, don't look so worried. If you're real quiet and play real dumb, you might live to get ransomed."

George looked at the white-faced Saxon and knew that the man had bought the lie.

It was a good lie. It was a lie that honestly made more sense than the truth.

He was tired. Walking back towards the horror of the battlefield, George barely noticed as the dagger in his boot sliced into his ankle.

Chapter Twenty-Seven

Sabra of the Lauathai, Crown Princess of Saline

The Otherworld

When day declines, and feasts renew the night,
still on his face she feeds her famished sight;
she longs again to hear the prince relate
his own adventures and the Trojan fate.
He tells it over and over but still in vain,
for still she begs to hear it once again ...
And thus the tragic story never ends.

Publius Vergilius Maro, 29 BC
The Aeneid Part IV

As Sabra drifted in and out of consciousness, the horrifying realities of the past day returned to her. Her father was dead, and the Cult now hunted them. What she knew was that Kahina was once again bearing her away from treachery. Yet where they were going she did not know.

As she rocked back and forth on her camel, she drifted into a deep sleep; finding herself again before the ethereal castle of the prince.

The castle had changed slightly since last she had been there. The walls were higher, and menacing stone statues now stood guard by the gates and on the parapets. However, this time, no voices challenged her as she walked up the steps of the shadowy fortress. It felt instead as if she was expected, and welcome.

She stopped for a moment, looking at the green, glowing orb that she remembered was called Gremlin. "You made this necklace did you not."

"Yes, my lady. It was made for the prince on the commission of the fairy queen."

"Someone I trust said that it was made by a djinn. That it would hide me from the dragon."

"Nothing can hide from the beast forever," the goblin buzzed. "But it might conceal you for a time if you wish the magic in the jewels to do so."

"It is very pretty," she whispered softly.

"Thank you, my lady. My prince is inside," the green, glowing ball said with a bob.

"You came back," the prince said, standing by the green, ethereal fire that flickered in the fireplace.

"And you're not dead," she said with a tired smile.

"Not yet at least," he said, looking over at her. "You look beautiful."

Looking down she realized she was still wearing her mothers dress. However, the blood, and dirt, that now stained it was gone. It was as white and clean as when her father had given it to her.

"It was my mother's," she said her voice catching in her throat.

"It is beautiful."

"My father gave it to me," she murmured, as memories of the battle flooded back and tears came to her eyes. "He is dead now. I was angry at him for so long, and now he's dead."

"I'm sorry," the prince said, gently wiping the tears from her cheeks.

"Before he died. He told me he was sorry, but he didn't say for what."

"Perhaps he didn't have time," The prince replied.

"He also warned me that the man who raised me was going to betray me."

"Was he right?"

"Yes," she said, her body convulsing in a sob. "Yes. I think he was."

"I'm sorry for that too. How did your father know?"

"The dragon told him," she answered.

"Then I doubt whatever he learned was the whole truth. It seems to me that the dragon says many things. Its words are truth told as lies and lies told as truth."

"The dragon has taken everything from me. You can't imagine what he has done to my people. I don't even think I can."

"I wouldn't be so sure. My people are a brutal tribe. Endless war has made us savage, but they say we were far worse once. There are stories of the time when a dragon ruled our island. A time when children were taken from their parents to be sacrificed and brothers waged war on brothers simply so the victor could offer up the vanquished to the beast. There are many I know that say that we were stronger then. That we have become weak and soft. They believe that we must return to the old ways and strive for even greater brutality. Some who believe this are simply evil, hungry for power, but others are my friends. There are even times I believe it myself."

"I know, the dragon told me. He ... showed me things," she said.

"What did you see?" he asked.

"Men dying badly... by your hand," she answered, as she rested her head against his chest.

"Then, the visions were probably true. My people have been at war since before I was born. War is a prison, and prisons eventually make beasts of all men," he spat.

"That sounds bleak," she whispered.

"War is bleak!" he replied sharply.

"Yes, but there is peace here. Do you think I could stay here for awhile?" she asked.

"This is a dream, my lady," he said sadly. "We cannot live in our dreams."

"Just for a moment," she pleaded.

"For a moment. But not forever. Not yet."

"I know," she said, listening to the slow thump of his heartbeat. "Did you loose many men in the battle?"

"Yes, and not all of them are dead yet. There were many wounded, soon to join the dead."

"Tell me about them?" she asked softly.

"I did not see how all of them fell-"

"No! No, don't tell me how they died," she said, looking up at him pleadingly. "I want to know how they lived."

Chapter Twenty-Eight

Gurzil

The Otherworld

*"Who are the Norns who govern childbirth and
choose who mothers what child?"
The Dragon answered, "There are many kinds
of Norns; they are not all of one family. Some
are god-born, some are elves, others come from
the dwarves."
"Tell me, Dragon, they say you are wise and
know much, what is the name of the island
where the gods and giants will fight their final
battle?" The Dragon answered, "It is called
Oskopnir; and there all the gods will wage
war."*
The Poetic Edda
Unknown
Recorded in the Codex Regius 1200 AD

ANGER AND JEALOUSY BURNED in Gurzil, feeding the fire that burned in what passed for his soul. He had watched as his bride entered the castle, the heavy doors of the ethereal fortress shutting behind her with a boom that seemed to shake the dream world.

Slinking like a snake, he moved towards the fortress.

There had been improvements made to the castle's defenses. Higher walls, with heavy iron spikes. More worrisome, however, were the carved stone gargoyles that now adorned the parapets, and standing guard at the gates sat two three-headed seraphim statues. Living things cast in dark stone.

Begone serpent, you are not welcome here, the stones whispered, as the dragon felt himself pushed back by an unseen force. Gurzil snarled, preparing to force his will against the guardians, but looking up he stopped.

Above the doorway sat a giant owl. Spreading its wings, it flew down to the drawbridge, and in a flash of light transformed into the silvery form of a woman.

The silver-skinned goddess before him wore molded, steel shin guards and carried a long heavy tipped spear. Her crescent moon shield bore a stone face, as hideous as the ones that now guarded the gates, mounted on its center. Other than this, she wore no armor, only a form-fitting black tunic, belted at the waist.

"So, the guardians are your doing?" the dragon hissed.

"Do you like them?" the pale-eyed goddess said with a smile.

"Stone scarecrows will not stop me from claiming what is mine."

"There are rules dragon. You know them as well as I."

"You are one to speak of the deep magics? Aren't Watchers, like yourself, not barred from interfering in mortal affairs?" Gurzil hissed. "Rules, it seems, are meant to be broken."

"Come now, they are dreamers, guests to this plane. You cannot harm them here, so why embarrass yourself?"

"What concern is it of yours, she-Faye?"

"I am the pale-eyed lady of war, Queen of Elphame, and the patroness of heroes," she said with a smile. "I like the boy. He's all smoke and blood and tricks."

"And you always the interfering bitch!"

"That's not nice. Bad dragon. Behave," the goddess said, lightly tapping him on the nose with her spear.

"Bargains were made. The woman is mine!" the dragon snarled. "As is the boy."

"Debatable, and not tonight," the fairy queen said, cocking her head with a coy smile.

"We both know you can't guard these gates forever. Other prophecies bind you. I have read the runes of doom that lay upon you and yours. I know the senseless death that even now comes for the one you cherish most. I know the field on which The War of Watchers, Makers, and Demons will be fought," the dragon hissed, smiling with satisfaction as the goddess's bemused smile vanished.

"What do you know?" she shrieked. "Tell me, Dragon!"

The dragon only laughed. "I know what is known. I know that war is coming, and the first casualty of the pointless confrontation will be the son who you cherish most. You can't stop it. It has been foretold in ages of old. And what has been foretold shall come to pass. Speak to the Spinners of Fates yourself, if you wish. Seek out the Norns or ask the Aiser who now shares your bed. You and your silent watchers will not long keep me from what is mine," Gurzil snarled as he took flight, his wings cutting a path through the ethereal fog.

Too long had he slumbered on his hoard of gold. He had become lazy and soft. He had left too many enemies strong enough to stand against him. However, he was patient, and he knew more than anyone imagined.

A seething fire burned in the dragon's belly. He would have preferred to avoid the involvement of other parties. That, it seemed, would now be impossible. There were many witches, and demons in the world, driven by an insatiable thirst for power, dominion, and blood. Soon the pathetic bottom feeders would come, seeking to reap a share from the field of blood he had so carefully sown.

However, In the short term, some of these scavengers might be usefull to his ends. Others would need to be eliminated. Doing so would cost him, and it would take time.

For now all he could do was wait for his enemies to reveal themselves.

Fidessa, Patrikia to the Empress Theodora

Carthage
July 25th 543 AD

Sergius was effeminate and unwarlike, very young both in years and in mind, excessively jealous and insolent to all men, luxurious in his habits, and inflated with pride. However, after he had become the accepted husband of the niece of Antonina, Belisarius's wife, the Empress would not permit him to be punished in any way or removed from his office ...

Procopius of Caesarea 555 AD
The Secret History of the Court of Justinian

FIDESSA HAD NOT WANTED to come to Africa, but then anything was better than the gilded cage of the imperial court.

If she had her way she would have returned to the circus. She'd been an acrobat. She lived for the thrill of sailing through the sky above the crowd.

The Empress did not approve. Theodora was of the opinion that anyone who would aspire to anything other than sitting around all day half-buried in purple silk was a naive idiot beyond all help. However, Fidessa was not as eager to forget the past. She had been around longer than most of the other coven members. Though she might not look a day over twenty, she had walked the earth for over a century.

Now she had come to the desert wasteland of the Empire. That said, it was also potentially one of the most valuable territories under imperial control. Yet, for some reason, it had been left under the control of a greedy sadist and his three idiot nephews. From what she had heard, the three sons of Solomon's brother, Bacchus, were like the character cast of a cheap tragic play. With the megalomaniac, the sadist, and the idiot. Fidessa guessed she should be grateful that she was being married off to the idiot. Better that way. If she decided later that the sadist suited her better, idiots were typically easier to dispose of.

It didn't take an overly intelligent mind to see the Emperor's end design in putting Solomon and his kin in charge of the province.

It was an old scheme. Find the most brutal bastard around, send him to a trouble spot, then let them off their leash to savage the population. The bloodletting provided an opportunity to kill off all the potential power players and troublemakers. Then, when the population had been brutalized to within an inch of rebellion, the ruler simply had to ride in on a white horse to rescue all the poor little people.

No doubt The Emperor would come to riding into Carthage on a great white horse.

"Oh, dear God, you poor people! What has this man done to you?" He would say. "I had no idea. Skin him alive, throw him to the lions, nail his hide to the wall!"

There would be cheers all around. The little people would all be so happy. And why shouldn't they be, no longer would they be raped, robbed and beaten on a regular basis, and they might even have food once in a while. No one would challenge it, since anyone with the intelligence to see the ploy for what it was would also be intelligent enough to know that the Emperor could always send another sadistic asshole to start brutalizing the population once again.

So why make waves? After all, Such purges always left openings for the intelligent and the ambitious. The Emperor would need people to run the province and balance the books.

It was simple, obvious, and crude, yet somehow, it always worked. That is unless you got the timing wrong. Ride in too early or too late and the whole thing tended to get messy, and bloody.

The whole plan also didn't tend to work out for anyone who happened to be standing next to the sadistic scapegoat when the hammer came down. This was especially true for the wives and mistresses of said sacrificial flunky. No, they tended to end up raped, murdered, and chopped into little pieces.

Fidessa was not blind to the possibility that she'd been sent to this shithole so that Theodora and Antonia could get rid of her, permanently. It was a messy and roundabout way of killing her, but that was certainly their style.

Fidessa was part of the old guard, a reminder of past defeats, and days when their people had been bandits, nomads, and circus performers. Theodora and her cronies were eager to have those days forgotten. However, she was not some pathetic fledgling to be thrown off.

She was a princess of the Szekely. She had ridden with Atilla the Hun. She might now be forced to defer to the Empress, but she did not serve her. Fidessa served a more powerful master, and he wanted her in Africa for other reasons. Therefore, she would make the best of it.

She looked around the room at her cats. Picking up the single white one, she stroked its soft fur as she looked behind her at the group of slaves who were carrying a pair of obsidian statues up the stairs. The figures had been carved in the form of tortured souls and were critical to her magic.

"Careful with those. They are worth more than your whole family. If I find so much as a scratch on them, I will pluck out your eyeballs and wear them for a necklace," she said, her voice sweet as poisoned honey.

She looked over as a well-dressed man walked up behind the porters.

"My Lady, I'm Sergius. You must be Fidessa," he said with a bow.

"My future husband. Good, I have to go make sure these idiots don't break anything. Here, take him for a moment," she said, dropping the large, white cat in the silk-clad nobleman's arms before heading out to make sure that the slaves didn't break or steal anything.

As she left to vent her frustrations on the servants, her husband-to-be looked down at the cat in his arms.

"Ok," Sergius said, dropping the cat on the table. "So, all in all, not so bad. Maybe a bit on the crazy side," he said, casting a concerned glance at her obsidian statues. "Definitely on the crazy side. But, at least, she's as attractive as she seems to be crazy." The line of cats stared at him. "Of course, the cats got to go. But that's no trouble. I'll just borrow a bottle of rat poison from the pantry. Yes, a big saucer of poisoned milk, and that will be the end of you lot."

At that, the white cat arched its back and gave a blood-curdling screech. Before Sergius could respond, the creature flew towards him, a snarling ball of fur, teeth, and claws.

Sergius shrieked as the cat raked sharp claws across his face and arms, shredding his silk costume as he hurled the homicidal feline off him. Red flecks of blood stained its white fur as it spat and hissed, its hooked claws having taken chunks of flesh with it.

Sergius grabbed a large candle stick and was about to swing it down on the cat's head when Fidessa screamed from the doorway.

"What are you doing to my cat?" Fidessa rushed forward and swept the animal up and into her arms. "How dare you hurt my cat?" she said, cooing softly to the beast that now purred sweetly in her arms while still managing to glare menacingly at Sergius.

"Me hurt it! The bloody thing attacked me," Sergius exploded, wiping the blood from his face as he looked at his shredded tunic.

"Well, serves you right. He tells me you were plotting to poison him!"

"I would never!" Sergius said.

"Are you calling him a liar? My cats would never dare lie to me," she said darkly, smiling as Sergius took a frightened step back. "Apologize to him."

"I will not apologize to a fucking cat!"

With a gesture of her hand, her nine other black cats hopped down from their various perches to encircle the imperial nobleman.

"What is this?" he said, his voice catching as the cats closed in on him.

"These are my cats," she said, fixing her hair in the mirror. "They tell me everything they see and hear, and they see and hear everything. They're not always the most loyal of servants. But that's what my white one is for. He keeps all the other cats in line. So, my dear husband-to-be, don't for a minute think you can keep things from me."

"Got it. You betcha," he choked. "Maybe, you can call off the cats."

"Of course, husband. Once you apologize to the white one."

Sergius gritted his teeth, backing up against the wall. One of the cats jumped up on the shelf next to him to yowl menacingly in his ear.

"Alright, I apologize!" he yelled.

Fidessa snapped her fingers, and the cats all scattered to various points of the room. "If you ever even think about harming my cats again, you will be sorry," she said, sitting down in front of a large obsidian mirror. "You may go now." She waved her hand to dismiss the terrified nobleman.

Sergius fled the room.

"I think that went well," she said, stroking the white cat's long, soft fur.

She looked up to where one of the black cats was perched above her. "Follow him," she said, pulling an obsidian orb from her pocket.

The orb was a powerful tool. Among other things, it allowed her to see through the eyes of any one of her cats. She seldom bothered with it since it was easier to just read their minds when the cats reported back to her. However, she was curious as to what her future husband's reaction to their first meeting was going to be.

"Ok, the crazy chick and her demon fucking cats are on the next boat back to Constantinople," Sergius exclaimed as he barged into the room where his uncle Solomon and two large, pale-skinned blonde men were looking over a pile of maps and papers.

Solomon looked up with a furious expression on his face. "Nephew, the barbarians in your district are in open revolt, one of my most competent and experienced tribunes is dead, Leptis Magna has been destroyed, and our outposts in eastern Libya will soon be overrun by desert savages. On top of all that, you have completely failed to secure our grain supply! The only thing you have done right to mitigate this catastrophe is to secure a marriage contract with that girl up there. She is likely the only hope we have of avoiding prosecution for this fiasco and is the sole reason I have not stripped you of your inheritance. You will marry that girl or—"

"Uncle, she talks to cats," Sergius objected.

"They all have cats, the Empress, Antonia, their sisters, all of them. The bloody imperial palace is infested with the vermin," Solomon bellowed.

"She doesn't just have cats! She talks to the cats! And she insists they talk to her, that they tell her things! And they're evil. Look at me! The white one. it attacked me," he said, casting a paranoid glance at the two black felines that were staring at him from the doorway.

"Oh, did the big bad pussy cat hurt you?" the large blonde man next to Solomon said with a thick Vandal accent and a taunting smirk. "It's always so sad when the honeymoon ends before the wedding even happens. And after you shelled out all that gold to buy her."

"Oh, don't worry. I'm getting my money back. They never told me the bitch was batshit crazy."

"Hey, at least, she's pretty. Most of the time, when you marry a woman for her political connections, she turns out to be a troll. Though, I will admit you Romans do somehow breed your noble women as pretty as gold pieces," the Vandal said, plucking a date from the fruit bowl next to him.

"Most of the women of the court at the moment all advanced from the ranks of the Blues. They're the daughters of charioteers, street performers and courtesans," Solomon spat.

"Well, I guess that explains why I have never seen an ugly Byzantine princess. Smoke-shows the lot of them," Gunthuris quipped.

"If you want her, she's all yours. Have fun with the evil cats!" Sergius snapped.

"Sold," Gunthuris said, turning to Solomon. "One attractive and well-connected imperial princess, that's a rare and valuable currency. That should cover my fee, but I'll still be needing gold for my men."

"That's not happening," Solomon snapped. "No, we must move to ensure our position here. So, my dear nephew, you will marry the girl before this debacle becomes known. We must ensure the Empress's favor now more than ever."

"What about my payment?" Gunthuris asked.

"I can't believe you really expect me to pay you for this disaster," Solomon snarled.

But Gunthuris only smiled. "You told me to assist your nephew with securing the grain from the Lauathai. He wanted to get the grain and keep the gold at the same time. I did tell him there were risks, but he insisted, and the customer is always right. I assisted. I even kept your nephew from being torn apart by the Berbers when he refused to pay them as promised."

"Your men ran and left an entire imperial garrison to die," Solomon hissed.

"You didn't pay enough for a death or glory charge. Your soldiers failed to secure their objective. How would my cavalry getting killed help you? Don't forget you need me, Solomon. Now more than ever. War is coming, and you don't have enough loyal soldiers. And now that you've lost eastern Libya, you don't even have land for your men's pensions. You need me. My rates, of course, are unreasonably high, but I'm happy to accept payment in whatever form you wish. Gold, grain, timber, stones... slaves."

"Fine! I assume you rescued your playthings," Solomon said, turning to his nephew.

"What?" Sergius asked, confused.

"Your whores! I expect turning them over to you will be payment enough to satisfy your expenses," he said, turning back to the Vandal chieftain.

"For now, his harem will fetch a good price."

"Uncle, you have no right!"

"I have every right. From now on, one bitch will have to satisfy you."

"What? That girl ... she's crazy and creepy," Sergius whined.

"You got to grant the kid the cats are creepy. It's going be a pain to herd them out the room before you bed the girl, or I guess you could just let them watch." Gunthuris chuckled.

"I am not having sex with her in front of the creepy cats!" Sergius objected.

"Listen, boy. I don't care if she wants you to fuck the cats. Right now, everything depends on you finding some way to make that girl up there happy! If she wants you to bed her day and night until she bursts with children, you will do that. If she wants you to sleep separately, then you will live as a monk with nothing but your right hand for company," Solomon bellowed. "What you will not do is spend your nights playing with whores! Nor will you go bothering kitchen maids and making sport of the wives and daughters of the officers. I strongly suggest you become a cat person. Because If that girl out there is anything other than the picture of domestic bliss, I will take a hatchet to your cock!"

"Why not have the gardener pick you a bouquet of lilies to bring her? They still bloom in the gardens here, do they not? Women love flowers, even the crazy ones. African lilies were my mother's favorite," Gunthuris added helpfully.

Solomon turned on the Vandal chieftain. "You would do well to remember your place."

"Oh, believe me, I have never forgotten it," Gunthuris muttered as he looked down at the palace gardens, where he used to play as a child, while his mother picked flowers.

As the men resumed their business, the two cats returned to their mistress.

"So, my idiot future husband has made one mistake too many and left his uncle a big mess to clean up. That won't please the empress," Fidessa said, stroking the white cat that purred malevolently on her lap, smiling as it looked down on the nine other black ones. "I need three of you to find out everything you can about the palace and the city, especially my future husband, his uncle, and that Vandal mercenary. Enlist local cats if you must, but make sure you dispose of them when their tasks are done. I have spent too many years getting out from under the shadows of my aunts. I don't want them infiltrating my circle through some stray alley cat. You will make sure of that won't you, my sweet?" she said, scratching the white cat behind his ears.

"As for the rest of you. You will proceed to our main objective and seek out this Gurzil and his followers. I need not tell you what will happen if any of you fail to please me."

At this, the cats before her quivered with fear. "Also, I need one of you to find your way onto a ship heading north.

Make for the island of Britain. There was a powerful cult of sorcerers based there at one point. If it still exists, find them. Reports are that the dragon has some connection to them. Learn what you can," she said, running her tongue over her pointed ivory canines.

She looked out the window of her balcony, to where her future husband was arguing with some men in the hallway. He was attractive, in a soft sort of way. There were certainly worse husbands to get saddled with. From her first impression, it seemed that he would be easy enough to control.

That would make things easier. After all, she had a job to do. And the faster she found the dragon Gurzil, the faster she could go home.

For there was more than one dark lord in the world, and the master she served would stand for no rival.

Made in the USA
Las Vegas, NV
13 August 2022

53217054R00187